OTHER BOOKS BY URSULA HEGI

Hotel of the Saints

The Vision of Emma Blau

Tearing the Silence

Salt Dancers

Stones from the River

Floating in My Mother's Palm

Unearned Pleasures and Other Stories

Intrusions

Trudi & Pia

SACRED TIME

URSULA HEGI

A TOUCHSTONE BOOK
Published by Simon & Schuster
New York   London   Toronto   Sydney   Singapore

TOUCHSTONE
Rockefeller Center
1230 Avenue of the Americas
New York, NY 10020

TOUCHSTONE and colophon are registered trademarks of Simon & Schuster, Inc.

Acknowledgments: The following chapters were previously published in different
form: "Belinda 1979: Ordinary Sins," *Five Points*, Winter 1997; "Floria 2001: The
Weight of All That Was Never Brought Forward," *Five Points*, Spring 1998; and
"Anthony 2002: Acts of Violence," *Story*, Summer 1994.

For information regarding special discounts for bulk purchases,
please contact Simon & Schuster Special Sales at 1-800-456-6798
or business@simonandschuster.com.

Designed by Joy O'Meara Battista

Manufactured in the United States of America

Library of Congress Cataloging-in-Publication Data
Hegi, Ursula.
Sacred time / Ursula Hegi.
p. cm.
"A Touchstone book."
1. Italian American families—American—Fiction. 2. Brooklyn (New York, N. Y.)—
Fiction. 3. Conflict of generations—Fiction. 4. Bronx (New York, N.Y.)—Fiction.
I. Title.
PS3558.E4185S23 2003
813'.54—dc22
2003059197

ISBN 0-7432-5598-4

for Gordon

ACKNOWLEDGMENTS

Many thanks to my wonderful agent, Gail Hochman, for her enthusiasm, support, and the Italian recipes. As always, I deeply appreciate my friends at Simon & Schuster—including Carolyn Reidy, Victoria Meyer, Marcia Burch, Doris Cooper—and especially my brilliant editor, Mark Gompertz, who understands my characters and vision, and who has taught me about the Yankees. In my research, I learned much about the Bronx from Lloyd Ultan's books: *The Beautiful Bronx 1920–1950*, and *The Bronx: It Was Only Yesterday 1935–1965*. Most of all, thank you to my husband, Gordon Gagliano, who took me to the Bronx and made it magical.

CONTENTS

BOOK ONE

Anthony 1953: *Elsewhere* 3

Leonora 1955: *Annulments* 53

BOOK TWO

Floria 1975: *At the Proper Hour* 105

Belinda 1979: *Ordinary Sins* 137

BOOK THREE

Floria 2001: *The Weight of All That Was
Never Brought Forward* 181

Anthony 2002: *Acts of Violence* 213

BOOK ONE

ANTHONY 1953

Elsewhere

That winter of 1953, stenciled glass-wax decorations appeared on nearly every window in the Bronx, and Uncle Malcolm was sent to jail for stealing stamps and office equipment from his last new job.

My parents were so busy fretting over Aunt Floria—who looked like a widow because she was married to Uncle Malcolm—that they got impatient whenever I told them how much I wanted a stencil kit. "Not now, Anthony," they'd say, and they wouldn't even glance at the commercial of the girl and her mother who opened their kit, pulled out stencils of comets and bells and Christmas trees that were cut from thick transparent paper. While the mother held a stencil against the window, the girl soaked a sponge in pink glass wax, dabbed it against the stencil, and they both smiled at the comets and snowflakes they'd created.

"All the other kids got stencil kits," I lied on the drive to Aunt Floria's.

Fordham Road was slick, and my father was steering cautiously in the icy rain that pelted our Studebaker. "Floria is my sister, after all," he said.

My mother tapped one painted fingernail against the St. Christopher medal that was glued to the dashboard. "Maybe you need to figure out who the hell your real family is, Victor."

"And what is not real about my sister?"

"Don't tempt me. Please."

"We already got glass wax for cleaning windows," I reminded her as we passed beneath the Third Avenue El. "So we only need to buy a stencil kit."

"Quit skutching, Anthony."

"Kevin has a stencil kit."

"Kevin always has everything you're trying to get. And when I check with Mustache Sheila, it's not true." My mother was always making up names that fit people just right, like the three Sheilas in our neighborhood, Pineapple Sheila, Bossy Sheila, and Mustache Sheila. Pineapple Sheila was Jewish; Bossy Sheila was Irish; and Mustache Sheila was Irish *and* Kevin O'Dea's mother.

"But all the kids have stencil kits."

"*Basta!* You know I detest it when you skutch. It's always the same. First you try getting what you want by being charming. Then you skutch."

I slid close to the wing window behind her, propped myself on the armrest to be tall. Inside my left mitten was Frogman, green and hard, and I curled my fingers around him. Frogman was a prize from a box of cereal I hated, but Kevin had finally traded Frogman for my two favorite baseball cards, Phil Rizzuto and Yogi Berra.

Kevin lived in the building across from ours on Creston Avenue, next to the back wall of the Paradise, where movies were air-conditioned and movie matrons shined their flashlights into your face if you talked. Summer evenings, when it was too hot and sticky to be anywhere else, our families would be at the Paradise, no matter what was playing as long as it wasn't banned by the Legion of Decency. At church, their movie chart was tacked to the wall of the vestibule: A-1 was morally suitable for all audiences; A-2 was morally suitable for all, with reservations; B was partially condemned; and C was condemned. Though we took pledges against condemned movies—not just to stay away from them, but also to boycott theaters that had shown them—Father Bonneducci still screamed from the pulpit that it was a mortal sin to see a condemned movie, and I could hear his voice inside my head whenever I passed the Ascot and tried not to glance at the posters of the condemned movies. Next door to the Ascot was a Hebrew school, and I wondered if the rabbi screamed at the boys about not looking at the posters. I liked the Swedish posters. Especially *Summer with Monika.*

I wished we had enough money to go to the movies every day, but at least Kevin and I could stand in the polished recess by the ornate ticket booth of the Paradise and feel the cold air, and retell the plots of our all-time favorite movies: *It Came from Outer Space; Invaders from Mars;* and, most of all, *Beast from 20,000 Fathoms.* We'd roar like the beast—"uuuughhh"—as it burst from the ocean near Baffin Island with its huge lizard teeth and lizard arms—"uuuughhh"— getting ready to squash Wall Street and the Ferris wheel at Coney Island. One day the movie matron came out and yelled, "Scat, you noisy kids, or I'll call your mother."

Some afternoons we'd spread Kevin's old quilt on his roof, and we'd spy on communists who might walk down Creston Avenue. So far we hadn't seen any, but we knew how to spot communists because they were mean and wore red uniforms. That's why they were called reds. They carried Jell-O boxes so they could find each other and trade secrets about the bomb. While Kevin and I waited, we'd read our Tarzan and Bugs Bunny comic books, or we'd scrape with Popsicle sticks at the tar along the seams where it bubbled in the heat. Some tar would get on our skin, our clothes, but we'd pretend we were getting a tan at Orchard Beach, even though we could see the Empire State Building from up here.

"I was talking about helping Floria too much while Malcolm is Elsewhere," my mother was telling my father. Elsewhere meant anything from jail, to England, to being on the run. Elsewhere meant never staying in one place for long because you're moving outside the law.

My father stubbed out his cigarette. "And who decides what too much help is?"

"You think you're just like Jesus walking on water. You think you can do anything without getting your feet wet."

"Feet? Jesus?"

"Well, let me tell you that Jesus got his feet wet. Plenty wet."

Feet wet. Wet feet. Feet cold. Cold car. Our car was so freezing cold, I could barely smell the leftover trays of veal scaloppine and eggplant rissoles next to me on the backseat. They were from the golden anniversary my father had catered, and he'd covered them with white towels that had the name of his business, Festa Liguria, stamped on them.

"What am I *not* understanding here about wet feet?" he asked.

"Forget it."

"No, no. Educate me. Me and the boy. We both may learn something from you that we've missed at mass."

I stared past our Palisades Park decal at the White Castle, gray now in the rain, where the twelve-cent hamburgers were as thin as Uncle Malcolm's playing cards; and as I thought of him being Else-where again, I pictured him *running, his lanky body tilted into the wind, one of his hands holding on to the green accordion he's strapped to his chest, the other to his ginger-colored hat.*

"I find it enlightening, Leonora, how you only quote the Bible to point out my shortcomings. Somehow I doubt the Bible was writ-ten for that purpose."

My mother jiggled two cigarettes from her pack of Pall Malls, lit them both, and stuck one between my father's lips. "It means . . . whenever you help Floria, you deprive your own."

"And are you my own then?" Though he grinned at her as if try-ing to joke her out of her mood, his voice was harsh. "Are you then, *mia cara?*"

She snatched a folded newspaper page from her purse. "If you're like that, I'll do my crossword puzzle."

———&

She couldn't sit still, my mother. Invariably, one crossed leg would bounce, or her hands would fidget for something to move. That's why she was too skinny, Aunt Floria had said to my father at my seventh birthday party a few weeks ago.

"I wonder if that's why Leonora can't hold your babies. Thank God she carried Anthony almost full-term."

I'd seen my mother hold plenty of babies and carry them around, but when I told Aunt Floria so, my mother came up behind her.

Eyes wet, she yelled, "Dropping a double litter does not make you superior."

But Aunt Floria yelled right back. "My twins are not a litter. At least I'm not starving my body to fit into a size six."

"That's the truth, for sure. If you quit eating macaroni for a year, you wouldn't get *down* to a size sixteen."

My aunt reached back and turned her black collar inside out. "I want you to check this label. Fourteen, Leonora. And I did *not* sew this dress. I bought it at Alexander's. Size—"

Quickly, my father turned on WNEW. "Listen . . . Frank Sinat—"

"Size fourteen. See?"

"You just sewed in a smaller size tag."

"Alexander's keeps getting bigger," I said, "just like—"

"Anthony—" My mother looked startled. "Don't you—"

"You told me Alexander's keeps getting bigger, just like Aunt Floria."

"I said nothing like that," my mother lied. "Floria—"

But my aunt was running up the stairs of my grandparents' house, and my mother was chasing after her.

"Floria, please—"

My grandfather reached into his pocket. "How about a peppermint, Antonio?" Just like the nuns at school who could whisk holy cards and erasers from their sleeves, my grandfather could produce whatever I might need from his pockets: rubber bands, money for paper candy or Nik-L-Nips, cat's-eye marbles, a whistle, peppermints, kite string. As a boy in Italy, he'd won a kite flying championship. Riptide Grandma complained that his pockets were always stretched out of shape, and the one thing he'd get angry about was when she cleaned them out.

I slipped his peppermint into my mouth. "The Alexander people keep knocking down apartment buildings to make their store even bigger."

"At home in Italy, people preserve old buildings instead of knocking them down."

"What if the Alexander people knock over the monkey bars in the playground?"

"In St. James Park? They're not allowed to build there."

"Promise?" I followed him into his music room below the stairs to the second floor. It smelled good in here from when it used to be a closet. On the floor lay wood specks that bugs had chewed from the beams.

"Promise. That park belongs to the city. Which means it belongs to you."

"Really?"

"To you and every child who plays there."

The window to the alley was on one wall of the music room, and on the other walls my grandfather had mounted candle-shaped lamps from his job at the salvage yard and a small picture of himself as a boy with a kite.

"I think it's funny when Americans talk about their historical buildings." He started cleaning a record with a folded undershirt. "Eighty years, Antonio? A hundred? Two hundred?"

Though he was a big man, the voice that came from his neck sounded little, as if it had to fight its way out, and I was sure that's why he loved opera so much, those big voices that came through the woven fabric in front of his golden-brown Victrola.

"In Liguria, we talk about thousands of years." His fingers curled a bit toward his palm, and he motioned with that hand as if asking me to come closer, to go way, way back with him, maybe a thousand years. "When I was a boy in Nozarego, a little younger than you, I helped my father in his vineyard that had belonged to his father and his father's father and so on . . . centuries of Amedeos, Antonio, before your time and mine."

"I almost got squashed at Alexander's."

He sat down on the wider of the two chairs. "*Oh Dio.* How did that happen?"

Upstairs, my mother and aunt were screaming at each other like opera divas, even though my mother had told my grandfather that opera was melodramatic. "They're always screaming, and it takes them half an hour to say, 'Come into my embrace,' or to recognize a long-lost brother. Then they scream the same thing again, and you can't even understand the words." My grandfather had listened closely, just as he always did, without rushing you, even though my mother went on and on, and when she'd exhausted herself and said she admired drama that relied on the power of words, the power of silence, my grandfather had smiled and said, "I like silence, too."

I climbed on his knees. "The Alexander people had their birthday sale and Mama and I were waiting for the doors to open but firemen were guarding them and people started shoving and squashing me."

"How awful."

"Some people got pushed through the windows and cut and mannequins got knocked over and then I heard sirens. I don't like Alexander's."

He nodded. "Have you considered trading time with your mother?"

"How?"

"You could ask her if, for every ten minutes in Alexander's, she'll give you ten minutes in the toy department."

"And for every hour in Alexander's I get one hour at the five and ten?"

"You could ask, Antonio."

"At Kress, not Woolworth, because it's bigger and next to Gorman's hot-dog stand."

For a while, the quarrel above us continued, but later that same evening, my mother and Aunt Floria danced to *Make Believe Ballroom* on WNEW, the way they liked to at family parties, my mother—despite high heels—not nearly as tall as my aunt, who had delicate ankles although the rest of her body was solid, like my father's. By far the best dancers in the family, my mother and aunt took pleasure in each other's grace and skill as they went spinning and dipping past us. And if there were words that passed between them, they must have been gentle.

Since the men didn't like to dance, they smoked and watched the women—including Riptide Grandma and Great-Aunt Camilla—do the rumba and the fox-trot and the tango. That evening, Uncle Malcolm wasn't Elsewhere yet. Sweating and laughing, he accompanied the radio by pumping long, shimmering breaths from his accordion as though he were part of Count Basie's orchestra. Uncle Malcolm was the only one in my family who wasn't Italian, and he seemed exotic to me because of that. His pale hair was damp, and his eyes chased Aunt Floria, who became girlish and light as she danced with my mother.

When my grandfather stepped next to Great-Aunt Camilla and whispered something in Italian, she laughed and, gently, pushed him away with her palm against his chest.

"It's true," he said, "even if I were a woman, I'd still rather touch women than men."

"That's brave of you, Emilio."

He sat down on the couch. "You go, Antonio. You go dance with the ladies."

My mother and Aunt Floria opened one side of their dance for me, and I rushed into the warm knot of their bodies, spinning with them. Spinning and dipping long after my father and Uncle Malcolm joined my grandfather on the couch, slumped toward him as if to make a triangle, and took the customary nap.

Afterwards, in the kitchen, Aunt Floria and my mother washed the dishes and argued, but we were used to them being quick-tempered with each other and then confiding and dancing as if they were the closest of friends. When they returned to the living room with brown coffee and black coffee and a silver tray of sfogliatelles and cannolis, the men stirred and uprighted themselves, and we all sat around and told stories the way we always did, with great passion, listening with equally great passion while one of us would take one thread of a story and spin it along, and the listening would evoke further memories, so that—with laughter or tears—we'd leap into a story and become part of its weave. It was best when the stories were already familiar, because then we could take delight in how they changed and yet stayed the same with each telling. And as we urged each other on, I felt the presence of untold stories—there already, beyond all of us in the future—shaping themselves within the body of my family, waiting for us to live these stories.

And to tell them.

Great-Aunt Camilla found her stories in foreign countries. Since she enjoyed traveling alone, she was a mystery to my family, but I liked mysteries, liked picking her up at the West Side docks, where the water was dark green and murky with oil slicks and trash, where the air smelled of tar and hot dogs, and where I got to see ocean liners when she returned with her faraway stories and faraway presents. One day, Great-Aunt Camilla gave me a tour of the *Mauretania*. Four other ocean liners were tied to the docks, and a barge with long rollers was alongside the *Île de France*, painting the hull. When my mother bought me a hot dog, I tossed the end of my bun to the seagulls, and as they fought over it, the horn of a tugboat shut them out. It had a big *M* on its stack. "That means 'Moran,'" Great-Aunt Camilla had told me, and I'd wished she would take me on one of her trips.

My favorite story of all was how my grandmother had saved my grandfather from drowning. My mother had named her Riptide. If it were not for Riptide, none of us would be alive. Not that she had rescued all of us, but she had rescued my grandfather when he was not my grandfather yet, not her husband yet, but just Emilio Amedeo, standing in the surf at Rockaway Beach up to his waist.

"The first day I saw him, I rescued him." That's how she always started the part of the story that was hers, the part where *she's sunning herself, wearing her new white swimsuit, when this young man suddenly topples and is pulled out to sea. One of his arms shoots up, then his face, open-mouthed. While she leaps up, races toward the water, dives in, and swims out to where he's drowning. "Hold on to me," she shouts and reaches for him. She's swimming on her back, one arm around him as if they were hugging, and he floats with her, resting on her body. "If we fight against the current, it'll tire us," she tells him. "All we need to do is wait . . . let the tide take us to where it weakens . . . then swim out of it." For a minute or so my grandfather floats with her, but when the tide sweeps them out farther, he panics, because it's obvious she's some rare kind of water-being, a manatee, or a siren, luring him deeper into her territory. As he struggles to free himself, she flips from beneath him, emerges behind him, grasps him around the middle.*

"I'm going to save you," her woman-voice shouts into his ear, "you have no choice there. But you . . . can make it easier for me to save you . . . if you quiet down. If you can't do that . . . I'll knock you out and . . . drag you to shore." He feels her breath against his left ear, against the left side of his neck, breath that rides on her shouting. "But save you I will. The one . . . choice you have is to make it look like we're swimming back . . . together. And then you don't have to admit to anyone that a woman saved you."

But it's my grandfather who revealed the story of his rescue. Who still liked to tell it, urged on by us.

"Let Emilio tell that part."

"He does it so well."

He'd wait till Riptide finished and then he'd continue the story from the moment when he quieted. *Against all panic. Because, out there, in this woman's fierce embrace, he understands that she'll make true on her promise to save him. In her fierce embrace, he understands that he'll ask her to marry him—water-being or woman—once they're back on shore. And because he's afraid of her slipping away from him forever once they reach the sand— more afraid than he is of drowning—he asks her name, Natalina, relieved to hear that she, too, is Italian, and then proposes to her while the tide is still pulling them out.*

It has become the story of their marriage.

And it was not long before they had their first child, Victor, named after Victorien Sardou, who'd written the play that my grandfather's favorite opera, *Tosca,* was based on. And since my grandfather loved Puccini's operas above all other operas, it only followed that the girl, born two years after Victor, would be called Floria.

My father and Aunt Floria liked to tease their parents about that first swim, how they had made it last because they got to touch each other in ways that would have been inappropriate had they just met on land.

"It would have destroyed Natalina's reputation," my grandfather would say.

Riptide continued to swim, one mile every morning, in the pool of the building where her sister, Camilla, shared an apartment with Mrs. Feinstein. Both worked as teachers in Manhattan, but Mrs. Feinstein didn't travel and saved her money for a Persian-lamb coat and elegant furniture. Their apartment had a fireplace and was two blocks from the East River on 86th Street.

Sometimes I'd wear my swimsuit instead of underpants to Sunday mass, and afterwards Riptide would take me to Manhattan. I liked being on the Jerome Avenue El because it went by apartments and I'd see people cooking or sleeping or watching television. Whenever there was a game at Yankee Stadium, people on the El would stand up and lean toward the windows on the right, catching a moment of the game.

Uncle Malcolm liked to take me to baseball games. Usually the twins would skutch, and he'd tell them, "No girls allowed at Yankee Stadium."

"I got us the best seats in the house that Ruth built," he said the first time he invited me.

Everything was exciting that afternoon: coming into the courtyard, where Uncle Malcolm bought me a program; going through the turnstiles, where he presented our tickets to the ticket takers; following him up steps so steep I really had to climb, steps to the top bleachers up in heaven; and squeezing into seats that were grimy and sticky from stale beer.

"From here we can see everything that's going on, not just part of the field—" He motioned to the box seats close to the third-base line. "—like those poor schmucks over there, who have to keep moving their heads."

I loved being this high up, loved the noise, the scoreboard with the numbers lit up, the vendors yelling: "Hot dogs, peanuts, soda, here."

Uncle Malcolm showed me how to fill out the program with a pencil, play by play, who got a strike, who got a ball. A couple of times he tapped the shoulder of the man in front of us. "Could I just borrow your binoculars for a second for my kid here?"

He bought us peanuts and Coca-Cola and beer, nudged me so I'd shout whenever he shouted. Such noise . . . I'd never heard such noise before, shouting and fighting and vendors yelling, while I sat in our best seats, feeling hot and stuffed and thrilled.

―ଦ

Great-Aunt Camilla's pool was in the basement, across the hall from the trash room, and the lockers were rusty and stank of chlorine and rotting swimsuits that people had forgotten. Riptide and I would dive into the murky green water, chase each other's toes, shriek with joy when we'd startle each other by surfacing unexpectedly.

My father laughed when I figured out one day that, by swimming one mile a day, Riptide could swim to Italy in nine years.

"She's the kind of woman who might just do that," my mother said.

"I'd rather take an ocean liner," Great-Aunt Camilla said.

Now and then Great-Aunt Camilla and Mrs. Feinstein would join us in their pool and swim like real grown-ups, their bodies long and narrow, so that they looked more like sisters than Riptide and Great-Aunt Camilla. Together, they'd do smooth and fast laps at the far side of the pool so that our splashing wouldn't frizz their curls.

I'd try to prolong our swim because I dreaded the men's locker room, where roaches and silverfish scurried when you turned on the light. According to Mrs. Feinstein, silverfish ate anything, even the glue in book bindings; and she'd point out dead silverfish in the light of her elevator when we took it up to the apartment for lunch.

―ଦ

The brim of my father's hat filled the rearview mirror. "At least instruct me how I am depriving my own and getting my feet wet at the same time, Leonora. Have you and the boy ever gone hungry? Without coats? Without crossword puzzles, God forbid?"

"Without the damn car heater."

I tugged the brim of my hat forward, then back. Forward again. Still, its rustling against my ears was not enough to smother my parents quarrel. They often fought about money. About not being poor. About not looking poor. Which meant keeping things clean and mended, saving scraps of leftovers for another day.

"I said I'll get the heater fixed."

"When?"

"When, she wants to know."

"Don't talk about me in the third person."

"Sorry."

I wound a piece of wilted lettuce around a button of my wool coat. We always had a few lettuce leaves or shriveled string beans on the seats, since my father used the Studebaker to transport crates with carrots and beets and lettuce and beans from the Bronx Terminal Market to Festa Liguria on East Tremont Avenue.

"People can get frostbite in this car." When my mother raised her thin shoulders, her back seemed half the width of my father's.

"I'll get the heater fixed once those chiropractors pay me for their convention."

"I rest my case."

"A lawyer in the family. All our troubles are over now."

"I promise not to use much of the wax," I said.

Why did the grown-ups always get to decide what was bought? Why should a car heater be more important than a stencil kit? Or a frying pan when the old one wasn't broken? I folded my hands and prayed to St. Anthony, my namesake saint, to let me live with the television girl and her parents. They never argued. I pictured the glass-wax girl, the glass-wax mother on the screen, *shown from outside their window as they decorate it while someone high up in a tree—maybe an angel—is pointing a camera at them. In their living room is a fireplace, ready for Santa to arrive.*

"We don't even have a fireplace," I said.

"Santa knows the route down our fire escape." My mother drummed the tip of her silver crossword pencil against her front teeth. "Light. Seven letters. A word for light . . ."

"I don't enjoy fighting with you," my father said.

"Now you want to fight and enjoy it, too?"

He let out an exasperated laugh.

I pulled off my itchy wool mittens and let them dangle from my sleeves on the cord Riptide Grandma had crocheted between them. The last time I'd heard my father laugh like that was when my mother had wanted to yank me out of Catholic school. She said it was bad practice to mix religion and school. But my father and grandparents said the nuns gave a better education, and I wanted to stay at St. Simon Stock because Kevin and my other friends were there.

Though I was sure I'd filled Frogman's leg with baking soda, I popped the metal cap off his leg. Some days, being sure only meant you had to double-check, because if you didn't, everything else would come undone. And I wanted to show my cousins how Frogman swam up and down when baking soda bubbled into water.

"Seven letters. Glow . . . too short." My mother reached up to fluff the speckled feathers on her red hat.

"Are you quite settled?" my father asked.

"Flicker . . . No, the fourth letter has to be *M*. . . ."

"If my sister hadn't married Malcolm," my father said, "we wouldn't even know the bastard."

I sat there, stunned, and for years from then on I would believe that—without marriage—men simply were not there. My father certainly proved that, because my mother kept him real during his absences by cooking his favorite meals, washing and ironing and mending his clothes, and, above all, talking about him when she picked me up from St. Simon's after school, so that, when my father came home at night, I'd feel surprised he'd been away at all because all day he'd felt nearby. Women were there without marriage, even Great-Aunt Camilla, who didn't have a husband. Women I saw all the time. In my mother's kitchen; at the beauty parlor, where the stink of permanents tickled my nostrils; at the Hebrew National Deli; at Joy Drugs; or in Ce'Bon, where a sprayer above the window filled the air with perfume. But men I only encountered when they were married to women I knew. What would happen if I couldn't get someone to marry me? Would I just disappear? And where would I be then?

I sat up tall. "Can I marry the twins?"

My mother turned and smiled at me as if I were still in first grade. "Both of them?"

"Maybe just Bianca. Belinda is funny, but I don't like her ugly boogers."

"I have asked you not to say 'ugly boogers,'" my father said, though he, too, knew to get away from Belinda when she sneezed because chunks of snot burst from her. "It is called a sinus problem."

"Marrying one's cousin is not a good idea," my mother said.

But if I married Bianca, she would have to let me wear her Superman cape. She used to leap off furniture with a bedsheet knotted around her neck, shouting, "Suuu-per-mannnn," until Aunt Floria sewed a cape from satin remnants with straps for Bianca's arms to fit through so she wouldn't strangle herself.

"Why is it not a good idea to marry a cousin?"

"Last week you wanted to be a bishop," my father reminded me.

"I can be a bishop first and then get married."

"You can't do both."

"Besides," my mother added, "you're too young to think about marriage."

My father slowed our car at the corner of Southern Boulevard, where the orange roof of the Howard Johnson glistened in the downpour, and the neon boy pointed to the tray of neon pies that the neon pieman offered him.

"Twenty-eight flavors," I read aloud.

"Always out of season," my mother said.

"Coffee is their most disgusting flavor." Whenever we went there, they'd just have vanilla, chocolate, coffee, and strawberry. Any other flavor we'd ask for was out of season.

"It's disgusting, all right."

My father glanced at her. "Malcolm probably considered those stamps another fringe benefit."

Fringe was the slinky stuff around the edges of my Ossining Grandma's piano shawl. She was my mom's mother. Rough and loving, she was sorry as soon as she slapped me or yelled at me, and she'd pull me into her arms; but it was the sting of her palm that lasted—not the kiss on my forehead. We didn't see her often, but when we did, I liked driving past Sing Sing, where my Ossining Grandpa had worked as a guard till he died from a burst appendix when my mother was ten. My Ossining Grandma prayed a lot for

her dead husband. Each prayer, she said, was a parking voucher for
God. She got one extra parking voucher for each votive candle she
burned in the red glass by the picture of Mother Cabrini, a new
saint who got to be a saint by working with emigrants from Italy.

But ever since last summer, my parents hadn't driven past Sing
Sing. Because of the Rosenbergs, my mother said. She felt sorry for
the Rosenbergs' little boys, who were orphans now. "I'm not that
sure the Rosenbergs really were Russian spies," she'd say. "The one
thing I *am* sure of is that McCarthy is a liar, a bully. Even President
Eisenhower is scared of him."

—⁓—

"Malcolm considers the world his very own fringe benefit," my father said.

I couldn't imagine the world with a fringe. My second-grade
teacher, Sister Lucille, had a map of the world above the boys' coat
rack, and my hook was beneath Africa, with the most crosses for
missions. During one of our air-raid drills, Maria Donez had cried,
and Sister Lucille had told us Maria was sad because her family was
going home to Guatemala. I forgot the name of her country, and
when I told my mother that Maria was going back to Palmolive, she
said Palmolive was soap, not a country. The following morning I'd
asked Sister and she'd shown me Guatemala on her map.

"What's fringe benefit?" I asked my parents.

"Remember now, Anthony—" my father said, "—whatever the
Amedeo family talks about in the car, stays in the car. And whatever the Amedeo family talks about in the house, stays in the
house."

I mouthed the words along with him. I certainly heard them often enough.

"Fringe benefits," my mother explained, "is what people get in
addition to their pay when they work. Like vacations. Or paid
holidays."

"Or stamps?"

"Never stamps. Never office equipment. Never tires or—"

"And never shingles?"

She started coughing, but it sounded fake.

"You're fake-coughing," I said. "You're really laughing."

She winked at me.

"Didn't I tell you the boy hears too much?" my father asked.

My mother leaned toward him to whisper into his ear, her lips as red as her hat.

Last summer Uncle Malcolm had been in trouble—"deep-shit trouble," my mother had called it—for selling a shipment of asbestos shingles he'd stolen from Quality Roofing, where he worked. The two brothers who owned Quality had waited for him one evening after dark in an alley off Webster Avenue, near Papa John's Diner. Both arms and hands in casts, Uncle Malcolm did much of his healing on the striped couch, opening his mouth for the pasta e fagioli and linguine that Aunt Floria fed him fork by fork, hunkering over him like a black-feathered mother bird.

One Sunday, while we visited, he made the twins stand in front of the couch and hold his bulky accordion between them. It glittered like the mother-of-pearl crucifix that Kevin's father had tied to the rearview mirror of his cab. Kevin's father used to drive a bus until he was blacklisted.

"Those Quality crooks stole the music away from your dear papa," Uncle Malcolm said. "Forever. Now the accordion is your legacy, girls." Usually he talked like the rest of us, but when he got dramatic, his British accent expanded, though he'd left England when he was sixteen and got fired from his apprenticeship with a roofing company.

The accordion was too heavy for the twins, too stiff without the motion of my uncle's body curving into it, without his fingers leaping across the keys.

"If you set it on the side," I suggested, "it'll be like a piano. Then one of you can press the black and white keys, and the other can push the buttons."

"That accordion is all your papa may ever be able to give you." Uncle Malcolm's fingers were wiggling, trying to fly out of the casts, to circle and dip as they usually did when he talked.

All he had taught the twins were two beginnings, not even the full songs—"I'm Chiquita Banana" and "Flight of the Bumble-bee"—and they'd play those over and over, singing along. To this day I can't bear accordion music. I'll leave restaurants if a strolling accordionist approaches my table. And I hate family gatherings if Belinda—now a music teacher—is coaxed into playing her father's accordion.

⁓

As our car passed the Bronx Zoo, I wished I could touch the green gate. Kevin had told me the gate felt warmer in winter. "Warmer than pavement and rocks. Because it's made of copper. And copper is warm and stays red beneath the green." Across from the zoo, the black spikes of the Botanical Garden fence filed past us, a thousand warriors with a thousand lances, and as I turned for one more glance at the zoo gate, I decided to draw a picture of it, not green, but red with smoke all around it.

"I must have been crazy to recommend Malcolm for that job," my father said. "Crazy to believe him when he said he was ready to start over."

"Not crazy," my mother said. "Generous."

"Crazy crazy crazy . . ." With each "crazy" his right palm slapped the steering wheel.

"Generous. You got him the job because you're generous by nature. And with those broken arms, he couldn't go back to roofing for a while. Besides, he comes across as polite, because with that accent he sounds like a butler from the movies. People misjudge him."

"He sells from an empty pushcart. A *scungilli,* that's what he is. A bottom feeder."

"Also very handsome."

"Malcolm Edmunds? Handsome?"

"Quite gorgeous, actually. He'll get another job roofing."

"Because he's gorgeous?" Smoke curled from my father's nostrils.

"Because roofing is the only thing he's good at. Agile and daring . . . that's why he always finds someone to hire him after he gets fired."

"It's not the only thing he's good at," I said. "He can whistle whole songs without stopping for air."

"And where would we all be without that talent?" my father asked.

"Too generous," my mother murmured and stroked the band of neck above my father's brown collar.

I could feel their quarrel yield to tenderness. It often was like that between them; that's why I believed nothing really bad could ever happen in my family.

He leaned into her palm. "Your hands are cold."

"So . . . want me to stop then?"

"Don't you dare."

As she tilted her head toward him, I saw where her left eyebrow, black near the bridge of her nose, changed abruptly to white. It had been two colors since birth, and my father liked to say that what saved my mother from being too perfect was that left eyebrow. With her black hair and pale skin, the contrast was startling, making her only more beautiful.

"I'll get someone to check out the car heater," he said as we passed the marquee of the Globe Theater.

"Can we afford it?"

"Soon." When her fingers kept moving across the back of his neck, he turned his face to kiss the inside of her wrist, the shadow of his beard blue below his jaw, and I felt a sudden and wild joy.

"So then," she said, "will you marry me, Victor?"

I loved it when he replied, "But I already did, *mia cara*, remember?" Once again, he kissed her wrist.

My mother laughed. "I've been thinking about the twins' names. Ever since Floria met Malcolm, she's been mumbling 'bastard' all day long. Picking names for them that start with *B* gave her a way to cover that up. BaBelinda. BaBianca."

"Not in front of the boy, Leonora."

But already I was trying out my cousins' names: "BaBelinda . . . BaBianca . . . Ba—"

"Anthony," my father said sternly. His hands covered the entire top of the steering wheel—wider than Uncle Malcolm's hands with their long wrists and fingers that could fix a bicycle tire or shuffle a deck of cards faster than my father could. Until that night outside Papa John's Diner, of course. He wasn't a real uncle, I reminded myself. Only a married-in uncle. Because of Aunt Floria.

—◌—

Black curls pulled back in a shiny bun, she opened the door of their first-floor apartment on Boston Road, looking as if she were in mourning with her black stockings and her black dress buttoned high on her neck. "Please, wipe your feet, darling," she said and took my cheeks between her palms. Her face hung above me, large and pale and beautiful. On one side of her mouth was a freckle, and as she kissed me on the lips, her folds of skirt released the memory of mothballs and lavender.

I kissed her right back, glad her face was all of one color. No sticky lipstick or creme. No raccoon eyeshadow like my Ossining Grandma's. I loved how Aunt Floria's scent changed with the seasons and also kept bugs away at the same time. Moths never dared live near her. And come summer, she would once again give off the sweet-sour scent of the citronella oil that she dabbed on handkerchiefs and bedsheets to discourage mosquitoes.

Beneath the gold-framed paintings of Pope Pius XII and Cardinal Spellman stood my cousins, round-faced and sturdy like their mother, wearing their patent-leather slippers and brown school uniforms. Still, I could tell them apart, because Belinda had gluey nostrils, while Bianca wore her Superman cape.

Aunt Floria lifted the towel from the eggplant rissoles. "You are an artist with food, Victor. I'll warm everything up right now."

In the kitchen, the dressmaker's dummy was wearing a half-finished wedding gown, so stiff it could have danced by itself. Cartons—some full, some empty—covered all surfaces that were not taken up by Aunt Floria's sewing business.

"You're moving?" My mother sounded alarmed, and I figured it was because Aunt Floria moved so often that my mother wrote each address in pencil, since she'd only have to erase it.

"The girls and I can't stay here. Not with Malcolm Elsewhere. Please, blow your nose, Belinda." Aunt Floria folded a piece of red velvet and two red velvet dresses with plaid collars and cuffs pinned to them. She sewed all the twins' clothes, dressed them alike. "We're five weeks late on the rent," she said.

"Why didn't you tell me?" my father asked.

"You know I don't like to burden you, Victor."

My mother rolled her eyes and walked to the window. Her back to Aunt Floria, she stared into the air shaft, arms crossed in front of her coat, elbows jagged beneath her sleeves. Rain smeared the glass, turning the living room mop-water gray.

I poked at my aunt's bolts of lace. She had customers from Manhattan and Brooklyn, even Staten Island, who came to the Bronx for their wedding and bridesmaids gowns.

"Better not touch that lace, Anthony," she said. "I have something better for you."

"Lemon wafers?"

"Too much sugar." My mother turned toward us. "It'll only make him skutchier."

"Nice corduroy pants, Anthony," my aunt said. "Where'd you get them?"

"Macy's."

"Turn around. Who did the hemming?"

"The old man with the sewing machine in the window of Koss'."

My father touched his lips where they disappeared into his beard, signaling me to stay quiet—*whatever the Amedeo family talks about . . .*—but that made me think even more of the old man who kept his long face bent over his sewing machine. My mother took our dry cleaning to Koss. Also clothes to be taken in, let out, or shortened, and the owner who stood behind the counter passed them to the old man who never talked.

"I would have hemmed them for free, Leonora," my aunt said.

"I didn't want to inconvenience you."

But I'd heard my mother say that, because of my aunt's situation, any favor you accepted obligated you tenfold. That's why I wasn't allowed to tell her when we took alterations to Koss', where steam from the pressing machine smelled of wool and yeast and starch.

"Girls," Aunt Floria told the twins, "why don't you go and play with your cousin?"

Bianca and Belinda—one year and one day older and heavier than I—took me into their bedroom, where we played the tickle game on the floor. You won if you didn't flinch while your toes or nipples got tweaked, or while you got tickled behind your knees or between your legs. In the months since we'd invented the game, we'd become bold. Stoical. I tickled Belinda, who then tickled Bianca, who tickled me.

When Belinda got both of us to laugh, she yelled, "I win."

"Nice girls don't play tickle games."

"Do so." Belinda crossed her eyes and stuck out her tongue.

"Sister Lucille says," I lied.

"Sister Lucille doesn't know."

"She knows." What I didn't tell the twins was that Sister Lucille said boys' hands did the work of the devil. Whenever Sister spotted a boy with his hands in his pockets, she'd smack his palms with her wooden ruler—one smack for each wound of Christ. If Sister found out about the tickle game . . . *Sixty smacks. At least sixty smacks with her ruler.* Sister Lucille also said waiting for chocolate was excellent training for waiting for heaven. Since Advent-calendar chocolate was the best chocolate in the world, Sister Lucille had told the class, "By not letting yourself have everything you want right away, you save up ten times that much in heaven."

Belinda pointed at my legs. "Sister Lucille says you got skinny legs."

"He does not have skinny legs," Bianca defended me.

"Skinny legs," Belinda hollered. "And it's my turn to play with him."

"No, mine."

"Mine. Anthony, tell Bianca you're my brother."

"No, he is my brother."

I watched them closely, trying to figure out whom to favor this time.

"Mine."

"No. Mine."

Often, they clung to me like that, fighting to impress me, to be my favorite, till I said I liked one of them better. Then they'd fight each other. Over me. I didn't like that adoration, but it was better than having both of them clobber me. To distract them, I pulled Frogman from my pocket. "Look. He can swim." I showed them the baking soda inside his leg. "If we put him into your tub—"

"But we have a rabbit in the tub."

"A new rabbit. A boy rabbit." Belinda gripped my hand. "You want to see? Papa bought him for me."

"Papa won the rabbit," Bianca corrected her. "My rabbit."

"Never mind her." Belinda pulled me toward the bathroom, where a rabbit crouched in the tub, eyes pink and scared.

"Don't touch him." Bianca was right behind us. "He's my pet."

But I was already stroking the white pelt between his ears, whispering, "Hey there, rabbit, hey—"

"He'll eat your finger."

"Does not," Belinda said as I snatched my arm away.

Bianca clicked her shoe against the side of the tub.

"Stop that. It annoys Ralph."

"His name is Malcolm."

"You cannot give Papa's name to a rabbit. You have to call him Ralph."

"Malcolm."

"Ralph." Belinda clutched the fur behind the rabbit's neck and heaved him into her arms. "Ralph likes to read comic books with me. You want to read comic books, Ralph?"

Prior to the rabbit, two painted turtles had lived in the twins' bathtub. My mother said they couldn't grow like regular turtles because their shells were painted with enamel. Bianca's turtle was pink and named Vanessa-Marlene; while Belinda's was green and named Bob. Their house was a turtle dish made of plastic, the size of a dinner plate, with curved sides. Inside, you poured gravel and snapped in a palm tree with six leaves. A ramp for the turtles led to that tree. The twins would have turtle races on the sidewalk and prod Bob and Vanessa-Marlene with twigs. If the turtles didn't budge, they'd lift them by their shells—the size of walnut shells, only flatter—and jiggle them hard to get their legs moving; but the turtles would pull in their claws and heads, hiding inside their glossy shells.

Before Uncle Malcolm bought the turtles, six baby chicks used to live in the tub. That's how you had to buy them at the pet shop, my uncle had said—"six chicks in a box"—and he asked my mother if we wanted to split the cost. But she didn't want to share our bathtub with filthy chickens. "I don't know how your sister can live like that," she'd told my father. I loved those chicks and tried to hold them whenever we visited. Though I was careful with them, they'd squirm in my palms, peck at my fingers. Aunt Floria fed them baby food, and the chicks would walk through the pablum and drag it all over the tub. Before anyone could take a bath, Aunt Floria would catch the chicks, set them into a carton, and scrub their pablum footprints from the cracked porcelain. Because they were so messy, they didn't stay long enough to get names. Uncle Malcolm gave them to the milkman, who had a farm in New Jersey. "They'll be so much happier in the country," he'd said. New Jersey was "the country," green and mysterious, with lots of trees and chickens and cows.

Of all the pets who'd lived in the twins' tub so far, my favorite was Ralph, and as I touched the velvet-soft pads beneath his paws, I swore to myself I'd never let Uncle Malcolm take Ralph to New Jersey. "I want to hold Ralph," I said.

"No," Belinda said.

"Why not?"

"Because you got skinny legs."

"And you are BaBelinda," I yelled. "BaBelinda with ugly boogers inside her head."

She reached into the tub, threw a fistful of brown pellets at me, and chased me from the bathroom, the rabbit bouncing in her arms; we ran up and down the dim hallway, dodging four suitcases, their bulging sides secured with rope.

"BaBelinda . . . BaBelinda . . ."

"Suuu-per-mannnn . . ."

As Bianca galloped past me, trailed by the cape Aunt Floria had patched together from various colors of bridesmaids' gowns, I was glad Riptide wasn't allowed to take my cousins to the pool. Aunt Floria was afraid they'd catch polio, even though we'd been vaccinated. At my school, the doctor with the syringe stood at one end of the cafeteria, and the lollipop nurse at the other. The only thing worse than polio vaccination was the screaming of sirens during air-raid drills, when we had to hide under our desks or got marched into a hallway without windows. "Just a drill," Sister would say.

"Skinny legs . . ."

"Ugly-booger BaBelinda . . ."

"Eggplant time," Aunt Floria called. "Time to eat."

"Suuu-per-mannnn . . . Suuu—"

"Girls. Anthony—" Aunt Floria stepped into our path. "Please? Do you have to be that noisy? You put that rabbit back in the tub. Now."

In the kitchen, the warmth of the oven was releasing the smells of my father's food: garlic and Parmesan cheese and tomato sauce. He was stacking wrapped plates in a carton I recognized from previous moves.

"I want to eat honeymoon salad," Belinda said.

"A house full of children for Christmas, Anthony . . ." My father gave me a warning glance. "Won't that be nice?"

My tongue felt sour. "But where do they sleep?"

My mother's cheeks looked pinched as she nested small pots inside big pots.

Carefully, my aunt asked, "Are you getting hungry, Leonora?"

"Not particularly."

"I just have to fix the dressing."

"I want to eat honeymoon salad," Belinda said again.

"What's that?" my father asked.

"Lettuce alone with nothing on. Get it?"

He shook his head.

"Let. Us. Alone. With. Nothing. On. Get it? Honeymoon?"

"I get it."

"That girl—" Aunt Floria turned to my father, who was winding string around her metal breadbox. "She makes me laugh."

"She's funny, all right. She got that from you."

"I don't always remember that part of myself." Aunt Floria set a few lettuce leaves aside for Belinda before she sprinkled oil and vinegar and Parmesan over the rest.

"You used to sew up the ends of my pajama pants," my father said. "Loosen the doorknob so it came off in my hand. Top my strawberry pudding with Dad's shaving cream."

"I did all that." Aunt Floria sounded pleased.

"Funny and mischievous . . . That's what you liked about Malcolm when you met him. The prankster in him."

"Childish and spoiled . . . The son of rich parents who's still waiting for them to come after him and force their money on him. My guess is his parents coaxed him into running away so that they'd be free of him. Their gain, my loss. He doesn't even care that I have to get Belinda to the doctor and talk about her surgery."

"I don't want my sinuses cut," Belinda cried.

"We're just getting your sinuses X-rayed."

"I can help with that," my father said.

"You've already done more than anyone else, Victor."

"Listen to your sister, Victor," my mother said. "She should know."

"I know." Aunt Floria's mouth twitched, and then the rest of her words tumbled out as if they were one: "And-I-hope-for-your-sake-that-you'll-never-have-to-depend-on-family-to—"

"I'm so sorry," my mother said.

"And you don't let me reciprocate . . . not even hem one lousy pair of pants."

"I really am sorry." My mother set down the malted-milk machine she was wrapping into newspaper and cupped Aunt Floria's face between her hands. "We'll get you through this." Gently, she stroked my aunt's face. Up to her temples. Down to her jaw.

Aunt Floria closed her eyes.

"And then we'll do the life . . ." My mother waited for my aunt to finish the sentence.

And my aunt did: ". . . we would like to become accustomed to."

I knew what that meant: a test drive in an expensive car. My mother and aunt loved to get dressed up and pretend they wanted to buy a car. Bianca and I enjoyed it when they took us along, but Belinda got stomachaches, because the cars smelled new—the same new smell that made her sick in fabric stores.

"Here." My mother lit cigarettes for herself and Aunt Floria.

Aunt Floria sucked deeply and tried to smile, but her voice sounded clogged. "I guess we'll bring the car back here, borrow it for a day or so, in case Malcolm messes up at his next job."

I'd heard her joke about that before, wanting to run Uncle Malcolm over and back up over him twice. "Till he's flat like a gingerbread man and has to be peeled off the pavement. Then I'll fold him up, put a stamp on his fanny, and mail him back to England." Only she hadn't done it yet. What would his parents do if they found him all folded up in their mailbox? They probably had a big mailbox because they had a big house. I wondered why she hadn't used Uncle Malcolm's car to run him over. Maybe because he never had a car long enough. One day he'd be dressed like the mayor of England, and the next day he'd be borrowing cigarette money.

When we began to eat, my father said, "I'll pay for Belinda's X rays."

"X rays at the shoe store are for free," I reminded him.

"Those kinds of X rays are different," Aunt Floria said.

Still, I imagined Belinda's face beneath the Easter-green light that exposed the skeletons of my feet at the shoe store whenever my mother bought me shoes that felt stiff at first, as if carved from the bones of children who'd fallen into the X-ray machine.

"Anthony—" My father set down his fork. "It's much harder for your cousins to leave their home behind than it is for you to share your room."

Aunt Floria served him another piece of veal. "I could stay with Mama."

"You stayed with Mama the last time Malcolm was—"

"Old Mrs. Hudak got lots of space," I offered quickly. "She likes company. You can make sure no one steals her."

When Aunt Floria frowned, her eyebrows, just like my father's, met in one black line. "What's that all about?"

"One of those neighborhood sagas." My father shrugged.

"Supposedly, our super was kidnapped when her grandson, the one who stays with her whenever his parents have problems and—"

"The one who's love-struck by Leonora?"

My mother laughed. "He's just a boy."

"Nineteen," my father said. "James is nineteen and old enough to be love-struck. And he's always ogling you in the lobby."

"He's a boy, Floria. Don't believe anything Victor says."

But my aunt leaned toward my father as if not to miss one word of his story.

"Supposedly, James helped his grandmother set up her lawn chair on our sidewalk before he went to the soda fountain, and when he came back, she was gone. Chair and all. What she claims is that two nuns drove up in a truck and—"

"Nuns? In a truck? Is that all you're going to eat, Leonora?"

"I'm done."

"Have some more eggplant or—"

"I know when *I'm* done, Floria."

My father raised his hands to distract them both. "Supposedly, those nuns grabbed the armrest of Mrs. Hudak's lawn chair, hoisted her into the back of that truck, and drove her to Van Cortlandt Park. Nobody believes her."

"I do," I said. "It was a blue truck."

"You saw it?"

"Mrs. Hudak told me."

"Sometimes Mrs. Hudak forgets things," my mother said. "Setting out the trash. Plus mopping the lobby and stairs. We need someone younger for the building."

"She's not that old," I said, alarmed, and resolved I'd help her more from now on, so she could stay in our building.

"You should see her clothes, Floria. John's Bargain Store, I bet. Because they fall apart after she wears them once. She's also been lying about the dumbwaiter, says it doesn't work just so she doesn't have to empty it. When her husband still was the super, the building was taken care of."

But I liked Mrs. Hudak much better than Mr. Hudak, who had died from hiccups last year.

"How did she get back home?" Aunt Floria asked.

"That's where this whole thing sounds made up." My father reached for the ashtray and nudged a few butts aside with the tip of a fresh Pall Mall. "Why would anyone want to kidnap an old lady in an old lawn chair?"

I could think of many reasons: Mrs. Hudak found kangaroos and eagles in the shapes of clouds; let me make lemonade in her kitchen; taught me to form shadow animals with my fingers against a lit wall; let me dust the banister in the stairway; kept big-boy bullies away from our sidewalk by yelling, "You goddamn bastard kids go back to where you belong."

Sitting by her open window, or outside on her lawn chair with the frayed webbing, Mrs. Hudak monitored what happened on our street. She told on kids who crossed without checking in both directions. From what she said, I was the only kid in the neighborhood she liked, and she yelled when Kevin and I played in our courtyard outside her window. I'd feel conflicted, singled out; but I also knew that she couldn't handle more than one kid. That's why she didn't want me around when James visited.

"Mrs. Hudak got two empty rooms," I told my aunt, "and she likes company."

⸺ᴄ꙳

Still—the twins moved into my room.

With their candy lipsticks and dolls.

With their father's accordion and domino game.

With the Superman cape Bianca wouldn't let me use.

With the onyx animals Great-Aunt Camilla had brought them from Africa.

With their real-life rabbit, who was banished to our bathtub.

With cartons full of dresses, always two of each, so they could look alike.

After they messed up my Tinkertoys, they opened the doors on my Advent calendar and ate every piece of chocolate after I'd been so strict with myself, not opening a single door till the day that was written on it.

My parents made me sleep across from my cousins on the cot

that Great-Aunt Camilla took on some of her journeys. "Camilla can afford to travel like that because she doesn't have children," some of my relatives would say. Not having children sounded selfish. As selfish as traveling alone.

Lying on the cot that night, I heard the twins breathing in my bed, filling my room with their breathing, and I thought that, if Great-Aunt Camilla took the twins along—along and away and real soon—it would stop those comments about traveling alone, and on the voyage back she'd still be traveling alone, just as she liked it, because she would have forgotten the twins somewhere far away, in Egypt, say, *in a canoe that floats down the Nile till the Pharaoh's daughter finds the twins and raises them as her own, the way she did with Moses.*

Mortified that Kevin would find out that girls were sleeping in my bed, I didn't let him come up, not even when he stood on the street five floors below our kitchen window and hollered, "Can Anthony come out and play?"

Aunt Floria made do with the couch in our living room. That's how she put it: "I'll make do with the couch." Since she always lived in furnished apartments, she didn't have a bed of her own. "Don't worry about me," she said, "I don't need much space." There was no space left anyhow, once her suitcases and slipcovers and that bride-dummy were stacked against the walls of our living room, hiding our boat picture made of nails and threads that formed sails. Even the landing of our fire escape was crowded with boxes and tarps, blocking Santa's entry into our apartment.

"Let's just hope the fire marshal won't come around for inspection," my mother said.

To be helpful, my aunt got up ahead of my mother to fix breakfast and school lunches, ironed sheets my mother had already ironed, scrubbed the floor behind our ice box, polished the black lid of our white stove, dusted the cookbooks on top of our cupboards. She took a splinter out of my swear-finger before I could bother my mother, and she played checkers with me, especially if I asked while she was writing a letter to Uncle Malcolm Elsewhere.

I'd sit on the counter between our gas stove and the cutting board while my aunt chopped basil for her pesto sauce. Or when she punched the pizza dough and then lifted and stretched it, and twirled it on her fingertips. It wasn't that her food tasted better than my mother's, but that I could feel Aunt Floria's joy inside me as she generously added ingredients instead of measuring them. To be able to cook like that! She kept the cupboards open to get what she needed. Taped to the insides of their doors were theater reviews and schedules. Although my mother didn't see most of these plays, she liked to know about them.

Since I loved the taste of raw spaghetti dough, my aunt would let me take a fistful before she cut it all into strips that she spread on wax paper across the cot and bed in my room to dry. At night, long after we'd eaten the spaghetti, I could still smell dough on my pillow.

Most mornings, she went to mass and helped my mother with the shopping. They didn't have to buy much because my father ordered wholesale—more than he needed for Festa Liguria—so that every evening he could shlep home one or two cartons of groceries. I liked the surprise, because whatever was inside was not what was written on the cartons: Bernice Peaches; Ajax Cleanser; Dole Pineapple; Hoffman Soda. It gave him such pleasure to announce, "Look what I got for you today." Though he only ate fresh bread, he sometimes brought a loaf of Silvercup, my mother's favorite; and whenever he'd ask me, "What does Buffalo Bob say to look for?" I knew he had the good bread in his carton, Wonder Bread, because on *Howdy Doody*, Buffalo Bob always said to look for the red, yellow, and blue balloons on the wrapper. I liked it even more when he brought Dugan's cupcakes or Drake's Devil Dogs.

Aunt Floria didn't want to come along when we went to the Bronx Terminal Produce Market to pick our Christmas tree. "I'll get some baking done while you're gone."

"I will take care of the baking when we get back," my mother said.

"You go and enjoy yourself, Leonora. Hear?"

"And you leave some work for me."

"I want to be helpful."

"I wish you wouldn't."

"I'll have dinner waiting for you. Fried cauliflower and chicken with fennel."

"I wish you wouldn't." My mother crossed her arms.

"It's the least I can do to thank you for letting us live here. How about if I make some cannolis for you, Anthony?"

I nodded. Cannolis were like giant pastry cigars. You could stick them between your lips. Suck the ricotta filling from their shells.

"Did you get rid of that squirrel in your storage room?" she asked my father.

"Even if I catch it, I'm not allowed to kill it. Squirrels are protected by the Parks Department."

"So what are you supposed to do? Feed it through the winter?"

"It's chewing its way into my supplies, making a mess."

"Squirrels are so pretty when they run up trees," Bianca said.

"That's fine," my father said, "but when they come indoors, they're just another type of rat."

"I can shoot it dead." I snatched a wooden spoon from our counter, aimed its end toward the floor. "Bang. Bang."

"We don't use guns, Anthony," my mother said, "including pretend guns."

"Give me that spoon, darling," Aunt Floria said, "and get your boots. Don't forget your earmuffs, girls."

It was snowing as we drove along rows of loading docks, their overhead doors closed, the produce inside, where it was warm. During the summer, when crates of produce were stacked outside and inside, you could still smell the earth on the vegetables. But today, on the docks, men who sold trees stood around fifty-five-gallon drums filled with red-hot coals; and after my father backed the Studebaker against the loading dock at Jack's, where he called mornings to place his produce orders, we stepped into the smell of pine and chestnuts and fire.

The men at Jack's wore gloves with the fingertips cut off, and they slapped my father's back and got the twins' names mixed up on purpose and gave us a newspaper cone with roasted chestnuts. Occasionally, sparks from the coals flared up, fusing with the shouts that hung above the rows of docks as people dickered, and when they carried away their wreaths or trees, they were pulled forward by the ribbons of their frozen breaths.

At Jack's, the men cut the rope from bundles of Christmas trees and showed us only the best ones, full around the base and tapering to a straight point.

They bellowed with laughter when my mother asked, "For that price, do they come with balls?"

"Bells." My father hid his grin behind his glove. "My wife means bells."

"Same thing," one said.

"That's what I've been telling you, Victor." My mother stepped close to the coals, let their heat reach up to flicker on her frosty breath. That flicker was the only thing moving while she stood motionless, spellbound by the fire.

None of the men spoke. But they were looking at her like you look at a dinosaur skeleton you long to touch in the Museum of Natural History, but know you're not allowed to, that you'll be punished, banished, if you were to try. Finally, one of the men sighed. "Lucky fellow."

And then the others remembered how to talk. "Lucky fellow," they teased my father when they tied the tree on top of our car.

On the drive home, my cousins started fighting with each other, and I felt them in my skin like an itch. I didn't want them on the seat with me, in the car with me. Bianca was accusing Belinda of stealing her onyx giraffe, and Belinda said that I had it.

"You're lying," I told her.

"I don't even like it," she said, though she'd been skutching Bianca to trade the giraffe for the bull that was just a chunk of onyx with stubby legs.

"You're lying," I told Belinda again. I liked the giraffe better, too, because the green streaks in the onyx made it look real fast.

"Anthony is being mean," Belinda chanted in her I'm-telling voice.

To keep them both away, I stuck out my elbows. Smoke from my parents' cigarettes coiled upward, flattened itself against the ceiling of our car.

"You don't want to give those fellows any ideas," my father was saying.

"They already got ideas."

"Well, yes, but—"

"You like my raunchy side."

"Not in public."

"Ah, just for you then?"

Belinda yanked at my elbow.

"Stop it."

"I want my giraffe back," Bianca whined.

My mother groaned. "Your sister has unpacked her Toastmaster. Her Mixmaster. Her—"

"The girls can hear you."

I leaned forward. "And her breadbox."

"Right. That hideous breadbox with those hideous flowers painted all over the front."

"The girls—"

"Your sister has hung the pope plus the cardinal. Our entire apartment reeks of mothballs."

"I didn't take your stupid giraffe," Belinda yelled across me to her sister.

"You give it back to me."

"I'll let you play with my bull."

"Floria needs to feel at home with us," my father said.

"She does. Believe me, she does."

"I don't want your stupid bull."

"It's not stupid."

"Stupid and ugly."

I kept my elbows out, pretending not to see the twins, although they bounced against my arms. What if someone else took what you'd been saving up? Would you get ten times as much Advent calendar chocolate in heaven? Or none? And how about purgatory? How much Advent calendar chocolate would you get in purgatory if you didn't tell on the kids who'd stolen it from you?

"While I *don't* feel at home," my mother said. "I can't take a bath without first cleaning after that goddamn rabbit. It's learning to jump from the tub, and I have to keep the door shut to make sure it stays in the bathroom. This morning I found it behind the toilet bowl. Your sister doesn't have a piece of furniture she can call her own, but she can always afford those filthy pets."

"What do you want me to do?"

"She's here to stay, Victor."

"It's just for a while."

"Like six months? Ten years? Whatever sentence Malcolm gets next? And you know what else? You complain about him and his schemes. But you aren't that honest, either."

"Don't you compare me to him," my father hissed.

"All this stuff you bring home—not just food, but plates and silverware and napkins and glasses and God-knows-what-else with 'Festa Liguria' written all over—someone's paying for all that, and it certainly isn't you."

"I don't know what to say to you when you get like that."

"Get like what?"

"You don't know shit about running a business, about writing off expenses."

Their harsh whisper continued while we carried the tree up our five flights of stairs, but when my mother saw that Aunt Floria had dinner ready, she got quiet—so quiet that, at the table, she didn't say "amen" when Aunt Floria finished grace. I wanted the two of them to get up, to start dancing and laughing; but there was no relief—not for them, not for any of us—and though my father praised the fried cauliflower and the chicken with fennel, he had the face he got when he was afraid of upsetting my mother. While I could barely swallow. Not even the sweet ricotta.

Before we went to bed, my father chopped at the sides of our Christmas tree until it fit into our living room with all of Aunt Floria's stuff. I hated how scrawny our tree looked afterwards. What spoiled it more was that we had to shove her fabrics and sewing supplies around the base of the tree, where we used to lay out the tracks for my Lionel trains.

—☙

The next morning, my mother's head was hurting, and she threw up. My father had to lead her by the arm back to the bedroom, where she lay with the door and curtains closed. She used to get a few migraines each year, but now she complained about them daily.

"Maybe you're pregnant," Aunt Floria suggested.

"No." My mother pressed one palm against her belly, her eyes afraid. "No," she said. "It's that smell of camphor that gets me sick."

"I'll air our clothes in the bathroom."

"Then the bathroom will have that smell."

"I'll hang them on the fire escape then."

But my mother took to her bed, yielding her kitchen to Aunt Floria. Light or sound or food made her migraines worse, and I was glad for her when she could sleep. Glad, too, that she didn't see how I enjoyed baking with Aunt Floria for Christmas: pignolata and taralli and mostaccioli. Three evenings in a row, my father put on his hat and took me along to Hung Min's, where we found some of the men from his backgammon club. While they played, I'd get to order my favorites for all of us: moo goo gai pan and fried rice and egg rolls and chow mein. Usually, my father only played backgammon on Mondays, but now he seemed anxious to be away from the apartment. The other men were far older than he, and they'd let me pour their tea and put lots of sugar into the little cups.

Around my mother he was careful. Quiet. Once, when I came into their room, he was sitting on the edge of the bed. "You want me to help you get rid of that migraine?" he asked her.

She hesitated. Then noticed me. "Anthony," she said.

My father kissed her throat. "We could send the boy into the kitchen while we . . . you know . . . ?"

"I couldn't. Not with your sister so close."

Some afternoons, the twins practiced the banana song on the accordion desperately, and with great tenacity, certain that those long-drawn squeaks would bring their papa back.

"Papa will hear us," they told me.

"And then he'll find us."

Since the shoulder straps were too long, they helped each other hold the accordion up and sang, "I'm Chiquita Banana and I'm

here to say: I ta-ke the bananas and I run-a away . . . ," while air
squeezed in and out of the bellows, causing dreadful sounds.

"Papa will find us."

In the meantime, though, the twins kept finding me.

Since Kevin's sister had the croup, I was not allowed in his
apartment, and Mrs. Hudak had just bought a television and
didn't let me talk while it was on. James had helped her move her
furniture so she could see the television from any part of her living
room. She used to sit across from me at her table, or she'd watch
our street from her window, observing more interesting things
than on television while also making our neighborhood safer; but
now I could only see her back and that television. Both Mrs. Hudak
and I loved lady mud-wrestlers because they fought dirty, but I
didn't tell my mother because she didn't allow anything violent on
our television.

I didn't visit Mrs. Hudak when James was around, and he'd
been there a lot since he'd graduated from high school. For a while
he'd worked at Sutter's, selling French confections, then at Mario's
on Arthur Avenue. So far James hadn't found a new job. He didn't
like me—not since I'd asked him why he got tomato-red when he
saw my mother.

The last day of school before Christmas vacation, I ran home to
Creston Avenue and locked myself in our bathroom before my
cousins could get home. Ralph was hunched beneath the sink pipes,
and I lifted him up. With my free hand, I cast shadows of snarling
dogs against the wall opposite the lamp, *dogs that snap at my
cousins' legs, bite off their heads,* but when I remembered how dogs
attacked rabbits, I stopped because I felt sorry for Ralph. Then I felt
sorry for myself, because all I had were shadow animals. I wanted
real animals. With fur and with eyes. Live animals. "You're not
filthy," I told Ralph and kissed the sleek fur on his face.

"Hurry up and flush, Anthony." Aunt Floria was knocking on
the door.

Nobody told her to hurry up when she took her long showers,

singing in Italian as if—so my mother said—someone were stab-
bing her ever so slowly.

I darted past Aunt Floria and out of our apartment. On the
front stoop in our courtyard, Kevin sat playing with his cars.
"Here," he said and handed me his yellow friction car. For himself,
he kept the red one, and we lifted our cars, chafed their wheels
against the concrete steps, again, faster, and again, till their racing
sound became a loud buzz and we let them speed away from us.

Mrs. Hudak banged against her window. "You're making too
much noise. Go back to where you belong."

We scooped up our cars and ran across the street.

"Supposed to check both directions," she called after us.

"Let's spy on her," Kevin said.

The stairway in his building was freezing, and the tar bubbles in
the roof had hardened and cracked.

"My Uncle Malcolm can fix that."

Kevin dropped to his belly and elbows. "Duck and cover."

"Duck and cover." I was Burt the Turtle, crawling behind Kevin
along the flat roof, past metal frames with washlines, past vents.
His corduroys were tight on his ass though his mom bought him
husky sizes at Fordham Boys Shop. We crawled toward the television antennas at the edge, where kids were not allowed, and took
positions for our spying game.

"Uuuughhh . . . uuuughhh . . . Mrs. Hudak . . ." we howled.
"We're going to get you, Mrs. Hudak."

But Mrs. Hudak was hiding from us.

"Uuuughhh . . . Mrs. Hudak . . . uuuughhh . . ."

Kevin had Nik-L-Nips, and we bit off the waxy tops and drank
the syrup while we scanned the sky and our street, especially
Smelly Alley, where anyone could be hiding. Smelly Alley was
down the block from us, a vacant lot with dog poop and broken
glass and sumacs and rusty cans and—most of all—poison ivy.
"Three leaves with a sheen, worse than mortal sin," my mother
had taught me. "Never touch those clusters of three shiny leaves."
"Sheen" and "sin" didn't quite rhyme but were close enough. Except poison ivy was worse than mortal sin, because mortal sin you
could confess to the priest and get absolution; but once you got

poison ivy, you had it for life, and you got it every seven years. But one Sunday last summer, after mass, Kevin—on a double-dare—rubbed a handful of those shiny leaves against his neck, and nothing happened to him. All he said was, "I'm immune." It was a shock to me, a revelation. Here someone had dared touch this curse of the human race, but nothing had happened to him, which meant that if you were immune to something, you couldn't get it. I felt giddy. Free. Because it had to be the same with mortal sin. And if you were immune to mortal sin, you never had to worry about hell. Not even purgatory. But when I touched the poison ivy, splotches of tiny bumps soon formed on my hands and where I'd rubbed sweat off my face. The bumps itched, turned red, and formed hot blisters that oozed foul liquid. Twice a day, my mother would stir half a box of cornstarch into the tub and I'd lie in the lukewarm water, feeling my skin get cooler while I envied Kevin, who had everything: immunity to mortal sin and to poison ivy.

"Mrs. Hudak is mean," Kevin said.

"Maybe she's a Russian spy."

"Uuuughhh . . . uuuughhh . . ."

"Let's play mass."

"I want to spy on communists. Uuuughhh . . . Mrs. Hudak . . ." Kevin's face was red, even though it was cold outside. Especially his big cheeks. My mother called him "lollipop face" because he looked like one of those red lollipops with a red face pressed into them.

"Let's just practice communion."

"We need crackers for communion."

"I don't have any." I pointed across the street and into our kitchen. "We can spy on my aunt."

Aunt Floria and the twins were eating minestrone at my table as if they belonged there. One floor below, we saw the top of Mr. Casparini's bald head, the top of his cigar, the top of his belly while he was sorting his stamp collection. On the third floor, Mrs. Rattner—Pineapple Sheila—was singing while rinsing her bowls and baking pans, and her son Nathan was studying so he could be a dentist. Last week, when Kevin and I had played spies, we'd shot rubber bands at Nathan's window and ducked before he could see us; but he'd still waved at us and stood up, stretching himself as if we'd reminded him to take a break. The next day, Nathan Rattner had left a squishy envelope in our mailbox. On the outside, he'd written "Enjoy, Anthony," and inside he'd stuffed rubber bands of different sizes and colors.

"There she is." Kevin ducked. "Uuuughhh . . . uuuughhh . . . Mrs. Hudak . . ."

I howled along. "We're going to get you, Mrs. Hudak . . . uuuughhh . . . uuuughhh. . . ."

But Mrs. Hudak didn't look up. She walked away from us, pulling her shopping cart.

"She's going to John's Bargain Store," I announced.

Kevin nodded excitedly. "To meet other communists."

—◌℈

Two days before Christmas, Riptide Grandma took me to Arthur Avenue—me alone, not the twins—my father's idea to give me time away from them. At the Italian market, Riptide picked a wrinkled black olive from one of the wooden tubs and laughed when I didn't want to taste it. "One day you'll say yes, Antonio," she said and chewed the olive, slowly, rolling her eyes sideways, just as she always did when she concentrated on tasting. Then she nodded and bought half a pound of those olives, broccoli rabe, tomatoes, and a tall can of olive oil.

At the dirty-feet shop—that's how it smelled—I pinched my nostrils while Riptide bought fresh mozzarella and chose one of the round provolones that swung from the beams above us.

Next we went to the poultry market, where chickens and turkeys watched me from inside their cages. Riptide told the poultry man she needed a turkey big enough for her family. "Everyone's coming over Christmas Day."

He took a turkey from its cage and hung it from the scale by its feet.

"No. I want a bigger one."

But when the poultry man brought a larger turkey, Riptide said it wouldn't fit in her oven.

As he opened the fifth cage, he whispered to me, "Last time I showed your grandmother seven."

The fifth turkey was dangling upside down from the scale, twisting its head as it watched the people in the market. Its face was right next to mine, and all at once it noticed me. Its eyes were curious and shy, and I thought it was a nice turkey.

"Look at that turkey looking at that little boy," someone said.

The poultry man laughed. "That turkey is looking at you, Antonio."

"Gobobobob . . ."

"Nice turkey," I told the turkey. "Nice—"

"Antonio has decided. *Questo.*" My grandmother nodded.

"No," I said. "Not this turkey."

But my grandmother decided this was the turkey I wanted, and when the poultry man took it from the scale and carried it behind the counter, I heard it go "Gobobobob." The counter was too high for me to see what was happening to my turkey, but I knew because I could hear something turning—it sounded like a wheel—and my turkey screamed so hard I got hiccups and I was sure they were plucking its feathers and when it quit screaming quit making any sound altogether I knew they'd plucked my turkey bare and chopped off its head.

"This is much harder for her than for you, Leonora," my father said.

"My soul bleeds for her."

"It's humiliating for her, needing our help like this."

"Oh, but she is so very fortunate to have your understanding. It's certainly more than I get from you." My mother sat up against the maple headboard. "More than Anthony gets from you. Let me tell you, having those girls in his room is miserable for him."

"Let me tell you then that staying in bed is not fighting fair."

"Oh . . . but I am not fighting, Victor." Her chapped lips stretched into a weak smile.

"I wish you were."

She didn't answer.

He touched her shoulder. "Are you quite settled?"

"I may never feel settled again."

He glanced at the stack of magazines on the dresser, *Life* and *Look* and *Good Housekeeping*. "Do you want something to read?"

When she didn't answer, I said, "*Life*. She likes it better than *Look* because it has more pictures."

"I don't want a magazine. Is that all right?"

"Hey," my father said, "I have work to do."

And he was gone, leaving his night socks on the floor where he'd tossed them. My mother made him wear those to bed because he rubbed the bottoms of his feet with sticky ointment.

I sat on the floor next to my mother's side of the bed and started a drawing of the zoo for her. I colored the gate red for her, with yellow and brown, so it was like copper. On top of the gate, I drew the lion, king of beasts. Then bears on top of one arch and deer on the other. The post on one side had a monkey sitting on it, the other a leopard. Tortoises supported the weight of my gate and all its animals, including the owls and cranes. Around the gate, I colored a halo of smoke. A path led through the gate, and at the end of the path I drew the African Plains where ostriches and lions moved freely.

My mother's eyes were closed, and all I could see between the white pillows and the white blanket was her white face, thinner than it used to be, and it occurred to me that she and I—so alike in the narrow shapes of our bodies—were hiding out from the people with sturdy bodies: Aunt Floria, the twins, even my father, who was wearing a tuxedo in the wedding picture above the dresser, squinting with absolute delight at my mother, who stood to his right in a long wedding gown, one arm joined through his. "Victor's sweepstakes smile," my grandfather called it.

Grouped around that photo were other family pictures, five of them showing me as a baby: held by my mother the day she brought me home from the hospital; by my father as he lifted me toward the ceiling fan; and then one picture with each grandparent except for my mother's father, who'd died when she was ten. As I watched her sleep, I felt sorry for her growing up without her father, and that made me wonder why the television never showed the glass-wax father. Maybe he was just in another television room—not dead like my mother's father—or maybe he was Elsewhere. All at once I felt certain that, if only I could decorate our windows with glass-wax bells and snowflakes, I would get my family back the way it used to be—one mother, one father, one boy.

While I was filling in the background of my zoo picture with a jungle just like the ferns on my parents' wallpaper, a loud crash came from my room. Then another. When I got there, Bianca was climbing on my bed, arms through the straps of her cape.

"Don't jump. You'll wake my mother."

She jumped. Tackled me. As I kicked and struggled to get out from under her, Belinda threw herself across my legs, and Bianca squatted on my stomach.

"Let me go."

"If you move, you lose the tickle game."

"I don't want to play your stupid game."

They yanked down my dungarees, my underpants.

"Let me go," I cried, feeling hot and queasy. To be found by the Pharaoh's daughter was too good for the twins. No, I wanted Great-Aunt Camilla to lose them in the desert, where *twin snakes coil around them and choke them, where twin buzzards eat what's left.*

"Let me go! Let—"

"Quiet in there, Anthony, girls." Aunt Floria's voice.

"I'm telling."

"Tattletale."

"Meanie."

The jingle "Don't be a meanie, bring me Barricini" floated through my mind. My mother loved Barricini's chocolates, and sometimes she would get all dressed up and take me for a walk along the tree-lined Concourse, where the wealthy Jewish families lived. We'd stop at Barricini's, nowhere else, to buy chocolate-covered almonds. Inside my head, I could hear the Barricini jingle,

"Don't be a meanie, bring me Barricini," and the jingle was pound-ing through me and I was the one yelling it, "Don't be a meanie bring me Barricini," yelling it faster, now, faster while the twins skittered from me.

"Don't-be-a-meanie-bring-me-Barricini!"

The twins hopped on my bed, watching me darkly through their father's leaf-colored eyes while I tugged up my underpants and dungarees, and when they edged forward I shrieked, "Don't-be-a-meanie-bring-me-Barricini, dontbeameaniebringme—"

"Girls. Anthony—" Aunt Floria again. "What is it now?"

"Barricini," I whispered fiercely while I backed away from my cousins.

In the hallway, Aunt Floria was opening the front door for two nuns. *Nuns know. Nuns know everything. They're here because of the tickle game.* I had the urge to confess though I was afraid I'd only get punishment, not absolution.

"Sisters, come in. Merry Christmas. Come in." Aunt Floria looked as if she were about to receive communion. "I'll get you some eggnog. Fresh yesterday. My brother made it at Festa Liguria. Or if you'd like some of my fig fruitcake—"

"No, thank you."

"We only have a minute."

"Anthony, darling, you get your mother out of bed. Tell her it's the Sisters of Mercy, collecting for the pagan children, and they're in a rush."

What if these are the nuns who took Mrs. Hudak away in their truck? Then they'll take the twins away. Aunt Floria, too. Take them Elsewhere. But not bring them back.

I jiggled my mother's arm. One side of her face was creased, and her hair was flat. Usually, before she went to sleep, she pinned her hair into curls and wrapped toilet paper around them. Slowly—as if she had to learn how to walk—she approached our living room.

"The twins started the tickle game," I told the nuns, "I didn't—"

A sudden sneeze interrupted me.

"Jesus Christ, Belinda." My mother wiped the back of her wrist against her chenille robe. "Bless you, I mean. I'm sorry, Sisters."

Aunt Floria was shoving two nickels and one dime into the slot of the cardboard collection box that had pictures of naked brown children squatting in a patch of grass, their faces sad. One had his head bent while the others picked through his hair for lice or worse. On back of the box was a mother in clothing with a child in clothing, both smiling at a cross. Clothing meant salvation, and what those naked pagan children needed for salvation was the clothing the nuns in Africa would buy for them the instant my aunt finished shoving her coins through the slot. Somehow, I expected those coins to make more of a sound, louder than a church bell.

I felt noble, picturing the pagan children with clothing and without lice, and I waited for my mother to help the children, too.

But she didn't. "Religion," she said to the sisters, "is only valid when it has to do with compassion, not with forcing your belief on—"

"Not now, Leonora." My aunt started apologizing to the Sisters. "I'm sorry, but my sister-in-law, she's been ill."

"It's arrogant to teach these African children that your God is better than theirs." My mother's eyes blazed. Trashing religion did that to her.

"My sister-in-law gets those migraines that—"

"For us," my mother added, "charity is close to home this year."

"If that's all we are to you, Leonora, charity . . ." Aunt Floria began to cry.

"That is not what I said." My mother pressed her fingertips against her temples. Her nail polish was chipped.

"We all do the best we can to be charitable in this earthly world," the older nun murmured hastily.

The other nodded. "In the eyes of our Lord, each act of charity is a prayer."

My mother shivered.

"I didn't want to do the tickle game," I confessed to the nuns. "The twins jumped on top of me and—"

But the nuns didn't glance at me. They were fretting about the chalices at their church. "Those chalices won't last much longer."

"Because they're worn so thin."

"Like a child's fingernails."

—೨

When my father came home with a carton of groceries, the nuns were long gone, and Aunt Floria had piled her belongings in the hallway. He had to climb around them to find her in the kitchen, where she was pacing between stove and ice box, trailed by the scents of mothballs and fish.

"I'll move out, Victor, right after I feed you and your family the seven-fish dinner. Mama says she'll take me and the girls in."

Already, I could see myself *back in my own bed. In my own room. Kevin and I are building bridges from Lincoln Logs. A crane with a real motor from my Erector Set.*

"Let's talk this over, please." My father set the carton on the table. From the hesitant way he unbuttoned his coat, I could tell he didn't want Riptide finding out about the troubles between Aunt Floria and my mother.

"Your wife—" Aunt Floria started.

"Great news," he said quickly. "That squirrel I told you about . . . it ran from the storage room today and out through the kitchen."

"Your wife doesn't want me here."

"One: that is not true." My mother stood in the kitchen door, the belt of her robe knotted around her waist. "And two: I have a name." She was talking in the frosty-slow voice I didn't like.

"Charity, Victor. That's all I am to your wife. She was ready to call a cab for me before you got home."

"Your sister ordered me to call her a cab."

"So now your wife has money to waste on cabs?"

"On an entire fleet of cabs."

My father held up both hands as if to stop an entire fleet of cabs.

The twins were leaning against the wall between the two windows: Bianca with her thumb in her mouth, pupils rolled up slightly; Belinda with both arms around the rabbit.

"Why don't we wait till tomorrow," my father said, "and then decide what to do?"

I stared at him. How could he, now that they were finally ready to leave?

Aunt Floria shook her head.

Let her go, I prayed silently. *Let her go.*

My father stubbed out his cigarette. "At least till tomorrow, Floria? It's getting dangerous to drive with all the snow."

"I have encouraged your sister to stay, Victor. I have tried to do my best with this . . . this situation."

"I have tried harder than your wife."

"I guess your sister wins. Again."

"I have a name too."

My mother groaned. "I can't do this."

Bianca's mouth made sucking noises around her thumb, while her other hand rubbed the side of her cape where the satin was frayed.

My father looked absolutely helpless.

Let her go. Let her go. Let her go. My prayer was becoming music inside my head, vibrating against my temples to the melody of: *Let it snow. Let it snow. Let it snow.*

"What are you humming, Anthony?" my father asked.

Everyone was staring at me.

I trapped my lips between my teeth. *Let her go. Let her go. Let her go.*

My father pulled a stencil kit from the side of his carton and held it as if he couldn't resolve what to do with it. "If you stay . . . the children can do glass-wax decorations together."

"But it's mine!"

"Anthony—"

"Mine alone."

Belinda set Ralph on the floor and got to my father the same moment I did.

But he handed her the stencil kit. "Don't be greedy, Anthony."

Mine alone.

Already, the twins were yanking my stencil kit open: comets and bells and snowflakes cut from thick transparent paper, holly branches and Christmas trees.

"For the children's sake then, I'll stay," my aunt allowed.

Above us, the white blades of the ceiling fan were motionless.

"You go lie down, Leonora."

"Yes." My mother started toward her bedroom. "Of course."

"I'll bring you a bowl of pea soup once I unpack," Aunt Floria called after her.

"Toastmaster Mixmaster breadbox," my mother recited. "Pope cardinal malted-milk machine . . ."

"Pope cardinal Toastmaster Mixmaster . . ." I whispered. "Malted—"

When she shut the bedroom door behind her without swearing at Aunt Floria, I knew it was up to me to restore my family. Otherwise my father would let the twins and Aunt Floria live with us forever, and my mother would get thinner and whiter till she'd vanish in the white bedding.

"Girls, you share with Anthony now." Aunt Floria lit a cigarette.

"You too, Anthony. Share." My father headed toward the bedroom.

But when I picked up the stencil of a bell, the twins edged me aside, and I wanted to take them by the shoulders, shove them out of my apartment, toss their dolls and earmuffs out behind them.

My aunt poured pink glass wax into a saucer, and the twins fought over that until Belinda managed to push one end of the dry sponge in it. While Bianca mashed the comet stencil against one kitchen window, Belinda squished the sponge into the comet's tail. At first it was gloppy, the stomachache pink of Pepto-Bismol, but as it dried it turned paler until it was the color of deep snow after blood has seeped through it. There's something odd that happens to the surface of snow after blood has fallen on it. If the snow is loose enough, blood will trickle to the bottom, leaving an almost white surface and, below it, layers of pink that get darker the farther they are away from you, until it looks as if a red lightbulb were shining up from within the snow. The one other time I would see anything similar would be the following winter, on Castle Hill Avenue, when the family in the house attached to my grandparents' would set up an electric nativity outside. After a snowstorm, Mary and Joseph would be covered to their waists, and between them, where Baby Jesus used to lie in a manger with real straw, a glow would come rising through the snow. All together it would be different, of course. Still, I'd start crying, because it would get me thinking about Bianca again—*I wish I'd never have to see snow again*—about how she lifted her stencil and looked disappointed

SACRED TIME   51

because some glass wax had seeped beneath, making her star messy. *All wrong.*

"All wrong," I told her.

"Less wax," Aunt Floria advised. "Remember now—take turns while I unpack our things."

Belinda grabbed the stencil of a bell and kept it flat against the window, while Bianca dunked the sponge into wax and swabbed it against the glass. From the living room came thuds as Aunt Floria and my father hoisted her stuff back onto the dark fire escape. I could tell the twins were not about to offer me the stencils, but I no longer wanted my turn, because I knew what we would look like from outside if Santa were to watch us. *The three of us. Here. Together. Forever.*

To separate myself from my cousins, I pulled a chair to the other window and knelt on it. In the snow, the water tower on the Paradise became the huge lizard beast, and on Kevin's roof, the antennas became people with hats waiting to cross the street. I pressed my forehead against the icy glass, and as I watched the lights of cars and trucks far below on the white street, I hoped the twins would be gone before New Year's Eve, my favorite holiday, because at midnight we'd put on coats, open the windows, bang spoons against the bottoms of pots in the cold air, and yell, "Happy New Year. Happy New Year. Happy New Year." All through my neighborhood, people would lean from their windows—the O'Deas and the Casparinis and the Weissmans and the McGibneys and the Rattners and the Corrigans—all of us together, kids and parents, all banging pots, all yelling, "Happy New Year . . ."

Not nearly as careful as the television girl, Belinda and Bianca were slopping pink wax on their window, stringing holly branches and comets and bells into garlands that looked like smudges someone had left by mistake, and I felt cheated for ever having wanted the kit.

"Girls," Aunt Floria called, "did you put that rabbit back in the tub?"

"You go," Bianca said.

"No," Belinda said. "You."

"Girls . . ."

"Anthony can do it."

"No. The person who just yelled will do it. You, Belinda. Now."

Belinda scowled at her sister. At me. "Don't touch anything till I come back," she warned, picked up the rabbit, and started for the bathroom.

Snow whirled into my face as I opened my window.

"Not supposed to," Bianca said, shoving herself next to my chair.

Icy wind snaked between my sleeves and wrists. "Listen . . . You hear that?"

"What?"

"Your papa."

"Where?" Her forehead was flushed, her voice eager. "Where is he?"

"Playing his accordion."

"Where? Papa—"

"On Kevin's roof. Sshhh." I touched one finger to my lips and tilted my head as if, indeed, I could hear Uncle Malcolm playing his accordion. Whenever I think back to that moment when I didn't stop Bianca from climbing on the chair with me, that moment when I first knew that I, too, was capable of being Elsewhere, of moving on the shadow side of all that is good, I can indeed hear my uncle's accordion, faintly, then swelling inside my soul. *But that is now.* And that evening it was silent, except for the muffled squeak of wheels on snow.

I raised my hand and pointed. "Over there."

When Bianca—arms hooked through the straps of her satin cape, elbows angled for flight—turned toward me, the warm strawberry breath from her candy lipstick struck my face. "Is it true, Anthony?"

I faltered.

"I really can fly to my papa?"

I still wish I could say I believed that Uncle Malcolm stood on Kevin's roof, playing his accordion, wish I believed that my cousin could indeed fly to him—if not every day, then at least on this eve of miracles. But I did not believe any of that when I told Bianca, "Yes."

LEONORA 1955

Annulments

Leonora spends the afternoon of her husband's engagement party in her bed with James, the grandson of Mrs. Hudak from downstairs. James has dark curly hair, and he works as a waiter at a downtown restaurant where he has to wear a tuxedo. But this afternoon, James is not wearing anything, and as he moves beneath Leonora, his face flushed, she feels distracted by images of her husband: Victor tiling the kitchen floor on his knees, his dungarees stretching over his firm ass; Victor balancing the checkbook for Festa Liguria, cursing as he discovers an error; Victor in front of the mirror dabbing one finger against his beardless chin; Victor kissing the throat of a woman whose voice Leonora would recognize.

Her friend Mustache Sheila has asked her if she's curious what this Elaine looks like, and Leonora had told her she's not. Still . . . she pictures Elaine as a blonde with small earlobes. For three months Leonora has known about Elaine, but not about the engagement party—not until Anthony mumbled something about needing new shoes.

"But I just bought you sneakers."

He pulled at his fingers as if yanking off invisible gloves.

It drove Leonora mad, seeing him like that, mad and worried. But she kept her voice gentle. "What is it now?"

The bones of her son's face lay so close to his skin they seemed to shine through, bluish white. He was receding from her. From the entire family. Often he went without speaking for hours, unless she forced him to say words.

It took him two days to tell her: "Dad says I can't wear sneakers to his engagement party."

───୧

James' hands take hold of Leonora's hips. "Almost—" he pants and turns with her till they lie on their sides, still joined. "I'm almost there."

Just about now Anthony should be sitting at a long table with Victor and Elaine and assorted members of both families. An odd concept—getting engaged while still married. Though Leonora has offered Victor a divorce, it's not what he wants from her. Victor wants an annulment, so that he and Elaine can have a proper wedding in front of a priest, exchanging eternal vows, the same vows Victor exchanged with Leonora twelve years ago. Perhaps one word will be different—"love" instead of "live": "As long as we both shall *love*"—so that Victor can move on to someone new when this love, too, wears thin. Once you have left one marriage, Leonora suspects, it becomes easier to leave a second marriage. Easier yet with the third and the ones after that. Already, she can see *a lineup of her husband's future wives, arranged behind a one-way mirror the way Jack Webb arranges a lineup of suspicious persons on* Dragnet *and questions a witness: "Look closely now. Is there anything you recognize about these individuals?"*

For herself, Leonora does not want to imagine a next husband.

A lover, however, is a different matter.

───୧

James prides himself on being a fantastic lover. He has told Leonora so. "I'm a fantastic lover," he said. But then he spoiled it by asking, "Right?" Still, it's true: sex is something James is very good at. Fantastic. Victor can get sort of Catholic around pleasure, but James is inexhaustible in exploring new angles.

James likes change: he has worked at a radio station, a grocery store, a garage, a bakery, and several restaurants. He wants to get back to being a dog breeder; but if you ask him what kinds of dogs he has bred, he'll admit to having owned one cocker spaniel. For a while. "With excellent papers. I was about to expand my kennel when I received this offer to work for a radio station in New Jersey and left the dog with friends in Queens. . . ."

What's constant in James' life is that he always returns to his grandmother, who won't let him pay rent. He is kind to his grandmother. Leonora remembers thinking that when James was just twelve and washing the outside of his grandmother's windows. When he hopped from the ladder to help Leonora carry Anthony's baby carriage down the front steps, he stared at her with the eyes of a man, not a boy, and she laughed, feeling vibrant in the post-pregnant lushness of her body, amused to envision her place in this boy's fantasies—*for him she is the first woman ever*—and as his greedy eyes fastened on her swollen breasts, she teased him, "What a beautiful boy you are," never anticipating that nine years later he'd become her lover.

Leonora keeps count of their different positions in bed, delighted with her body, the body of a woman whose lover is far younger than she, this lover who has been staring at her ever since he was a boy. How she enjoyed making him blush by smiling at him. Until he grew up and no longer blushed but still stared at her. Like that morning Victor moved out with his cartons and suitcases while she stood in the bedroom, incapable of walking. Afraid she'd stay frozen in that one position, she made herself set one foot forward, then the other, out of the room and out of the apartment and down the stairs, determined to keep going till she no longer had to concentrate on each step. In the lobby, James was leaning against the wall by the mailboxes as if waiting for her, and she stared right back at him.

They didn't speak as he followed her up the stairs, climbing through layers of fresh and stale smells that drifted from apartments as if they were traveling through various countries: fish on two, though it wasn't Friday; cinnamon on three, where it usually smelled sweet from baking; on four, chicken soup, gamy after simmering too long.

They didn't need to speak as she led him into her bedroom, because their fantasies overlapped as though they'd watched themselves countless times in a movie of their own making.

———⟳

The first time Victor returned to the apartment, Anthony locked himself into his room.

"Don't you want to go to the zoo?" Victor shouted through the solid door.

No answer.

"Afterwards I'll take you to the White Castle . . . get hamburgers with lots of chopped onions."

While he was coaxing Anthony to come out, he whispered to Leonora, "I've spoken with Father Bonneducci. Father says the church has become more lenient about annulments."

She motioned him away from their son's door. "How can you annul a marriage when there is a child?"

"That's what I asked him, too. But according to Father Bonneducci, it's done quite frequently."

"You just nullify a child then?"

"Don't do this."

"How can you think of nullifying any child, considering that your sister's child died?"

"Don't bring Bianca into this." He followed her into the kitchen. "Father says—"

"Don't you hide behind *Father-says*." Leonora has grown up within this religion that claims to be the path to God. She's skeptical of any group that considers itself superior, especially Catholicism, which offers you priests as tools to cut out the impure parts of your soul with confession—the killing of your sins—and demands your sacrifice. But to Leonora, sacrifice is poison: it comes at you in the shape of giving and is clotted by resentment.

"Well, what Father says . . ." Victor worked two fingers inside his collar, tugged at the fabric. "Father says he can't marry me in church if—"

"Now you and *Father-says* are getting married?"

"Don't do this."

"Your mother will be so happy. A son in the clergy. Well . . . almost *in* the clergy."

"You know what I mean."

"Then *say* the name of that woman you intend to marry. Unless you're ashamed of that woman."

"Anyhow, he can't marry . . . Elaine and me in church if I'm divorced. Because his loyalty is to his bishop."

"Not to God, but to the bishop?"

"Don't do this."

"And where is your loyalty, Victor?"

"Don't do this."

"Why don't you tell *Father-says* that at least divorce is honest. Because it acknowledges that there once was a marriage."

"But if we annul—"

"It's part of my history, too, Victor, this marriage to you. And I'll be glad to end it with divorce—believe me—but I won't pretend it didn't exist."

"That is not what annulment means."

"What does annulment mean then?"

"That . . . I guess, that it was never right. . . ."

She felt her arms tighten, and when she tried to speak, he stepped back from her as if he could feel her rage.

"Never right in the eyes of the church," he said quickly.

"How about in your eyes?"

"Don't ask that."

"Was it right in your eyes, Victor?"

"Was it right, she asks."

"Yes, because *she*—if you must talk about me in the third person—deserves to know if it was right in *her* husband's eyes."

"Yes."

"Yes what?"

"It was right."

She didn't respond.

"For a long time. All right?"

"Right all right?"

"And now it no longer is right."

"Then how can you annul it? Look at the word. Annul. Invalidate. Void—"

"This is not one of your damn crossword puzzles."

"Too bad. Those I usually solve. Nullify. Cancel. Disclaim—"

"It's only a word."

"A word, yes. That's what Judas thought, too, and of course that led to a bag full of money, a sore throat, and betrayal."

"Here you go with your lopsided Bible stuff. Listen, I'm not crazy about how they uphold their rules by maneuvering around them. But they have to."

"Why do they have to, Victor?"

"Why?" He looked miserable.

"Yes, why?"

"Because . . . those rules have been there for centuries."

"And so they ask us to live a lie by invalidating that we had a marriage? What does that make our son? Illegitimate?"

"Don't ever say that."

"They're screwing with lives. And with truth. Don't you see that?"

"Then where do I go from here?"

"To Elaine. *Father-says* gave you his blessing to fuck her."

"Wine or hot chocolate?" she asks James.

"Hot chocolate."

"That's what I guessed. Still the tastes of a boy."

"Really." He looks sullen.

"In bed you have the tastes of a man."

"Tell me more."

When she returns from the kitchen with his cup of hot chocolate and her glass of wine—a fine bottle of white Bordeaux she's bought for today, not the wholesale Chianti Victor shleps from work—James has fluffed her pillows against the maple headboard so she can sit next to him in bed. He has moved the ashtray—Anthony's first-grade project, seashells from Bermuda glued to a saucer—and he has tilted her reading light so that his flat hand makes a shadow across the wall. His thumb is up, his index finger bent, and when he slants his little finger down and up again, the shadow becomes a barking dog.

"Don't," Leonora says sharply.

"Just something my grandma showed me."

"To you and to Anthony."

"So?"

"It makes you seem like . . ." She lights a cigarette, holds the smoke as long as she can to keep from saying what she knows she'll say anyhow. "It reminds me that you're closer in age to my son than to me."

"Want me to make a shadow cat instead?"

"You don't get it."

"It's because I get it." He drinks from her glass. "Tastes of a boy, my ass."

"Does that mean I'm stuck with your hot chocolate?"

"It means I get both." He laughs. Settles himself against the pillows, tells her about a restaurant he plans to open in Southampton: "French cuisine. One of my friends from work, a chef from Paris, is coming in on it with me."

Grandiose plans. As always. It's impossible to keep track of where James has lived while doing what, and Leonora no longer tries to separate the things James has done from the things James would like to do. Most of Anthony's little friends have made that distinction between fantasy and reality, but for James they still fuse. Yet it's exactly this quality that makes James safe. Because she will never lose herself loving him. One of the best things about their affair is that it is temporary.

James starts rubbing his feet against her hardened soles.

"Now what are you doing?"

"You have calluses."

"You bet." She crouches next to him. Dips her tongue into the hollow of his collarbone. Tastes the salt of new sweat.

He skips a breath. Mumbles, "Calluses . . ." without the earlier conviction.

"Plus, I am a thousand years older than you."

"Good."

She follows his scent down his belly but bypasses his groin, teases him, though he heaves himself toward her. When she inspects his feet, they're soft and narrow with long toes. Hairless. Victor has stubby toes with thick hair, chafed soles he massages with Vaseline and covers with baggy socks he wears to bed so he won't stain the sheets.

"You have the feet of an infant," she informs James. "You *are* an infant."

"My grandmother always bought me expensive shoes . . . never too tight."

After Victor moved out, she found one of his socks under the bed, still shaped by his foot, and she felt his loss abruptly as if it were happening that instant. Even though she'd been done with him ever since that afternoon last February when Anthony was doing his homework at his desk, and she left his room to answer the phone in the kitchen.

—ဒ—

A woman's voice, deep, like a man's almost. "I wouldn't be calling you if I weren't so worried about my sister."

"Your sister? Who—"

"Elaine. You don't know her. But your husband does. And I can't bear to see her like this. Waiting for you to let him go."

Leonora's face felt cold. The phone felt cold. And around it, her hands felt cold. It was the familiar cold that was hers in emergencies, slowing everything and freezing it so that panic had no way in. Leonora loved that cold. Loved its insulation. Its clarity. Loved being able to count on its dignity to be there for her. And within that cold she knew the woman was telling the truth. Not because Leonora didn't trust Victor—it was more complicated than that, had to do with punishment. So much had felt like punishment since Bianca's death. Punishment of the parent who had not lost a child. *At least not an already-born child. After you have been spared that, you are willing to give up almost anything, even your belief in your son. And live instead with a measure of suspicion.*

Not that anyone blamed Anthony.

"Poor boy . . ." they'd whisper.

"That girl wanted to be Superman."

"Talk to me, Anthony."

"There's nothing you could have done to stop Bianca."

"To witness her fall . . ."

"She was always trying to fly."

"You must eat something."

". . . so terrifying for him."

Even Floria, disoriented by grief, said, "Let him be. Don't make him relive it."

After you have been spared that loss of your already-born child, you are even willing to give up your husband. Insurance against losing still more.

"Mrs. Amedeo?" Deep voice. Hesitant voice. "I'm sorry to be the one to—"

"Tell me about your sister," Leonora's cold, slow voice said.

"They love each other. They've been wanting to be together. Except Vic says you won't give him a divorce."

"How long have . . . Vic and your sister been lovers?"

"A little over a year."

"What month?" Leonora had to know if it started before or after Bianca's death.

"Why do you—"

"What month did it start?"

"January."

A year and one month ago . . . just after we bury Bianca. Victor goes to the funeral alone, stands in for the three of us, because we don't want Anthony to see the coffin. I keep him with me that day, take him to the Museum of Natural History. The weeks after that, trying to do other things with him that are normal. A movie at the Paradise: Abbott and Costello Go to Mars. Reading together in the library on Bainbridge Avenue. Inviting Kevin and Mustache Sheila along to Jahn's and sitting beneath a stained-glass lamp eating banana splits. And then—late one evening—laughing, suddenly laughing, because Victor comes home with his beard shaved off.

Feeling ashamed for laughing because of Bianca, and yet making it last because laughing makes me feel alive. Telling Victor I wouldn't have recognized him if I'd seen him on the street. Where before his jaw was squared off by the edge of beard, he now has a round chin, pale. But at least no sloping jawline for him, though I baited him once, "Is that why you have a beard?" A valley between his upper lip and nose, quite defined. I rub my cheek against his, tease him. "Like having a different man. How safe . . . having an affair within our marriage." His sleek face against mine reminds me of my first kiss—Stevie Klein in high school—and I feel vaguely unfaithful. But it's a degree of unfaithfulness I can handle. Enjoy, even. But Victor dodges my embrace, gets skittish when I try to seduce him. I take my distance, figure I'll wait till he grows a new beard, because that's the man I know. Not this stranger whose sleek face makes him elusive, evasive. Makes him Vic.

Whose reluctance had nothing to do with Leonora's eagerness, but rather with this Elaine, who either had a sister or was pretending to be her own sister on the phone. If so, Elaine's willingness to fight for Victor impressed Leonora, who was not willing to fight for him at all. "You don't like beards, do you?" Leonora asked her.

". . . No. But what does that have to do—"

"When do they see each other, your . . . sister and Vic?"

"Thursdays. Thursday evenings."

Thursdays. Those evenings that separate Victor's weeks. Evenings when he prepares lists for his busiest days—Saturdays and Sundays.

"And usually Mondays. For lunch."

"Of course." *Monday. His one day off. A day to do errands.* "And what is it you want from me?"

"Just to tell you."

"Yes."

"So you can be aware."

"Yes."

"And to find out if you're willing to let Vic go. Or if he's lying."

"Vic never lies. Believe me."

"He wants to be with her."

"With your . . . sister, yes. So you're telling me. And you? What do you want for yourself?"

"I'm her sister." The voice, higher now. "And I want what's best for her, but I'm worried—"

"My soul bleeds for you."

"I'm worried about—"

"Worried about Elaine. Frantic about Elaine. Distraught. Anxious. Shaken—"

"He hates it when you get that way with the words."

"He said that to you? Or to your sister?"

"I have to go."

"You have asked your questions. Now grant me the courtesy to answer mine. How did you and Victor meet?"

A pause. Longer than a minute. But she was still there. "A dinner he catered at . . . at the place where Elaine works."

"How did it begin between you?"

"I can't."

"How did it begin?"

"Ask him." And she was gone, Elaine or Elaine's sister.

Leonora hung up the cold receiver. Tucked her hands beneath her armpits to warm them. Picked up the phone again and called Mustache Sheila. "Can Anthony stay with Kevin overnight?"

"Sure. What's the matter?"

"Just something Victor and I have to take care of."

"You don't sound good. Are you—"

"I can't talk about it, Sheila."

"Send Anthony over. Anytime. You hear that?"

Thin neck curved over his marbled notebook, Anthony was sitting on his bed next to his favorite toy, Robert the Robot, silvery gray, with wheels and arms that could move.

"You should be at your desk," Leonora reminded him. "Otherwise you'll ruin your spine and your eyes."

Without looking at her, he slid off his bed.

"It's not that important," she said, hating his obedience. "You can stay on your bed."

He stopped moving. His eyes darted from the bed to Leonora, then back to the bed, and when she touched his cheek—his triangle of gaunt cheek—he flinched but didn't say anything. He'd been trying to get by with shrugs and nods. In school he did well enough with his written work. That's why the nuns didn't try too hard to make him talk. "We have other children who are shy like your Anthony," they would assure Leonora.

"But he wasn't like that before," she'd say. What she couldn't explain to the nuns was how he'd been wrapping himself around the memory of Bianca falling, wrapping that memory into a space so tight and small that the rest of him was left pulpy, easily smashed.

Leonora knew what that was like, because she, too, had that tight, cold space inside her. Ever since she was a child. Except within her it had grown tighter by and by, while for Anthony it had happened all at once the moment of Bianca's fall; and he hadn't learned yet to use that space to protect himself the way she used to whenever her father had raised his fists. *Fifty-four days of my life. Spaced far apart. Over four years. Then not so far apart. You count them. Mark them in the back of your photo album. One flat line for each. Fifty-four days of fists without warning. And the fear that waits for you every dawn—"If you tell, you'll really get it"—until your father dies.*

Not now. She kissed the top of her son's hair. *Don't think of it now.* "Guess what?" she said. "Kevin's mom says you can stay over."

Anthony crossed his skinny arms.

"Hey . . . you like Kevin. You're his best friend."

He nodded.

If she'd known a way to blast his cold, tight space open without injuring the rest of him, Leonora would have. Instead, she gently coaxed him. "Take your school things along."

He slipped his pencil into his Davy Crockett pencil box, slid the wooden top closed.

"Pajamas. Clothes for the morning. Do you want to eat something before you go?"

He blinked as if incapable of deciding.

Lately she'd been waiting him out till he had to make a choice for himself; but today she rushed him. "I'll make you a salami sandwich while you pack your things."

He grimaced as if food were repulsive, an obligation that kept him prisoner at family dinners. To think how he used to enjoy eating, but now even sweets no longer interested him. Sweets and words.

“You don’t eat enough. See, now I’m sounding like your Aunt Floria.”

Still, he didn’t eat, and when he was gone—reluctant he was in leaving, so reluctant—Leonora filled the bathtub. Washed her hair and dried it, letting it fall over her shoulders. While all along her heart—slow and cold—beat inside her chest. She drew a narrow line of black along her eyelids as if she were getting ready to go downtown for a show. She darkened her lashes, painted her lips deep red, buttoned the silk dress Floria had sewn for her; and when she sat down in the living room, facing the entrance hall, she saw herself as if on stage—this woman waiting for her unfaithful husband—and she was able to appreciate the drama, as well as the potential of even greater drama. That’s what she looked for the instant the curtain rose: drama in setting and costume; drama within the first words. She wanted drama to sweep her onto the stage until she was so much part of it that she forgot she was sitting in a darkened row.

She wanted it to be that real.

As real as Victor’s surprised expression when he came in and saw her dressed up and quiet.

“Hello,” he said heartily, acting as if there were nothing unusual about her waiting for him like this.

She looked at his naked face—looked steadily, solemnly—and felt articulate without words.

“How was your day, *mia cara?*” Victor asked.

“Where’s Anthony?” Victor asked.

“Probably at Kevin’s. Right?” Victor asked, still playing his part.

She wondered if not speaking was like that for Anthony. To have all of them dance around him with words? Not all bad. A certain power, pleasure even, in letting others do the words for you.

“I get it. You didn’t feel like cooking tonight?” Victor asked.

“Are we going out to eat?” Victor asked.

“Tell me about Elaine,” she said quietly.

His face arched up. Ashen. Startled. “What do you mean?”

That moment, Leonora learned how to wait. Learned all a woman as fidgety as she would need to learn about waiting in a lifetime. While her husband unbuttoned his left cuff. While he folded it up twice. While he started on the other. While she noticed a speck of lint on the carpet.

Slowly, Victor lowered himself into the chair farthest away from her.

She counted the frames that hung on the wall behind him: five.

Counted the faces of family in Anthony's first-communion photo: ten.

Counted the nails in the string picture of the sailboat: seventy-four.

Said: "I know, Vic." And felt him struggling. Resisting. But she pulled him in. Felt strong and beautiful and cold as she pulled him in. "I know about you and Elaine." She was both—on stage and in the audience—being and watching this woman who looked extra-ordinarily calm; this woman whose black hair framed her thin neck; who didn't look at him directly, just let her eyes follow the vines and leaves in the carpet, follow the vines out to the fire es-cape, along the washlines and back in, along the walls and to the frames above him. Five. "But I want to hear about her from you, Victor."

She pulled him in closer yet, until his words slopped on the floor between them and froze into ice thick enough to keep him from reaching for her, ice fragile enough to make any crossing treacher-ous. She let him talk. The habit of confession. Of trading sins for absolution. Sitting as still as a priest in the confessional, she con-cealed all shock, all sadness, all rage, and whenever Victor hesi-tated, she said, "I know," and bludgeoned him with her brutal silence till he said Elaine had seduced him.

"Oh, please," Leonora said.

"I swear I didn't intend for it to turn into sex."

"What did you think it would turn into? A cartwheel? A Ferris wheel? A—"

"It's the truth. She seduced me."

"And you held still while she seduced you. Of course. What else could you have done? Now that was the first time, right? Tell me, how many times did she manage to seduce you over the months?"

"I'm ending it with her."

"Don't do it for me."

"What are you saying?"

"That you're on your own. That you've already left me," she said, and felt stunned by utter loneliness. "At least have the decency to admit your part in that affair. Not that decency has anything to do with it."

"I'm sorry. I am. I want us. You and me and Anthony."

"And Elaine. And Elaine's sister."

"She doesn't have a sister."

"Right." Leonora was reminded of a documentary she'd once seen about one afternoon in a marriage. The conversations between the woman and man were bizarre—their incessant probing of each other's thoughts; their fussy competition for the affection of their five dogs; their inept cooperation in tidying their grimy kitchen—but once Leonora got beyond wondering why they'd let any filmmaker into that private mess of their lives, she realized that for them all this was normal and that, if a filmmaker were to follow any two people who were close to each other—follow Victor and herself—just for a few hours, they, too, would come across as bizarre: the things they did in private; the way they talked private-talk; the words and the gestures and the habits. Except that most people knew not to expose all this to a filmmaker. Still, the impact of the film on Leonora was her amazement at what people took for ordinary, because, for this woman and this man, what they revealed about themselves was not bizarre at all. At least not half as bizarre as this conversation with Victor.

Not even ten percent as bizarre as hearing Victor ask: "You want me to call Elaine now? Tell her I won't see her again? I will. If that's what you want me to do. I'll call her in front of you. To prove to you that I'm ending it with her."

"You expect me to take one phone call as proof? After you've been lying to me for one year and one month?"

His lips moved as if he were doing the math.

"How many seductions were you exposed to in one year and one month?"

He reached for the phone. "You can listen to what I tell her."

"You would do that to her? Have your wife listen in while you break up with your lover? Don't you think she deserves more?"

Victor stared at her.

"At least have the balls to tell her in person. You can't just fuck someone—"

"I hate it when you use that word."

"And I hate it when you *do* that word with someone else."

"I am sorry. I said I was sorry."

"You can't just fuck someone for one year and one month and then end it over the phone."

"You're sending me back to her?"

"Are you afraid she'll seduce you again?"

———⟶

Leonora runs her hand through James' hair—hair so curly and lush it snags her fingers—then down his spine, across his buttocks, flatter than Victor's. As she tightens her fingers, she feels him squirm with pleasure. Away from James, she barely thinks of him.

"What happened between you and Mr. Amedeo?"

For an instant, she thinks he means Victor's father, then realizes he's talking about Victor. "What name do I have when you think of me?" she teases him. "Mrs. Amedeo?"

"Leonora. I thought of you as Leonora whenever I thought of doing this with you."

"Good answer . . . I'll tell you what happened between me and Mr. Amedeo. Another woman got involved in my marriage."

James laughed.

"It's not intended to be funny."

"Just how you said it. Like you invited her into your marriage."

"Most definitely not."

"You know what's nice?"

"Tell me."

"That we're using each other without pretending that it's something else."

"I'm not using you. I don't believe in using anyone. And I'm—"

"'Using' is the wrong word. What I mean is—"

"Fucking?"

"Yeah . . . fucking."

"Fucking each other without pretending for it to be love . . . I like that."

———⟨⟩———

They did try, she and Victor. Tried with their marriage after he left Elaine. Tried to be together more. Tried to talk and tried to listen. But Leonora made the mistake of wanting to understand—not only why Victor had been unfaithful, but also what her own decision would be. That's why she encouraged him to take her inside his dreams, his fantasies. "No secrets between us, Victor. No lies."

And he made the mistake of making her his confidante. All for the sake of honesty. Also because she was the only one he could talk to about Elaine.

She barricaded her jealousy inside her cold calm heart; didn't flinch when he confided how often he thought of Elaine; witnessed his exquisite pain at saying the name of his beloved aloud: *Elaine*; understood that he needed to feel that charge at hearing himself say: *Elaine*. Because it had been like that for her, too, when she had started loving Victor: tasting the sound of his name, *Victor*; needing someone to witness that sound: *Victor*.

He offered her more than she wanted: how he envisioned Elaine thinking of him at the exact moment he was thinking of her—

"Thinking what?"

—how he'd dreamed that Elaine was getting on the El in front of him at White Plains Road while it was raining—

"Did she look back to see you?"

—and that he'd followed her, without her noticing, to the Crotona Park station and from there to her apartment—

"What is it like, her apartment?"

—with the green kitchen cabinets and the purple carpet, purple leaves on purple, and that they'd barely gotten inside before they'd made love—

"Fucked," Leonora said. "That's not love."

—in their wet clothes, standing against the door—

"You didn't take anything off?"

—and how he'd imagined pulling off his shirt and Elaine kissing the dimple on his shoulder and—

"You do not have a dimple on your shoulder," she whispered, the rage harsh in her throat.

"Well, I do."

"No, you don't."

"I do." Stiffly, he pointed to his right shoulder. "Here," he said.

"I would know if you had a goddamn dimple on your goddamn shoulder."

"Want to see?"

"Spare me."

Because he had torn the marriage vows that were sacred to her, she questioned his faith, his relationship to his God, trying to tear what was sacred to him. Whenever he'd wrest himself from those raw and strange conversations, she'd remind him that she'd rather know than speculate. What they created between them was a greedy and nightmarish honesty. Days and hours they spent on feeding this honesty with their pain, with their satisfaction at keeping their marriage alive, until the honesty got so fat that it craved more.

—⟨⟩

"I'm crazy about your body," James tells her.

He *is* crazy about her body. He has told her. Many times. Leonora used to think he was merely saying it the way some men believe they have to tell you they love you once their hands get inside your clothes. Not that she has a lot of experience, but she reads enough to know that, indeed, James is crazy about her body.

"You are fantastic in bed," he tells her as he straddles her. "I've never been with a woman who likes sex as much as you."

For an instant she feels ashamed. *Insatiable.* She doesn't like to feel insatiable around food or sex.

But already James is pushing himself inside her. "Am I the best lover you've ever had?"

"The best," she says, resolving that not even shame will distract her as she yields to the urgency between them.

———∽———

When Victor arrived that morning to get Anthony, he was wearing a tux and carrying a Hoffman Soda carton. "Look what I got for you today."

"I can't believe you're shlepping groceries to me on your engagement day."

"I got you Dugan's chocolate doughnuts and a butter dish and—"

If she didn't stop him, he'd pack two cartons every day at work, one to drop off with her, the other to take home to Elaine. "Why, Victor?"

"Because we need a butter dish."

"We?"

He glanced around the room as if making sure she hadn't moved the furniture without consulting him. It made her want to drag the couch into the bathroom, her bed into the middle of the living room. Just to unsettle him.

"Anthony . . ." she called.

He opened his door as though he'd been standing behind it, wearing a new suit plus the black shoes Victor had bought for him.

"Your father is ready to go."

"I'll get him back to you early evening, if that's all right with you," Victor said, but he waited as if hoping she'd prevent him from going through with this foolishness. The collar of his new shirt pinched his skin, pressed a ridge into his neck.

She felt a strange sense of finality, more definite than on the day he'd moved out. It made her temples ache, and she pressed her fingertips against them.

"Another migraine?" Victor asked.

"Nothing you can do."

"Well . . ." He got this nervous little grin on his face, the grin she'd found charming when she'd first met him.

"Don't even think about it."

"Well now . . ." He ruffled their son's hair.

But Anthony jerked his head aside. He usually was edgy before Victor picked him up, angry after he was back home.

"What have you told the boy about me?" Victor had asked her. "He's content when he's with me, and I can't understand why he's so aloof between visits, why he refuses to talk to me on the phone."

"Don't blame me," Leonora had said. "He makes his own observations."

One afternoon last month, when she'd taken the bus to retrieve Anthony from Victor's tiny apartment off Westchester Square, she'd found them sitting on the sunny front stoop, Victor's arms loosely around Anthony, who sat with his back to him. Victor's left palm lay against Anthony's chest, and she wished that they both would harbor that touch, Victor's palm against their Anthony's chest just like this, and that they would turn to that memory whenever they'd miss one another.

———ᘓ———

"Well now . . ." Victor said again, moving one hand across his jaw as if searching for his lost beard. "Anthony, the two of us better be off."

As Leonora bent to kiss her son's cheek, it gave her some measure of satisfaction that he did not shrink from *her* touch, and that Victor noticed. "Have a real good day with your dad," she told him as if it were a regular visit, as if she were not worried about him. At least her father-in-law had promised her that he'd sit with Anthony. And there'd be others in the family, including Belinda.

She listened to their steps in the hallway, on the stairs, until she could no longer hear them. Eyes closed, she rubbed her temples. Orgasms were the best remedy for migraines, but James was still at work, and she didn't feel like masturbating. She was restless.

Searched for something to occupy her till he arrived so that she wouldn't think of Victor with Elaine. She turned on the radio, filed her nails, flipped through copies of *Look* and *Good Housekeeping*, and when she came across instructions for decorative centerpieces, she chose to make the most ludicrous one, an edible basket.

At Russ' on 183rd she bought the vegetables she needed, then got Pall Malls at the candy store. As she crossed the street, the old tailor in Koss' window looked up from his sewing machine. At the Hebrew National Deli, she waited in line for pastrami on rye and a bottle of Dr. Brown's cream soda, which she drank while working at her kitchen table, weaving strands of dough into a basket. But she didn't feel like eating the sandwich because she was filling up on dough. Like Anthony, she preferred raw dough over anything baked, liked how it swelled inside her like light, adapting itself to her shape without making her feel heavy.

While the basket was in the oven, she got out her rolling pin to flatten red and yellow peppers, and then pressed flower shapes from them with cookie cutters. She carved radish roses, fashioned stems from asparagus, leaves from peapods. Her ferns were scallions and celery, cut into long strips, and she was arranging those around the flowers inside the warm basket when James rang the bell. She took one last look at her creation and was stunned into disbelief. Nothing was what it seemed: her braided basket was not rattan but bread, and her flowers were not flowers but vegetables. Altogether, her centerpiece looked exactly as it had in the magazine: false.

─୬

As she strokes the insides of James' thighs, he curves himself toward her. She is amazed that she is capable of having sex without love. Amazed and a little smug. An added benefit is that, with all these orgasms, she's hardly had any migraines.

He touches her left eyebrow with his ring finger. "How did you get this?"

"I was born with it."

"Looks almost like lightning struck you here."

"Lightning . . ." She smiles. Sees herself *standing still beneath a tree as it is split by lightning. While she stays intact—the one change her eyebrow. Like the signature of lightning. Daughter of lightning. Lightning herself. Fast and hot and powerful.* As a girl she used to turn the left side of her face away from her mother's camera to hide this eyebrow that was almost entirely white except for a few dark hairs where it began. But Victor loved what he called the light side of her face, and she came to love it, too. The picture she framed of their wedding is the one with her face turned fully toward the camera, her eyebrow as white as her gown.

As James traces her eyebrow with one thumb, it moves her that he, too, appreciates that uniqueness in her. Even though he is so young. Maybe all along he's been more mature than she thought.

But he destroys that illusion. "Have you ever thought of dyeing it black like your other eyebrow?"

"I don't want to dye it black."

"Don't get so mad. I mean, you paint your fingernails. And you wear lipstick. And—"

"That eyebrow defines me."

"Sure it does. It's only that—"

"What?" She sits up. Reaches for the wineglass.

"Never mind."

"It's only that—what?"

"That you'd be a real knockout if you dyed that eyebrow."

"Maybe I don't want to be a real knockout." She hears the sharpness in her voice and thinks how much quicker this man retreats from her edges than Victor. James cannot match her there. Cannot grind his edges against hers and set off fire. Not like Victor. It makes her feel sorry for James. Makes her wonder how many men she will scar with her edges. *I hope there'll be many.*

Setting down her glass, she reaches for James, traces the dark curls on his chest with her tongue, draws him close to her skin, aroused by his swift desire that blots out images of Victor walking toward a distant and deceptive altar.

Minutes after James leaves comes a knock on the door, and she opens it in her robe, thinking he must have forgotten something. But it's Victor's sister in the black party dress that used to fit just right but now hangs on her with the darts in the wrong places and the scalloped hem drooping.

"What is it?" Leonora shifts one hip into the opening of the door to keep Floria out.

"I want to be sure you're all right."

"I am very much all right."

"May I come in?" No makeup ever. Just planes of pale, mobile skin. And that wide, mobile mouth with one freckle on the left side.

"I'm about to take my bath."

"Only for a few minutes? You don't even have to talk to me."

"Did you go?"

"He's my brother."

"So . . . how was it then, his engagement party?"

"Sickening. I couldn't stay."

"Oh." Leonora steps aside. Lets her in. "Anthony . . . How did he—"

"Quiet. The way he gets, you know? But not unhappy."

"To think I'd ever settle for having him 'not unhappy.'"

"He and Belinda were playing dominoes. My parents are sitting with them. Malcolm, too."

"I want a bath. I'm so . . . tired. And—"

"I figured we might want something special." Floria rummages through her big handbag: the smell of mothballs . . .

Leonora fans one hand in front of her nose. She hates that smell.

. . . a pack of Lucky Strikes . . . two half-empty bottles, one black, one clear. She hands them to Leonora. "Sambuca. I stole them."

Leonora grins. "From Victor's party?"

"You mind?"

"Let's drink to that." From the mahogany buffet, Leonora gets two of the gold-rimmed shot glasses with the logo "Festa Liguria" that Victor brought home after catering a bar mitzvah.

"Coffee beans. You got coffee beans for good luck?"

"Only ground coffee. I'll get it. You stay here."

But Floria follows her toward the kitchen she hasn't entered since Bianca fell. She has never spoken to Leonora about Bianca's death. For a while, she couldn't even bear to be on this block of Creston though she lives five minutes away on Ryer Avenue, in a ground-floor apartment for which Riptide put up the deposit and Victor the first month's rent.

"I'll get the coffee." Leonora stops her from entering the kitchen. "Really."

Floria passes her. "I think—I think I'm ready to be in there." But in the open doorframe she falters, her back slumped, before she pulls herself inside, one hand reaching for the wall as if she were walking on an ocean liner. Leonora has never been on an ocean liner, at least not at sea—just the *Queen Mary* and the *Mauretania* when she'd picked up Aunt Camilla—but she has read how, even after you're back on land, you'll hold on to walls for days because you'll feel the ground beneath you slanting. And that's how Floria is walking.

Leonora grips her arm. "Here." Leads her to a chair with its back to the windows. "Sit here." Gently, she presses Floria down, feels her shoulders through the fabric of the dress like planks. "You know what I'd like to do soon with you?"

"No."

"Go downtown and try on the most expensive clothes we can find." Leonora knows that what gives Floria more of a lift than anything else is the feel of expensive fabric against her skin, the kind of details you'd never find at Alexander's.

"All right," Floria says without enthusiasm. Above her, the fan cuts the light, makes it blink as if the entire room were breathing. But it's really Floria's breath, the kind of breath you have to strain for.

Leonora reminds her, "You used to love those excursions, the two of us, no children along, all dressed up." She reminds Floria of walking into the most exorbitant stores on Madison or Fifth, trying on clothes that cost more than a year's rent. Floria would comment on the quality of the work, compare it with her hems, her seams. In the dressing room, she'd study the design, get out the notebook with her drawings and fabric swatches and pictures from magazines, and sketch rapidly: the way in which a dart might angle, or a waistline might gather, or a collar might drape.

"I still remember when you sketched that hem at Bergdorf Goodman's."

"I don't copy everything I see."

"Of course not. Only details that appeal to you."

"To steal an idea in its entirety would be unethical."

"But to be inspired by someone else's idea is different."

"We need coffee beans."

"We'll do it like this." Leonora licks her right index finger, dabs it into a can of Chock-full-o'-Nuts-is-the-heavenly-coffee, and licks off the brown granules. "Pretty bad. See?"

Floria tries it. Grimaces.

"It'll be better once we chase it with Sambuca."

"Which one do you want?"

"The black. It's thicker. Like oil almost."

"You wouldn't drink oil."

"Okay, not oil. How about like coffee liqueur?"

"The black is not thicker."

"What are you? A Sambuca expert?"

"The black only seems thicker because the clear Sambuca looks like water."

"It also flows like water. Faster than the black."

"We simply must conduct some experiments then." Finally, Floria manages a smile.

If this is what it takes, Leonora will play along. "We simply must." She knots the belt of her yellow robe. "Let me get a few extra glasses." But she can't move, can't look away from the smile, an inward smile that brings some of the light back into Floria and reminds Leonora of the love that used to link them, love for each other's children while they bent across the twins' stroller, across Anthony's baby carriage; while they took their children to the carousel in Palisades Park and strapped them between the swan's angel-wings, safe for children too small to ride the horses that moved up and down on poles. "Glasses," she reminds herself and darts into the living room. Returns with the two bottles and four shot glasses. She fusses with them, lines them up on the kitchen table in front of Floria.

Who sits there so stiffly.

Who says, "I have missed you."

"I've missed you, too."

Who says, "I get afraid of sleep."

"Of nightmares?"

"Of not being able to sleep."

"Have you tried counting backwards?"

"I used to look forward to sleep. Now I'm tired all day and all night and I still can't sleep."

"You will again," Leonora says.

From Malcolm—who has been amazingly devoted to Floria, who has managed to stay out of jail since his release four months after Bianca's funeral, who has been holding the same job with Solid Roofing—Leonora knows that sometimes Floria stays in bed for days, once as long as eleven days, seldom bathing or eating. Whenever Leonora visits her during those spells, Floria seems slow, inert, forgetting what Leonora said the moment she said it, forgetting what she was about to do. She doesn't let Leonora help her get up, doesn't want to talk, not even sit up in bed, just lies there without a pillow beneath her head. She, who's always been on time with her sewing business, now neglects deadlines. Her sadness can be set off by a crooked seam, say. By a cracked eggshell. A lost glove : . .

Last October, Malcolm dragged Floria out of bed and to Montauk for an off-season special, three nights for the price of two, hoping that walking on the beach would make her feel better. And it did. For a while. Until the sadness claimed her once again. It always got bigger than what had started it. Immobilized her.

People in the family took turns staying with her while Malcolm was at work and Belinda in school. Once, Leonora arrived to find the apartment open. She followed the short hallway into the kitchen, where Floria had squeezed a brown, lumpy couch between the stove and her sewing machine. There was no living room. Sounds of weeping came from the bedroom behind the kitchen.

Then Belinda's voice. "Don't do that. Please, stop—"

Floria was sitting on the floor, rocking herself, moaning.

Quickly, Leonora knelt in front of her, brought both arms around her, started rocking with her. "Don't you have school?" she asked Belinda.

"I didn't go." Belinda's eyes were frightened. "Mama found Cuddles on the bottom of the bird cage." From the way she said it, Leonora knew the parakeet was dead.

"What did you do with it?"

"I wrapped him in a dishtowel."

"I'll take him with me."

Belinda looked alarmed. "But don't flush him."

"Of course not," Leonora lied. "I'll give him a burial."

Heat climbed from Floria's scalp into Leonora's face. The grass-and-vinegar smell of tears.

Rocking, and gradually slowing the monotonous back and forth, Leonora whispered, "It's all right," knowing it never would be all right again—for Floria or Belinda or any of them.

"About that Elaine . . ." Floria lights a fresh cigarette from the butt of her last one. "She salivates when she speaks."

Leonora laughs aloud.

"You want a description?"

"No." Leonora shakes her head. Shrugs. Says, "Yes."

"Makes you want to wipe her mouth."

"More," Leonora demands.

"She has gangly legs and forward features."

"Forward features?"

"Well . . . those lips. And then her forehead and chin stick out."

"Neanderthal style?"

"Not quite. But the general direction."

"I am so happy for Victor." When Leonora opens the black Sambuca, its licorice scent hits her before she can pour it. "It *is* thicker," she insists, watching it fan out in two of the glasses.

Floria opens the clear Sambuca. Splashes some into the other shot glasses. "Same consistency."

"She's a blonde, right?"

"Mouse-blonde. Thin hair."

"Mousy . . . thin hair." Leonora leans forward, lets her abundant hair tumble across her face. Shakes it back. Sighs. "My hair is too heavy."

"Poor you." Floria yanks pins from her bun. Lifts her hands beneath her lush mane. "Too heavy. Mine, too."

They grin at each other, raise their glasses, sip.

Leonora shudders. "The clear one has a medicine smell. The black one is like licorice."

"They smell the same."

"Okay." Leonora lights one of her Pall Malls. "Since you believe they're the same, you may as well drink the clear Sambuca."

"I'm drinking both." Floria dips one finger into the yellow-and-black coffee can. Hers is a face Leonora would trust if she were to meet her now for the first time, a face that's angular without being narrow, plain without being ugly. And out of all that emerges an odd loveliness.

"You look lovely," she tells her.

Floria makes her eyes go crossways, aims the tip of her tongue toward her left ear.

"How much tasting did you do before you got here?"

Floria takes a sip of clear Sambuca, sucks on her finger, sighs, and takes another sip. All at once her face is somber again.

"Hey . . ." Leonora tries to pull her in and away from herself, from the sorrow, from that window. She's good at pulling others to her when she chooses to. *Cold fire. Brilliant fire.* Equally good at keeping others out. *The cold without the fire.* She leans toward Floria. "Let me explain what's wrong with the clear Sambuca. It bites you after you swallow. Like the serpent of Eve's Paradise."

"Now I understand where Anthony gets his creativity."

But Leonora doesn't want Floria to mention Anthony. Not in this room. Because to mention him is to evoke Bianca even more. Already, she feels her niece's death rising, here, between Floria and herself, and she tries to keep it down, because she's terrified Floria will blame Anthony. *I would. If Anthony were the one who'd died, I would blame Bianca forever.* She feels the effort of keeping it down. Because, along with it, there is so much more she must keep down—not just Bianca's loss, but everything else connected to her. *Bianca and Belinda as infants, dark and tiny and lovely,* curled toward each other in one crib, *twin babies whose combined birth weight is to the ounce what Anthony will weigh at birth one year later. Eight pounds and six ounces.*

One child to equal two.

To finally equal one.

———

With the last one Leonora didn't even realize she was pregnant until Floria and the twins moved in that Christmas. Migraines, she thought she had, and when Floria said, "Maybe you're pregnant," Leonora said no, but felt it—that instant—the heaviness, familiar and frightening, *weighing you down, though you know that you're merely one week late and that the child forming weighs close to nothing. And though you picture yourself holding it, feeding it, you cannot feed yourself. Whatever you force down, your body heaves up. You vomit, hot and sudden. Feel nourishment shoot through you in a hot, dark stench. While you stay hollow. And yet, you believe there has to be room for whatever is forming in you, child or tumor or abyss, and so you hold yourself still, so still, a cradle for your child. You don't dare admit to your husband or his sister that you're pregnant because you don't want them propping you up, fretting you'll lose this one, too, already grieving, though you may be able to hold on to this child and watch it be lifted from between your thighs. You wave their concern away, tell them you have migraines. Gentle and safe you keep yourself. Because you want it, want this child. And you make yourself believe that you can. You order your body to contain this child. After all, it's not for long, your child's life within you, compared with the lifetime it will live outside you. Yet, already you feel your body refusing, hoarding its selfish heat for no one but yourself, though you want to give shelter to your child. Already something within you is shifting, closing off to anyone but yourself. You feel your child sliding away from you, exiled from your body, from life. Because you are too selfish. Though the doctor says that it's not so, that you have no control*

*over this, you know in the depth of that dark nastiness how it's al-
ways about you. About your selfishness, that you can't turn around
though you want to. The selfishness that caused your father to pun-
ish you. The selfishness that leads to yet another child falling from
you. Falling just weeks after Bianca falls from your lives. Following
Bianca on her bloody path. That's why you don't admit to anyone
about losing yet another child. Not even to Victor. Because how
can your grief possibly compare to his sister's?*

Leonora can't imagine what it must be like to have your already-
born child die before you. Out of natural sequence.

Now, she and Floria each have only one child: Anthony who
has become timid and quiet; and Belinda who seems frantic as she
watches over her mother, whose bridal gowns are no longer ready
when promised, who is preoccupied with making dolls. It started
when Floria made a large doll for Belinda to keep her from being
afraid at night in a room set up for two. Although the doll was
made from linen, it looked remarkably like Bianca. Its hair was
brown yarn, and Floria embroidered the mouth and cheeks and
eyes like Bianca's.

Creepy as all hell, Leonora thought when she first saw the doll.
But Belinda adored it. Named it Belinda-doll. Took it to bed. To
school. To the doctor. Whenever Floria sewed an outfit for Belinda, she made a matching one for the doll. *Creepy as all hell.*
Then Belinda's teacher, Sister Marguerite, wondered if Floria
would enjoy making a doll for her niece. Floria worked from photos, made the doll skinnier and shorter than Belinda's doll. Yellow
yarn for the hair, braided down the doll's back. Matching green
dresses for the doll and for Sister Marguerite's niece.

Her payment: five weeks of prayers. The first customer who
paid with money was Belinda's doctor, who admired the doll Belinda clutched while getting her sinuses examined, who asked if
Floria would be interested in sewing dolls for both his daughters.
Gradually, other inquiries came in from people who'd seen one of
Floria's dolls. They gave her photos. Snips of hair to match the
color. The doctor's aunt from Connecticut wrote. Asked if Floria
ever sent dolls out of state. Someone else had relatives in Texas. In
Wyoming.

So far, Floria has sent dolls to nine states, each different in appearance and age, depending for whom it is: toddlers, five-year-olds, even a twelve-year-old whose parents wanted to lure her back into childhood.

Leonora thinks making those dolls can't be healthy for Floria; but when she told Floria what everyone else in the family didn't dare say, Floria didn't want to hear. "It has nothing to do with Bianca," she said.

Malcolm's the only one who's grown stronger, and he's been wonderful with Floria, except for encouraging her with these creepy dolls. He does all the shipping, decides on the prices. "Never give your talent away," he told Floria. "Except to the church."

———————

Floria is sampling the black Sambuca with great concentration. Dips her finger into the coffee can. Licks it off and drinks again.

"What I was saying about this clear Sambuca," Leonora explains, "is that it bites you after you swallow. And then it rises like fire into your brain. Try a sip of the black. Just to compare."

Floria compares. Smacks her lips.

"Can't you feel that the black is more compact?"

Floria shakes her head. "Please, tell me I am hallucinating."

"All right. You're hallucinating. Why?"

Floria motions toward the counter where Leonora's centerpiece sits in questionable splendor. "Whatever is that . . . thing?"

"An edible flower basket I made from vegetables."

"Why?" Floria shakes her pack of Lucky Strikes. When nothing comes out, she crushes it and lights one of Leonora's cigarettes. They both have one. "Why would you do that? It's ghastly."

"Not as ghastly as your creepy dolls." Horrified at what she's said, Leonora gets up. Bends across her basket: nothing is what it seems to be, only more so now that her braids of bread have split and her scallions are wilting and her radish blossoms have turned scabby. "Quite ghastly," she says. "You're right."

Floria doesn't answer.

"I'm sorry."

Floria nods.

"So then, to make this up to you, I'll send the basket home with you."

"I couldn't."

"It's yours."

"I couldn't bear looking at it."

"It's yours, along with all those pots and dishes and baking pans and napkins and tablecloths and glasses your brother dragged in here because he could write them off."

"We could take the centerpiece to his party."

Leonora starts laughing. "Let's. It's as fake as his promises."

"Ultimately, though . . . that basket is too good for him."

"True." Leonora sits down and takes one long sip. Closes her eyes. "Feel how the black curls up behind your nose but doesn't go any higher, not into your brain like the clear stuff."

"Your brain. Not mine."

"I was talking brain in general. Not yours." Leonora takes another sip, coats her fingertip with coffee, sings the Chock-full-o'-Nuts-is-the-heavenly-coffee jingle, ". . . better coffee millionaires' money can't buy."

"If you had millionaires' money, what would you buy?"

"A new pope. New bishops. New *Fathers.*"

"I would buy a house. With an extra room for my sewing. With a front porch and a garden."

"And I'd buy black Sambuca. Because it goes through the roof of my mouth, and then curls back. It's like licorice."

"More like anise, really."

"So we're really agreeing. Because licorice comes from seeds of the anise plant."

"No. From the licorice plant."

"You don't ever want to agree with me. It's an attitude that has nothing to do with facts."

"Get the encyclopedia."

"What do I get if I'm right?"

"If you're right . . . I'll tell you about the worst lover I've ever had." Floria covers her mouth. "Forget I said that. Have another drink. Then you'll forget for sure."

"And here I thought you went into marriage pure as communion wine."

"Wine is wine."

Leonora hauls her chair to the cupboards, steps on it, and tugs the encyclopedia from her stack of cookbooks above the cupboards. "Licorice . . ." She flips pages. "Lic . . . lic . . . lic—"

"Get down before you break something."

"Only if you tell me about your worst lover."

"You first."

"Who says I had a worst . . ." She teeters. Balances herself. "Worse than what?"

"Worse than other lovers."

"Oh."

"Every woman has at least one."

"How many have you had?"

"Get down from there or I won't tell you about Leopardman."

Leonora climbs from her chair and drags it back to the table. "Yes?"

But Floria is stalling. She is tilting the coffee can, is shaking it till she has a pile of coffee on the plastic tablecloth, is pushing a crater in the middle as if she were about to add yeast to flour.

"Leopardman?"

"Leopardman." Floria dabs her fingers against her tongue. Follows with black Sambuca. Traces the purple-and-gold lettering on the bottle, its round body, its neck that's as long as its body.

Leonora loves seeing Floria like this, funny and a bit wicked. And without any trace of that sadness. "Let me guess. Leopardman swung from chandeliers."

"If only . . . He came dressed the part. Skimpy underpants in leopard pattern. Like those flimsy scarves at the five and ten."

"Your mother gave me a blouse in that pattern, and I had to write one of those wretched thank-you letters she insists on, even though I hated the blouse."

"You wore it every time Mama came over."

"*Only* when your mother came over."

"At least you weren't coached in writing thank-you letters *until* you married Victor. I had to do it from the time I knew how to write, and I had to mention how each present was used. Like, 'Dear Aunt Camilla, I'm writing this letter with the beautiful pen you brought me from Spain for my ninth birthday. . . .' Or: 'Dear Mrs. Cohen, Today I'm wearing the yellow cardigan you knitted for me. It's so fluffy. . . .' Victor and I had to include a drawing of each present with our thank-you notes. Photos if available."

"Photos? Let me tell you about photos. Four days after Anthony was born, your mother came over with manicotti and a camera, made me dress Anthony in every damn outfit people had given him, and propped him up between the sofa pillows—four days old he was, Floria, four days—while she took snapshots of him. A different outfit in each. Strip the baby, click the camera, strip the baby, while I had birth blood down my thighs, and when Anthony got cranky, she allowed him half an hour for a nap, then woke him up and went at it again."

"Strip the baby, take a photo. . . . I got one of those photos. 'Dear Floria, Thank you so much for the darling cotton outfit with the lemon-yellow duck appliqué. As you see in this photo, it's one of Anthony's favorites. . . .'"

"That sappy? Jesus Christ, your mother stood right over me while I wrote those notes. 'Dear Mrs. Bennett, Thank you so much for the darling white jacket you knitted for Anthony. As you see in this photo, it's one of his favorites. . . .'"

"Strip the baby, take a photo, strip the baby. Mama was so pissed at you."

"At me? I wrote those damn thank-you letters."

"But you didn't write *her* a thank-you letter."

"Because I thanked her in person."

"Doesn't count. You also signed notes to others with your name and Anthony's on the first line, but Victor's underneath."

"So?"

"Mama said it showed where you thought Victor's place was in your family."

"Your mother—" Leonora slaps both palms on the table, into

the shadow of the fan as it hunts itself on the clear plastic that covers the flowered tablecloth. She feels snared in the Amedeos' family patterns, in that tight circle of everyone getting together to celebrate every piddling occasion or to repeat the same tiresome gossip. "I want to get an annulment from your mother. Now here's a relationship that deserves an annulment. A relationship that was never right. At least that's Victor's prerequisite for an annulment."

Maybe getting rid of Victor is her chance to get rid of his entire family. She can get away from anyone. She proved that to herself when she got away from her father by wishing him dead.

If only it had been all bad.

Then she could put her father behind her altogether. But when Anthony was two, she took him to Rockaway, let him taste his first cotton candy, rode the carousel with him. When she walked with him to the edge of the water, a man on a horse rode toward them. In the shelter of his arms sat a girl of five or six, singing in the smooth light of the sun. And what Leonora wished that moment was that she, too, could remember a summer afternoon when she felt *her* father's arms protective around her, the swaying of the horse beneath them—father, child—or any other memory, good, before the others started. She, a girl of five or six, singing within the circle of his arms, singing in the smooth light of this acquitting sun.

It could have happened.

And as she turned to watch the horse pass, she was struck by sudden bliss, remembering. *It did happen. The bliss of being little and riding—not on a horse—but on my father's thin shoulders beneath a red umbrella. He is rushing to catch the streetcar while I'm singing to myself, my hair against the fabric of the umbrella as street lamps from above light up my red-red world. . . .*

It's a moment of pure bliss, a moment to sustain Leonora for the rest of her life if she'll make a pact with herself to forget the fear of her father, to forget his fists falling on her. *Fifty-four days of fists without warning. Fists without reason. Fists that could kill you if fifty-four days were to turn into fifty-four weeks. Or fifty-four months.*

"His appendix," Leonora's mother explained when he died.

It had to be a sudden death. Of course. A death he couldn't pre-vent. His appendix bursting inside him. That. Rather than shooting himself in the parking lot of Sing Sing.

—⟨⟩—

"Have some more Sambuca and listen to me," Floria says. "Please. Mama is that way with everyone. Loves you one moment. Picks on you the next. And believe me, she's been easier on you than on me and Victor."

"I'll make sure to send her a proper thank-you note for that." Leonora tilts the clear bottle, gingerly pours for both of them. Only a finger's width of liquid is left beneath the blue label with its pic-ture of the Colosseum.

"Think how you call her Riptide. Think about it. A riptide will sweep you out, ignore your screams, determine the direction you're being swept. The one thing you can do is wait her out. Let her take you along and relax, and then use the first chance to swim out of the current."

"Very good."

"It's something she taught me . . . about swimming."

"I'll never force Anthony to write thank-you letters."

"On some level, Mama admires your spunk."

"Because it gives her more to grind down?"

"I thought you wanted to hear about Leopardman."

"Why did you only bring two bottles?"

"Slow down."

"Is that what you had to tell Leopardman?"

"Don't I wish. . . . No, he was all costume and gymnastics. I could never get past feeling embarrassed for him. I mean, he didn't quite swing from chandeliers—"

"Why not?"

"—and he didn't pound his chest, and he didn't jump up and down on all fours . . . but I always felt he was at a costume party, and that any minute he'd realize how foolish he looked."

"So—did you do it with him?"

"Sure. It was just not . . . very exciting. He worked at a Horn & Hardart's Automat, stocking food behind the little glass doors. Whenever I went downtown for a show, I used to go there for the creamed spinach that Mama likes."

"Their petits fours are the best. Even just looking at them through the cellophane in the lid of the box . . ."

"Have you tried their rice pudding? So soft, and those raisins . . ."

"Too runny. Now stop distracting me with food talk."

"Tapioca?"

"Fish eyes."

"Leopardman was older than I was, but I'd had two boyfriends before and knew it could feel better."

"You did it with them, too?"

"And then I went to confession."

Leonora stares at her. "I'm envious." She feels aglow, as if someone had bathed her in licorice. Inside and out. It's floating throughout her head. Glowing. Coating her toes and the backs of her knees. "I had a worst lover, too." She is thinking fast, trying to outdo Floria's Leopardman, but truth is she never had a lover before Victor, had only kissed one boy in school, Stevie, that's all they did, that one kiss, and she never strayed from Victor during their marriage—he was the one to do that, son of a bitch. Her only other experience is with James. Except James does not belong in the worst-lover category. And he's very much part of her present. Of today. "My worst lover . . . only perfected himself in that one area—in bed."

"And that made him your worst lover?"

"Because as soon as he starts talking . . . I mean, he talks so big that I feel . . . embarrassed for him. He'll say things like: 'I work in transportation,' when he really just drives a cab. Or he'll say: 'I'm breeding dogs,' when all he has is one lousy cocker spaniel. An expert in everything and in nothing." Just thinking about James makes Leonora feel wide open, delicious and swollen.

"You look how I feel in the dentist's chair."

"That awful?"

"Depends."

"Victor says you've always been weird about dentists."

"So, what else have you found out about me?"

"Lots and lots. That you enjoy having your teeth drilled. And I keep finding out more."

"That Hudak boy in your building—"

"That you kept your girdle on the first time you slept with Malcolm."

"Malcolm told you that?"

"Victor, who heard it from Riptide, who—"

"I don't even want to start guessing where my mother heard it."

"Why wouldn't you fuck Malcolm after you'd fucked others?"

"Just because I fucked before doesn't mean I have to fuck on demand."

"This is the first time I've ever heard you say 'fuck.'"

"You say it often enough for both of us. Oh, fuck it—now you're the one distracting me. That Hudak boy . . . didn't he have a cocker spaniel?"

Leonora makes her face go indifferent.

Floria is smiling to herself, making patterns with coffee on the tablecloth, following the vines and flowers on the fabric beneath the clear plastic. She licks two of her fingers, washes the coffee dust away with a sip of Sambuca. "You aren't doing it with that boy. Tell me you're not. You *are,* Leonora. Right? I know that boy has driven a cab. That he used to have a cocker spaniel. You *are* doing it with that boy?"

"He is *not* a boy."

"Christ, Leonora." Broad laughs rise from Floria's belly like bubbles from the bottom of an aquarium. "You're getting yourself some baby pudding."

"He's twenty-one. And a lot harder than pudding."

"Then why are you so uppity about Victor?"

"Because at least I waited till the marriage was over."

"I'm not so sure it's over. Victor would come home in a minute if you let him."

"You got that one wrong."

"He talks to me, Leonora. He's my brother."

"So let your brother talk. And you can listen. I've done all the listening I'm going to do. I don't want your brother telling me how he had a dream about Elaine, or how Elaine likes to fuck in the middle of the day on some stupid rug."

"He says you didn't care when you found about him and her. That you didn't cry or anything."

"He wants that, too? Watch me cry as a good-bye present to him?"

"I told him you were hurting. That you just couldn't show it."

"I *chose* not to show it. And I really don't want to talk about him, Floria."

"As long as you understand he'll come back to you in a—"

"Whatever would I do with him?"

Floria looks at her, steadily.

"Did *he* send you here with those bottles?"

"I told you I stole the bottles. But I know my brother. He and that . . . woman, they're no match."

"Well, I don't want him."

"Want . . . You want to hear about the one man I wanted."

"In addition to the men you *had?*"

"I met him just once—on my wedding day. He was Malcolm's best man."

"Julian."

"You remember him."

"Julian Thompson. I danced with him."

Floria's eyes sharpen.

"He was a sensational dancer." Leonora arches her back. "Not half as handsome as Malcolm. But what a dancer. He builds furniture, right? Mostly I remember him because Victor got jealous. It was only our second date. So . . . Julian Thompson . . . Did you do it with him, too?"

"Of course not. It was my wedding day."

"Well . . . how about the day after?"

"That's enough."

"Or you could have waited a week or two."

"I'm not a slut."

"Of course not. I'm sorry. Will you still tell me about Julian Thompson?"

Floria hesitates.

"I'm sorry I teased you like this."

"All right . . . Malcolm rented a room in Hartford from Julian's parents for a while. You know . . . after he left England, when he lived all over the place."

Leonora nods.

"He stayed in Hartford for almost a year. Became friends with Julian. Years later, he invited him to our wedding. To be the best man and to drive the limo. Typical Malcolm—renting a stretch limo without a driver—grandiose and cheap. It was snowing when Julian drove me to St. Nicholas of Tolentine, and when we arrived, he opened my door and reached for my hands. I tell you, a jolt ran up my arms, down my entire body and through my legs into the earth—something that's never happened with Malcolm, and I knew I was about to make a huge mistake, marrying Malcolm. Julian was looking at me with such regret, such tenderness, that I was sure he felt the same. But here I stood, shaking all over—supposed to walk up the church steps in this wedding gown I'd sewn, walk down the aisle on Papa's arm toward the altar, where Malcolm waited in a suit he'd borrowed from a neighbor—and what else could I do?"

"Run the other way?"

"It never occurred to me that I could." Floria draws her lower lip between her teeth. "Maybe now." She nods. "Maybe now I would."

"What happened to Julian?"

"I haven't seen him since. He married the following January, and we couldn't afford to go to his wedding. But we used to exchange Christmas cards, sometimes photos, their son, Mick, our girls—" Floria pulls her head into her shoulders as if she'd been struck.

Our girls.

Quickly, Leonora covers the back of Floria's hand with her palm.

"It's always there." Floria turns her hand beneath Leonora's, palm to palm. "Except sometimes I forget and hear myself say 'the twins' or 'the girls.'"

"There are no words to tell you how terribly sorry I am," Leonora whispers. "Every day. Every hour."

"Every day . . . every hour . . ." Floria curls her fingers upward, laces them through Leonora's. Her nails are perfect ovals without polish. "Do you know how often I wonder what would have happened if I had stayed in your kitchen with her? Or if I'd come back a few seconds sooner?"

"I keep doing the same thing. See myself screaming at Bianca to get away from that window."

"Screaming at her to take off that cape. Slamming the window shut. And it all becomes so real that I feel the cold air on my arms . . . see the snow."

"I am so sorry. . . ." Though Leonora has waited for Floria to mention that day, has imagined this, it doesn't restore what she hoped for, that quirky, dependable closeness. "So very sorry." Lowering her head, Leonora presses her lips against the knot of fingers between them, tightens her fingers. And still Floria feels unreachable. Unforgiving.

Ever since Bianca's death, Leonora has been afraid that her father's violence may live on in her son, confused because it's a violence that doesn't fit her son. But, then, it didn't fit the father from before the violence started, the father *who carries me beneath the red umbrella, the father who takes me to Far Rockaway, to his favorite restaurant, which is no wider than a hallway. Fried chicken and home fries and creamed corn. As I finish eating, a tall black man comes in, bends across my plate, looks closely at the chicken bones and skin. "What have you been eating, girl? Was it splendid and tasty?" I tell him yes, tell him it was splendid and tasty, and he's laughing along with my father. "I'll have the same," he tells the waiter. And my father winks at me and says, "Excellent choice."*

She believed she'd left the fear at her father's grave, but it's here with her now, fear for her son, and there's a sadness in Floria's face that makes Leonora certain that she, too, is fearing for Anthony.

Floria's fingers are longer than her own, rounder, causing wider gaps than when Leonora laces her own fingers, and when Floria disengages her fingers those gaps feel carved, feel forever, and Leonora readies herself for any accusation Floria will make against Anthony.

"He's divorced now," Floria says.

"Oh—you mean Julian."

"Don't you think he has forgotten me?"

Leonora divides the last of the clear Sambuca, a few drops more for Floria. "Maybe he's waiting for you."

"Don't be silly." Floria rests her forehead on the table. "I'm so tired."

"Want me to get the couch ready for you?"

"No. I'll close my eyes for a few minutes before I leave. Sometimes I'm sure it's the most significant love I've known. Because it . . . stayed like it was that one day." Floria's voice fades. "We . . . never had a chance to disappoint each other or . . ."

"In a marriage you would have found plenty of chances for that."

Floria sighs. Takes a deep breath. Another. Lets out a delicate snore.

⎯ ⌒

She's still fast asleep at the table when Victor brings Anthony home. He frowns when he sees her here but doesn't say anything. Neither does Leonora. They're silent as they untie Anthony's shoes—wet from rain—and help him out of his suit. Limp with exhaustion, he allows them to lead him to his bed, tuck him in. Leonora suspects he is acting younger than he is to keep them both here with him.

Victor kisses his forehead. "Sleep tight." He follows Leonora into the hallway.

"Go now," she tells him.

"Can't we sit down for a while?"

"I already sat down today."

"I mean sit down and talk."

"I already talked today."

"Please?"

"What for?"

"I don't know. I don't even know what I want to say to you. Only that I don't want to go yet."

"Want want want . . ."

"It's not like that."

"Why don't you go home to Elaine and—"

"It's not home."

"—and figure out with her what you *want.*"

"This has nothing to do with Elaine. And it's—"

"That's one hell of a statement to make on the day of your engagement to her."

"I know," he whispers.

"I can't help you with that, Victor." Leonora steps around him, places both hands against his shoulder blades—*How long since I've touched you? How long?*—and shoves him toward the door. All day she's been by this door, waiting for someone to leave or to arrive. Opening it. Closing it. Opening it now for Victor, who is still talking.

Talking about talking. "How do I know what I really *have* to say to you until I start saying it?"

She seals his mouth with her palm, and doesn't yank it away when he kisses her fingers, her arms, her neck. She pushes the door closed, shakes off her robe, helps him with that ridiculous cummerbund. There, with her back against the front door, it's urgent between them, rougher than ever, lust and danger, while Floria and Anthony are sleeping nearby. She feels weightless as he lifts her, heavy as she opens herself and sinks around him—*and it could always be like that, like that again*—yet, just as she's about to come, she feels disoriented because, it's all new and it's not.

And then she knows. And is livid. "You've learned from that woman."

"I love you."

"You have fucking learned from that fucking woman."

"The only one I want to be with is you."

"Why don't you try fucking her with both of you standing on your heads?" She snatches her robe from the carpet. Wobbles for an instant and, absurdly, finds herself thinking how it's almost time for the bare floor of summer, and she reminds herself to call the carpet man to pick up the rugs and clean them, keep them till fall. "Remind me to call the carpet man."

"Let me stay?"

She flings the cummerbund at him.

"You have learned, too. Think about that. We both have learned."

She's jostling him out the door. Locking it behind him. When she checks on Anthony, he's sleeping on his stomach. At the kitchen table, Floria is snoring softly, and Leonora covers her with the orange-and-green afghan that Riptide crocheted for her.

In her bedroom, Victor watches from the wedding photo, his eyes burning her skin.

"No," she tells him.

We both have learned.

"Don't you dare," she tells him, feeling smutty though he's her husband. Though she did not feel smutty with James.

But his eyes remain on her, probing.

And so she makes him stop. Lifts the silver frame off the wall, lays it face-down on the maple dresser. There. Now he can no longer see her. He's out of her life. Even more so after tonight.

In the morning, her head feels light with an almost pleasant Sambuca headache that floats behind her cheekbones like part of her breath. She wraps the wedding photo in an old towel, but as soon as she slips it behind the records in the living room, she starts missing herself, missing how she looked as a bride, graceful and substantial. She reaches for the photo, unwraps it. And there she is. *Graceful. Substantial.* The only thing wrong with the photo is that Victor is in it. It makes her think of the used-furniture shop on Jerome Avenue. She has never been inside though she passes it on the way to the beauty parlor, and she has noticed a hand-printed sign in the window:

RESTORE YOUR BELOVED PHOTOGRAPHS!
INDIVIDUALS, PETS, FURNITURE, PLANTS,
AND SETTINGS CAN BE REMOVED OR ADDED.
WE REPAIR CRACKS, TAKE OUT STAINS,
AND REPLACE MISSING PARTS.
YOUR ORIGINALS ARE SAFE WITH US.
ALL WORK DONE ON PREMISES SINCE 1921.

She used to wonder what kind of people would remove others from their photos; but when she steps across the puddle in front of the shop and opens the door, she has no trouble at all handing the intricate frame to the man behind the counter and asking him to remove Victor.

When the man nods, his hairpiece slides a tiny bit forward. Shiny and black, it looks as if cast in one piece. His eyes are knowing and sad, as though he spent all his hours doing away with unfaithful husbands, and Leonora has a feeling that, the instant you enter his shop, he can tell if you've come from the end of a marriage. What gives you away? The slant of your lips? Your bitten fingernails? That rage in your eyes?

For his services, he asks a high price, but Leonora reminds herself what Victor is spending on engagement parties, on new suits and shoes. While she's been saving money on little things, feeling cheap. Saving money forever. Storing a box of ice-cream cones in the car, so that, when they drive to the Carvel's on Webster Avenue, Victor can buy just two vanilla swirls and take some off each top to put into a cone for Anthony. Three for the price of two. *Pennies saved.* And nail polish—how she uses bottles right down to the dregs and then adds polish remover to make them last longer, even though the polish won't coat her nails evenly and always flakes off. *Pennies.*

As she pays to have Victor eliminated from her wedding, she promises herself to buy the most extravagant bottle of nail polish on her walk home.

That evening Victor calls, asking to talk.

Every evening he calls.

Every evening she tells him to talk to Elaine instead.

Every evening he says he has broken it off with Elaine.

Every evening he says he wants to come home to her and Anthony.

At the end of the week Leonora returns to the used-furniture shop. In the filigreed frame, she's the only one left, still graceful and still substantial in her white gown; but where before Victor's arm was linked through hers, stands now a waist-high pedestal, the kind you see in museums, and her left elbow—forever angled in that initial position—rests on the marble top. In back of the pedestal hang the airbrushed folds of a long curtain.

"Is this how you wanted it?"

For an instant she thinks he's asking if this is how she wanted her marriage all along. "It's how I want it now," she tells him.

As she walks out, the wrapped photo under one arm, a woman in a flared coat comes out of the coffee shop at the end of the block, raising her face into the mild wind, smiling to herself. Leonora sniffs the air—buds and new green. The woman's stride is graceful, fluent, and Leonora can tell this is a woman who enjoys being alone. It makes Leonora want to be alone like that, too. Already she sees herself stepping from some coffee shop or theater, wearing a flared coat, her face radiant with the pleasure of being alone. She feels her stride getting lighter, and as the woman approaches, her smile deepens, as if she knew Leonora's thoughts, and her arms rise in preparation for a hug. A bit too effusive for Leonora. Still, she slows down, bracing herself. Just then a thin man with sunglasses—he must have been a few paces behind her all along—rushes past her and into the arms of the woman, whose light was all along for him. *Because of him?*

It takes the breath from Leonora, and she has to lean against a brick wall as the two embrace and kiss. Traffic moves past her, women with strollers, people with pull carts to do their shopping, while Leonora is trying to preserve that first glimpse of a woman rejoicing in being alone. But where before she'd only been aware of the woman, she now is overwhelmed by all else around her: the stutter of a jackhammer, a shrill argument in a courtyard, two little dogs yapping. The scent of spring carries soot and exhaust fumes. Against the left side of her body, she feels the silver frame, and as she tightens her arm to keep it from falling, she feels as though she's the one who has stepped from one frame into another and has ended up behind an airbrushed curtain. Where she'll find Victor.

And that's when she knows she'll call him.

The first evening they're back together, he arrives with a Bernice Peaches carton full of groceries as if he'd never been away. That part of being together feels familiar; but in bed his body feels unfamiliar, and she won't let him near her. Despite the sex in the hallway the day of his engagement. Because of the sex in the hallway.

After she switches off her bedside lamp, she adjusts her pillow, punches it as she usually does to get it right, waits for him to ask.

And he does. "Are you quite settled?"

It comforts her, the ritual of that question—*Are you quite settled?*—makes her realize how she missed the history of the ritual, starting with that same question years ago. When Victor repeated it that following night and the night after—*Are you quite settled?*—or even in the car if she was fidgety, she got annoyed, as she does whenever he repeats himself, but out of that annoyance a certain tenderness arose, until she finally came to expect that habit. *Are you quite settled?*

It's like that between them with other things that have changed from the incidental to the frustrating, from the frustrating to the endearing. And that's why she has let him come back. Because of the habits. Because of Anthony. Because of the inevitable tenderness between them. Because time will not be theirs forever. Because of the woman in the flared coat. Despite the woman in the flared coat.

She knows she will be hard on Victor. Will make him sweat his way back to her. It's for herself she'll do that—not for him. Quite likely, she won't trust him when he is away from her, at least not for many months. Until, gradually, she won't have to remind herself to be hard on him. And maybe there'll be a day when she won't question where he's been without her, a day when she won't need to hold back with her love.

When she wakes before dawn, he's lying on his side watching her as though he hadn't slept at all. Moon paints his slick face, *face of the moon, slick and bleached, face of a man whose skin is slick and bleached as moon*—

He lays one fingertip against the base of her throat. "You turned to me while you were sleeping, *mia cara.*"

She swallows. Feels her throat against his skin.

"Your body turned toward me. I didn't move. Your throat—" He stops. His eyes are on the wedding photo above the dresser.

She waits for him to question why it no longer includes him.

"Your throat," he says, "came to lie against my wrist. I felt your pulse in my wrist. It was . . . beautiful."

Her pulse flickers against his fingertip the way he must have felt it in his wrist—beautiful, airy—and she's suddenly glad he's here. His touch makes it possible for her to imagine what it'll be like to have his entire body against hers, soon, a hundredfold the sensation of her skin against his fingertip now. Not yet, she decides. And feels herself opening up. Opening—

But he says, "I thought this is what it must feel like to carry a baby."

"Don't," she warns him. He has been so careful with her. Grateful to be back home with her and Anthony. And he still doesn't understand how these words are slicing through her.

"That kind of nearness"—*face of a man whose skin is slick and bleached as moon*—"like the baby is already living beneath your own skin . . ."

She sees herself alone, in this very bed, after Victor's death, reminding herself how his face looked the first night he was back after cheating on her—*face of the moon, slick and bleached, face of a man whose skin is slick and bleached as death*—

"I was thinking," Victor murmurs, "how that's something only women experience, but when your throat was against my wrist, I understood what it must be like, being pregnant."

"You can't," she says. "You can't understand." Is this what their marriage has been like all along? Even during those moments when she believed they knew each other? Is it all that simple to him? What about the nuances? The grooves and the folds?

"Not the same, of course," he says. "Just almost like it."

"It is nothing like being pregnant," she tells him firmly.

What she does not tell him is that pregnant means afraid. *After losing the first one, you no longer know how to carry a child without fear. The child and the fear start living inside you at the same instant, and both grow within you until the child will bleed from you. While the fear recedes to your womb, ready to swaddle the next child. The shame of having yet another child fall from you. The whispers: "Leonora lost another one. . . ." Each child falling from you sooner. Four lost. Only one born: Anthony. Who was your first pregnancy. An eight-months baby. Living. A pregnancy still untainted by fear. Anthony, who started inside your womb one month after you married Victor. Since then, all others have fallen from you: after five months; after three months; after two months; and the last one barely taking root in your womb before your body cast it out. Amazing to think you could be raising five children so far. God forbid. Given the choice—*

Don't think it.

Still, given the choice—would you want to raise one or five? But what if you had other choices? Two children? Three? You could handle two or three children. But the question you must push yourself toward is this: five or one? And the answer is savage. One. Given the choice. Given the four babies that fell from you. No. You would have chosen the one.

"Feeling your pulse in my body," Victor tells her, "was sacred."

⌒

BOOK TWO

FLORIA 1975

At the Proper Hour

The Italian words of her childhood that come back to Floria have to do with music and food. Her father listening to his opera records: sacred time. Her mother cooking: sacred time. *Un bel di vedremo. Fragole. Scarola. La forza del destino. Costoletta. Una furtiva lagrima. Insalate. Tarantella. Dolce.*

It's her first trip to Liguria, and she has come alone to Santa Margherita, to this hotel that was a convent for centuries. Perhaps the nuns scattered during the war years and forgot to reconvene. Some may have married. A different altar. No longer a bridegroom in spirit only.

There is an odd allure to being inside this convent as a woman who has conceived and borne children. Cats approach her window as she rolls down her black stockings, as she empties her suitcase. She has packed lightly: her black nylon slip doubles as a night-gown, her black raincoat as a bathrobe, and her black sandals as slippers.

Two cats lean against her window as if expecting the glass to yield to the pressure of their bodies: a ginger cat with white paws; and a brown cat whose fur, beneath the brown, reveals the blurred markings of a much wilder and larger cat. Far below the cats lies a courtyard, and across the courtyard rise the clay roofs of red-and-ocher buildings. Beyond them curves the harbor, where veins of land fuse the hills to the sea.

Sundown blurs into dusk, and an old woman appears in the alcove of a nearby roof: first her head, then her arms, her waist, as she climbs laboriously from a stairwell. Her shawl—the same implausible shade of turquoise as the scalloped bay behind her—shrouds her hair and the shoulders of her red bathrobe. As she flings food scraps into the dusk, pigeons plummet from all directions of sky like falling children, flicker around her till they become extensions of her: one body with countless heads and wings, easily startled into separate birds if anyone were to move abruptly.

In the hills beyond the old woman, Floria can make out the village where her father was born. Nozarego. The name reminds her of Nazareth, conjuring olive groves, money changers in the temple, donkeys on dust-brown paths. In Nozarego, the largest structure is the church where her father celebrated his first communion. The following year his family moved to Mestre, a city as sprawling and ugly—so he has told Floria—as Nozarego is contained and beautiful. When his family took a freighter from Genoa to New York, he believed he'd eventually return to Nozarego; but he hasn't been back, though he likes villages better than cities and sees the Bronx as temporary. Too noisy, he likes to say, too confusing, too drab. And yet, he came to love the Bronx for giving him employment in a salvage yard, for letting him afford an attached house on Castle Hill Avenue, where he renovated the deep space beneath the stairway into a music room with an angled ceiling.

Two years ago, when Floria turned fifty, her parents gave her this trip to Liguria, but it's taken her this long to get here because her father asked her to visit the grave of his grandparents, because she has already enough dead people in her life.

"In many of these villages," her father told her, "the cemeteries are situated where the earth rises to its highest point. To make it easier for the dead to start their way to heaven. By carrying them up as far as earth will allow it, we can be part of their journey for as long as possible, and we ease that part of the journey they will have to take alone. But first we have to leave the dead."

Floria knows that from burying her daughter. At Bianca's grave, her father took her hands, his face parched, his eyes glistening as though they hoarded every drop of moisture from his body. "When I was a boy—" His voice clogged. "All that separates Bianca from heaven is that layer of earth. The dead can only ascend when no mortals watch. And we must let them. . . ."

Floria takes out the photo of her father she's brought to Italy: the day of his first communion, and he stands in front of the stone church, the ground one large mosaic of widening circles. His eyes are turned toward the cemetery high above, and his hands hold his communion candle as if it were the string to his kite. Floria props the photo against the television on the desk next to her bed, picks up the vase with mimosas, their tiny yellow globes wilting.

"Not yet," she tells the boy in the photo.

In the bathroom, she throws the mimosas into the wastebasket, and as she rinses the vase, her body heats in a sudden blush that leaves her damp from thighs to hairline. Ever since she stopped bleeding, these flushes have come to feel like a trade-off she prefers over the days of blood. She knows how to let it pass, by yielding, by reminding herself that the abrupt heat will be over for her in fifty seconds at most and that the dampness—especially beneath her breasts, where the soft weight of flesh against flesh hides her sweat as if it were forbidden—will dry.

She imagines Malcolm next to her, curved sideways, not spooning, but toward her, knees against her knees, palms against her palms. And she envisions herself taking her husband's hand and guiding it to the damp skin beneath her breasts, whispering, "Feel this. Just feel this, Malcolm," letting him warm himself on her mysterious fire.

The husband of her youth would be fascinated by her scent, her taste.

The husband of her youth would touch her without hesitation.

But the husband Malcolm has become in the sum of their years together would pull away from her, no longer curious, no longer inventive.

The husband Malcolm has become would be repulsed by her sudden heat.

Floria wonders if the nuns, too, were they too seized by this sudden heat? Did they speak of it to each other? Would they, in a community of women? Floria can feel the nuns, *praying and sleeping within the walls of this convent, walking across the terra-cotta tiles of the courtyard, leaning against the white columns, sitting on the edge of the marble fountain, where water dribbles from the hands of naked baby angels. Some of the nuns are still young girls. Not a loss to their mothers, but a blessing. At least some mothers pretend. A daughter in the convent. A son in the clergy. Blessed art thou among women. Blessed for losing your child. Young girls falling or drowning or walking from villages where they grew up, away from stone houses the colors of dunes and of earth, stacked against the hills amidst deep-green vineyards. Echoes of pigeons—their purring, their claws on tile roofs—crawl along stone walls, stalk the girls through narrow streets that smell of mangoes and recently gutted fish.*

When Floria was a girl, the nuns at her school feared the passion of flesh and converted the girls' passion to a chaste ecstasy that was as pristine as the white gowns of the young postulants, who floated toward their eternal bridegroom on the cross above the altar. Like many of her classmates, Floria dreamed of becoming a postulant, but she found two reasons against that. One: she was afraid of turning into a nun like Sister Gabriella, who believed she'd been carrying the baby of the Archangel Gabriel inside her for eighteen years because the other sisters were jealous and wouldn't let her give birth to the Archangel's baby. And two: she couldn't imagine what she would be like after she'd shed the white robe of the postulants. Not that it had anything to do with wearing black forever. Black made her feel elegant. Most of her clothes were black, as much a part of her as the scent of her skin. Or her name.

"You're named after Floria in *Tosca*," her father told her when she was old enough to understand, and Floria imagined Puccini and her father deliberating names, while sitting knee to knee in her father's music room, where he had just enough space for two chairs.

Singing swelled the curves of his Victrola, streamed through golden threads, and slid down the angled ceiling toward the window that faced the alley.

When her father was at work, he kept the door locked; but in the evening he'd let Floria in—not her brother, though she was two years younger than Victor. "Because you know how to be quiet around music," he told her. What she loved even more than the music was to look at his face go wide as he listened to his operas, so wide that light poured from his skin.

No one touched dinner, not even guests, till he emerged from his music room, and even if Floria's saliva pooled around her tongue, she knew not to eat until he'd sat down, nodded toward her mother, and raised his soup spoon.

This early in February, the hotel is empty except for Floria and the signora behind the reception desk, who is Floria's age and has a strong face with broad lips that are closed in a mysterious and evocative pout. The signora wears suits like the ones Jackie Kennedy had when she still lived in the White House, but, unlike Jackie Kennedy, who owned many short jackets with matching fitted skirts, the signora has two: a stone-colored tweed with silver buttons, and a red wool the shade of strawberries before they're entirely ripe. For three days the signora wears the same suit, then the other suit for three days. That's how Floria is reminded of time passing.

And she will remind herself: *Now it's six days since I arrived here.*

Now it's nine days.

In the breakfast room that used to be the chapel, a holy-water basin still hangs by the door. On the marble altar, the signora has set out enough food for a dozen people who will never arrive—cheeses and wafer-thin slices of ham; flaky pastry spun around air; juice squeezed from blood oranges—as though she were waiting for the nuns to return.

As Floria eats, she wonders if the signora owns the hotel. If so, how can she afford to operate it for just one guest, providing all this food and the fresh flowers? The floors between the lobby and her room below the roof seem to be empty. Perhaps the hotel is only open for repairs, and any guest is incidental. Yesterday, an old man replaced some tiles in the lobby, and this morning, two men are erecting scaffolding in the courtyard. They shove and hammer scuffed rods into brassy couplings, lay boards across each width of two rods. The shorter of the two, heavyset and deliberate, scales the layers of boards like a gymnast, with much grace and little effort, while the other man moves with a self-consciousness that reminds Floria of Anthony. He, too, has that habit of touching his face or neck as if to make sure he's still there.

She used to love Anthony as if he were her own, and through him, learned to love his mother, too. When she met Leonora, she didn't like her at all—too thin; too irreverent—but once they both became mothers, a friendship grew between them, impulsive and confident. And this is another loss for Floria: no longer loving Anthony as if he were her own. Instead: feeling uneasy around him. Not knowing for sure what he had to do with Bianca's fall. And yet knowing. Feeling ashamed of that knowing. And keeping that knowing her secret. So many things to keep secret in this family. *Things-we-don't-talk-about.* Not talking about the first time she felt uneasy around Anthony.

Twenty-seven years ago, but she can still see him, a toddler in an orange jacket, playing with Bianca and Belinda at the St. James Park playground, patting sand into cakes, digging holes for his car. When he clambered out of the sandbox, he smiled angelically and wobbled toward the monkey bars, where a little boy was playing with a toy truck. In his outstretched hands, Anthony offered his yellow metal car, but the moment the boy reached for it, Anthony seized the truck.

He howled when Floria took it from him. "Wherever did you learn to offer something just to get something bigger?" To distract him, she plopped him back into the sandbox, and for a few minutes he played with Belinda and Bianca, but soon he clambered out again and—with that same angelic expression—headed for the monkey bars, extending his car. He was about to grab the boy's truck when Floria scooped him up, and while he squirmed and kicked, she worried about him beyond that hour, that day.

———⟆

Some days, Floria eats in small trattorias, where her aloneness spreads beyond her body, so visible that it makes couples and families at other tables uncomfortable. It's not at all like the aloneness she felt that long-ago spring when she took a vacation without Malcolm and the twins. Five days in Montauk, in a small hotel near the ocean. How she relished sitting by herself in a restaurant, ordering only what she alone craved, that very instant, without having to plan, to prepare, for her family. And since she knew she would return home in five days, her aloneness clothed her, strengthened her. Because this aloneness was what she'd chosen, she felt a fierce connection to Malcolm and her daughters that did not take away from her aloneness.

But one evening, when she feels glances of pity from people at other tables, even from the waiter, it strikes Floria that here, in Liguria, she carries that aloneness without the connection: a woman who has only one child left; a woman uncertain about staying with her husband. *Without Malcolm?* It's the first time she's thought it, like this, so directly, but it doesn't shock her, that thought, is already familiar as though it formed itself inside her over years.

Without
Malcolm
Without Malcolm

The waiter crosses the room, a large tray on one shoulder. He wears expensive shoes without socks. Looks like an actor who could play a lover or a thug, fuck your brains out, as Leonora would say, or cut your throat in an alley, with equal passion and skill. When he stops to look at Floria, probably because he's felt her staring at him, he smiles, shifts his tray from his shoulder, raises it with both hands, and drops it, startling everyone in the restaurant. But he bows as if indeed an actor, sweeps one arm across his chest and into the air, invites applause. Floria laughs and claps her hands, certain that it's not an accident, that he's done this before, his way of flirting; and already a man at the next table is applauding, then others, applauding and laughing with her, while the actor is sweeping his stage. Afterwards the hum of conversations, animated before, becomes livelier, encompasses her, now.

At the hotel, the lightbulb by her bed has burned out. When she calls the desk, the signora comes up to her room, argues that Floria has enough other lamps.

"But this is the lamp I use for reading in bed."

With a quick swish-swish of nylon thighs, the signora exits, and when she returns, her sullenness is like a coating against Floria's skin, and she doesn't bother with words while the signora replaces the bulb.

Toward dawn, half awakened by soft snoring, Floria stretches to reach for her first smoke. She likes that velvety rattle high in her throat just before she wakes fully, savors the vibration of the snore where it tickles the roof of her mouth. Occasionally it goes away as soon as she listens to it, as though it had an identity of its own, but usually she can spy on it, let its delicate strength fan into her voice. Mornings when she wakes up snoring, her voice feels stronger, and that strength affects her walk, her thoughts for the entire day.

On her way to breakfast, Floria is prepared to ignore the signora, but she already stands by the holy water and greets Floria, palms raised as if about to absolve her. I can do this, too, Floria thinks, raise my palms like that. And she does. The signora smiles, guides her to one of the elaborate tables where each white napkin is folded into the shape of a bishop's hat. As every morning, Floria is the only guest. It's obvious that the signora likes this work better than her maintenance duties. So would I, Floria thinks, suddenly ashamed for insisting the signora climb back up all those stairs, for one lightbulb.

—☙

When she returns to the trattoria a few nights later, the lover-thug-waiter is not there. Two women and a small girl arrive after her, but grab the table she's been waiting for. All in ivory, they're like characters from *The Great Gatsby*: ivory hats and skin; ivory dresses and hair. Their profiles: studied elegance and indifference. Reluctantly, Floria lets the waitress seat her at their table. Without glancing at the menu, she orders a plate of *trofie*. But the women are discussing the menu in rapid Italian, choosing *antipasti, primi piatti, piatti secondi,* practicing their indifference on Floria and on the girl, who's playing with a rubber shark and a Barbie doll.

While lamplight bounces off bottles with olive oil and peppers lined up on the bar, the girl is shoving Barbie's legs into the shark's jaw. Like elements of different centuries colliding, Floria thinks. When her pasta with green beans in basil sauce arrives, she eats hastily. The women are passing binoculars between them, peering through the window into the deep-blue night, while the small girl tries various shark-and-Barbie combinations: Barbie's hair between the shark's rubber teeth; one of Barbie's legs down the shark's throat.

After finishing barely half of her food, Floria pays and steps into the dark street. All at once, the familiar fear is back. *Afraid of being afraid.* She walks faster, trying to fight it off. Ahead of her is a woman, her hair covered, and when she enters a church, Floria follows her. She dips her fingers into the stone basin of holy water, crosses herself—"In the name of the Father and the Son and the Holy Spirit"—and kneels to pray as one should in places that are holy. But ever since Bianca's death, prayer has eluded her. Church has become bad theater: repetitive gestures and words without meaning. Still, she is not like Leonora, who cultivates irreverence and loves to rant against the church. She wishes Leonora were with her, now. Then she wouldn't be so afraid.

Another woman enters. Genuflects and begins to cry. Floria's father has told her about women like that in Italy. "They enter a church, any church, and start crying instantly. For them it's a reflex, like salivating before eating." But Floria envies that ability to cry. She cannot cry. Cannot pray. Cannot return to what she knows now—but did not know while Bianca still lived—was a state of grace. Afterwards, the dark sadness set in. Not being able to get out of bed, to put on her slippers, to dress. She could envision exactly what to do:

> *slide my legs out of bed*
> *push my feet into slippers*
> *stand up*
> *walk to the closet*
> *pull my bathrobe from the hook*
> *lift one arm into a sleeve*
> *then the other*
> *button the front—*

But it was too much to do. Too much to consider doing. Over and over, she pictured the sequence, but the link between her will and her body had snapped. Overwhelmed by all she couldn't do, she stayed in bed. Deciding if she wanted a pillow was a major task. Some days it was the only decision she could make. To get from her bed to the door was an insurmountable distance. And even during those hours when she managed to get up, everything she used to enjoy—sewing, listening to music, reading, shopping for fabrics—became a mountain to whittle down. And for what? She had nothing to look forward to. Except to keep whittling down that mountain of all she hadn't done so that it would not fall on her.

Unless it had already fallen on her. Because she felt as though she lived beneath it—without air; without light. Not every hour, though. She was not like that every hour. Sometimes she crawled from beneath that mountain with tremendous effort, forcing herself to slide her legs out of bed; push her feet into slippers; stand up; walk to the closet; pull her bathrobe from the hook; lift one arm into a sleeve, then the other; button the front; brush her teeth; wash her face; cook; sew, even.

She discovered that when she was away from home, she could sometimes follow through on what she needed to do. Other days, all she accomplished was to get out of the apartment, and she'd wander her neighborhood, farther and farther away from home, relieved when it rained, so that others wouldn't see her face.

What mattered was to get from one hour to the next. From one day to the next. In the beginning it was because of Belinda. Who forced her to get up. Who demanded that she read to her, or at least string words together. Though Floria tried, she forgot the beginning of a sentence before she got to its end. She reread it. Forgot it. Stared past the book. Past her daughter.

"Try again," Belinda tugged at her.

"Don't . . . I am so tired."

"Read to me, Mama. Now!"

But she didn't trust herself to take care of her daughter. Was afraid. *Afraid of being afraid.* Afraid of others' seeing her afraid of being afraid. The fear was unlike anything she'd felt before, and she didn't know if her life would ever be ordinary again. With sleep and silence she shielded herself from others. Sewing orders were not completed. A wedding had to be delayed. She was bad luck.

The mother of the bride told her so: "You are bad luck. Don't you know that a wedding postponed means the marriage won't last?" She took the unfinished wedding gown from Floria, pins and all, though Floria had fretted which neckline would be best for this bride with the bony chest who wanted a neckline far too low. "I'll find another seamstress to finish the gown," the mother of the bride informed Floria. "Your reputation is ruined. I'll see to that. Because you're ruining my daughter's life."

"Be grateful," Floria whispered.

"For what?"

"Be grateful your daughter is alive."

"Don't you threaten me."

"Grateful. Be grateful." Floria slipped past the bride's mother and the bride's half-finished gown, leaving her door open.

When Malcolm found her, she was sitting on a swing in Slattery Park, clutching a pebble. "Hey." He sat down next to her, laid one palm against the rigid valley between her shoulders. "What do you have there?"

As she tightened her fingers around the pebble, she felt its shape, its color, imprinting itself forever into her skin.

He bent closer. "Tell me." His voice kind, urgent.

She let him peel back each finger to open her hand. Listened to herself as she told him how she'd walked from the bride's mother, how suddenly she'd had the thought how much easier it would be to not be alive. "That's when I picked up the stone. Because it scared me, the thought. And I held on to the stone and promised myself to live."

"That's good." Malcolm reached for the stone.

But Floria snapped her fingers shut. "You weren't even there."

"You know I begged them to let me be at her funeral, to send me with someone from the sheriff's office. You know they told me decisions like that are never made quickly, that there's a process to follow."

"I know . . . you weren't there when she died."

He flinched.

"And *that* you cannot blame on process and regulations."

"I only blame myself. If I'd been there that day—"

"No," she says. "I've done the same, wondered . . . what if I'd been in the kitchen with the girls and Anthony. . . ."

"If I were to promise you that I'll never be back in jail again— would you believe me?"

"If? You either promise or don't promise. Don't ask for my belief just in case."

"I promise. I promise you I'll never do anything to end up in jail again. And I won't ask for your belief till I've proven that to you." He enveloped her fist with his hand. "We'll take it home with us, your pebble."

"No."

"You'll have it as a reminder."

"Of misery?"

"Of knowing that you'll survive this."

Though she didn't want to keep the pebble, she didn't have the energy to stop Malcolm; but when he opened the apartment door, she wouldn't go inside. "I'm scared of having it in there."

"It's just a stone."

"It'll remind me how . . . I felt when I found it."

"You want me to throw it out?"

"Oh no. That's . . . dangerous. Because it means both—the not wanting to live, and the promising myself to stay alive."

"Then let me take it back where you found it."

"Not to the playground."

"Someplace in the park where you don't go. I'll figure something out." Gently, he opened her fist. Took the pebble, egg-shaped, a mottled sand-yellow.

For two hours he was gone, and when she asked him where he'd left it, he said, "I considered several hiding places, but none of them felt right till I found a crevice between some rocks. I pushed your pebble in there for safekeeping. Maybe, someday, you'll want it back."

"No." But already she imagined going there. Felt the danger. The promise. "Would I find it?"

"I'd find it for you," he assured her.

In the half-light of church, others are kneeling—most of them women—fast lips murmuring, belief a habit, a birthright. Above the side altar, a faded Madonna is nursing Baby Jesus. For a moment Floria feels exhilarated—she hasn't seen a bare-breasted Madonna before—and she wonders who the artist is. She's glad it's not Michelangelo. Her mother has urged her to visit his tomb in Florence, but from what Floria has read about Michelangelo, it would be exhausting to be around him. Too much like her mother: capable and demanding.

All around Floria, women are praying. Have any of them known the kind of sadness that will never just be ordinary sadness again, once you know what waits for you beneath? Sadness is the trapdoor to the void. Not that it will open each time you walk across it. But you'll be aware of the void. Terrified of the void. Terrified of love. Terrified of anger. Because of that awareness, the border has changed. Though, gradually, you'll have days when you trust that the ground will hold.

As Floria rests her forehead on her linked fingers, she notices the

floor with its ancient stone mosaic: worn shades of gray and terra-
cotta. That pale dove-gray . . . she'll make slipcovers in that color,
sew curtains and pillows in terra-cotta. Instantly she feels shallow.
She's in a church, for Christ's sakes, surrounded by prayer and tears
and holy statues. Still . . . she can get some fabrics. Ask her mother
to crochet a matching afghan. And she already has a vase that
would match.

When she leaves the church, shreds of mist hang above the piazza like wings of colossal birds, and coming toward her in that
mist is a family, exquisitely dressed, the parents' hands linked to the
child between them, a girl of eight or nine, who's laughing at the
shadow-sky from her velvet collar, bouncing like a marionette,
knees knocking and elbows flailing, like children will swing from
their parents' hands. The woman's fur coat flows around her like a
cape, and within that fluidity, that playfulness, the family seems
privileged. Mist and the arches of the piazza separate them from
the rest of the world, from anyone who has not sampled that degree of happiness.

If I could be certain—

*If I could be certain Bianca is with parents like these—no longer
mine but taken care of so exquisitely in a world where, for now, I
cannot touch her—maybe, then, this is the closest I will know of
heaven. Or maybe that's what heaven is meant to be all along, that
glimpse of someone you love being safe forever.* But as the family
gets closer, Floria is stunned to see that the girl's marionette
dance—suspended like this between both parents—is the only way
she can walk. Her crooked limbs twitch as she propels herself forward, mouth open to the sky, not in laughter, but in one unending
wail.

In her hotel room, Floria undresses without turning on the light,
slips naked between the sheets. She shakes a cigarette from the
pack, strikes a match in the dark, throat greedy for that gasp of
smoke, and wills herself to believe the parents were bringing the
girl to the church at nightfall to be healed.

And that she will be healed.

Must be healed.

But all at once the girl is Bianca—*forever suspended; forever falling*—and Floria crushes her cigarette, jams one palm against her mouth. *Cheated.* Cheated out of her first glimpse of the girl: so playful and lucky and protected; cheated out of imagining a lifetime for the girl as she has imagined a lifetime for Bianca in all these years. Measuring her—what she looks like, what matters to her—by the changes in Belinda. Embarrassing herself by clinging to her surviving daughter. A mother who tries too hard, offers too much. But Belinda has learned to dodge that sticky love in school, in college, in marriage. Instead of living at home while taking classes at NYU, Belinda moved into a dorm. And after she married Jonathan, they rented a back three-room apartment in the West Village instead of returning to the Bronx.

What used to be Belinda's room is Floria's sewing room, but she keeps fresh sheets on the bed in case Belinda ever wants to stay overnight. But Belinda is perpetually in flight from Floria, planning her escape before she arrives. If Floria struggles against that flight, revs up to offer more, the flight becomes urgent, immediate. Recently, though, Belinda has also been in flight from Jonathan, who is clean in an aggressive manner, brushes his teeth after every meal, takes several showers a day; and from what Floria can tell, Belinda is getting ready for a flight more drastic than anything she has attempted before.

As the signora pours juice for Floria, she opens her lips to smile, and her lovely pout is no longer a pout, but the way her lips have to arrange themselves across her protruding gums and teeth.

"*Grazie.*"

Sun slices the red pulp in Floria's glass—*Blood of Christ; Blood of the Lamb*—and she wonders what it would be like for someone from another planet to walk into mass. Flesh of Our Savior eaten by priests and sinners. Amen. Barbaric rites. Definitely a Leonora thought. Floria reminds herself to tell her.

From the lobby comes the peck-peck of the signora's quick heels as she checks on flowers, perhaps, or deliveries. Light peels shadows from the white columns in the courtyard, and angels spill water from their palms. Did the nuns really choose those naked angels? Or did the signora? Leonora's vote would be for the nuns: *"To make up for all those clothes they have to wear. But why didn't they choose grown naked angels?"*

A few days ago the hammering ceased, and after enclosing the scaffolding with green netting, the men went away. Yesterday, the painter arrived with pails and brushes and floated behind the netting as if he were inside the watery glass of the aquarium in Coney Island, where Floria took the twins. While Belinda loved the aquarium, Bianca wailed, "It's going to break," pointing at the glass. Right away, Floria picked her up and promised the glass wouldn't break, but Bianca was inconsolable. "The glass will break . . . and then the fishies will break . . . and then—" Floria brought her nose against Bianca's, eyes against eyes. "Nothing will hurt you. I promise."

As Floria lights her third cigarette of the morning, she wonders what promises the signora has broken. Quickly, she rolls up two slices of ham, hides them in her napkin, and rushes up the stairs— sixty altogether—to her room, with its massive ceiling beams that support the clay bellies of the roof tiles. She opens her window, feeling mischievous, because the signora would disapprove of feeding the cats, and as she tosses shreds of ham onto the clay tiles, she clicks her tongue—"here . . . here . . . here"—and cats pour onto the roof in long, fluid shadows, three, then eight, a graceful swarm in the shape of a fan.

She steps from the polished door of the hotel, leaves the bay behind, and feels the town open around her in its maze, the hushed shade of yet another narrow street, the sudden brightness of yet another piazza. Some of the foundations smell of camphor and damp stone, of cat piss. She doesn't mind the camphor. Like her mother, she ties mothballs and sprigs of lavender into squares of muslin

that she tucks into out-of-season clothing, and she advises her customers to do the same. "That's how things last," she tells them.

She likes to turn corners, to come upon the unexpected, to observe faces. Shopkeepers have set out crates with vegetables and
fruits. She loves hearing the Italian words. In high school, she and
Victor felt embarrassed by their parents' accents, and it wasn't till
they both had children that they valued the Italian customs, the
language. Holding the produce in her hands makes her think of her
mother, who is a goddess with food, a priestess with food; whose
hands move gently, precisely, while she rhapsodizes about soaking
chestnuts in red wine, skinning broccoli, separating cloves of garlic.
Who becomes poetic, brilliant.

"It's where your mother's soul lives," her father likes to say.

Victor, who has inherited that gift for food, knew he wanted to
have a traveling restaurant, as he called it, when he was still in
grammar school and watched two women cater his parents' tenth
anniversary. At seventeen, he began working for a caterer in Throgs
Neck, and he had his own catering business before he was thirty.

A scrawny woman is shouting at three boys who're playing
kickball around her vegetable stand. Her ankles are frail, unsteady,
and whenever the ball gets too close to her, she shakes her cane at
the boys as if she were a conductor trying to prevent her orchestra
from escaping. Quickly, Floria positions herself between the
woman and the boys, lingers while she buys a handful of dried figs,
but when she gets nudged by the cane and the woman yells at her,
she walks away, eating her figs as she passes a fish market. She
walks beneath washlines strung between windows, sagging with
sheets and towels and underwear, all white, except for one red
blouse. As a girl, Floria wanted a blouse like that.

A man comes toward her with a tiny dog on a leash. "Rat on a
string," Victor would say. He's quick to notice rats in parks, in subway tunnels; compares them to squirrels, to tiny dogs; to pigeons:
flying rats. He hates the small park near their parents' house, where
people toss bread crumbs to the pigeons despite his warning that
feeding pigeons attracts rats. In winter, when the weeds have
shrunk to the ground, you can see the rats in the petting zoo. That's
Anthony's name for the park. Usually he's so quiet, but if he makes

a joke, it's bizarre. Petting zoo. You just stare at the ground till you see it moving, and if you clap your hands, rats scurry away, and the dead plants shiver long after the rats have passed. It's almost like dropping a stone into a pond and watching the water ripple outward from that point.

_____

Some of the streets don't have sidewalks, and she has to share the pavement with cars and motor scooters. When a bus advances, she presses herself flat against a shop window. Inside, on a satin cushion, lies a cameo brooch that resembles her own profile, as if she'd come across a lost ancestor. She hesitates. In Italy—so she has been warned—shopkeepers expect you to buy once you enter. Still, she goes into the shop. Buys the brooch for herself. Pins it on her collar, amazed at her extravagance. Enters other stores, as though buying the brooch had melted all frugality. Buys shampoo that smells of apples. Fresh mimosas wrapped in cellophane. Lotion three times as expensive as what she usually pays. An oval platter in a pattern of terra-cotta and dove-gray.

In the window of a shoe store, she notices elegant black pumps and asks to try them on. Though even the largest size is too tight, the saleswoman tries to force Floria's right foot into the stiff leather, her flying hands suggesting in some universal language that Floria can cut a few slits into the leather—there and there and there—to make the shoes fit.

"No, *grazie.*"

But the woman is already undoing the straps of Floria's other sandal, ready to crush that foot, too.

"No, *grazie.*" Floria is certain the woman would cut off a toe or two to make those shoes fit. She can see her *motioning toward the back of the shop. "Come into our special fitting room." Positioning her in front of a basin stained with blood where previous customers were fitted.*

"No," Floria says and gets away, her sandals loose, flapping around her. She bends to tighten them, and as she heads downhill, she values the solid connection to the ground her feet give her. To think how it used to bother her that her shoe size is larger than Malcolm's. *No more.*

To find her route back to the hotel, she aims for the open sky above the bay, where sounds of pigeons and motors don't get snagged as in narrow roads but travel upward. From the bay, she can orient herself by walking along the promenade, and through the side street by the *farmacia* that leads to the hotel, and to the signora with the elusive pout that's there as long as she doesn't speak and remembers to laugh with her mouth closed.

From outside the hotel window, the ginger cat stares at Floria while she bathes. Even with cats back home—smaller specimens than these Italian cats—Floria is never quite at ease. Cats, it has seemed to her ever since she was a child, have the potential for danger that flexes beneath their sleek manners, beneath their speed that's only matched in intensity by their stillness. Whenever Bianca and Belinda begged her for a kitten, she told them cats hunted other pets—especially chicks and parakeets.

As Floria opens her new bottle of lotion, she feels watched. She glances toward the window, where a black cat crouches, as if the ginger cat had been transformed. Its black fur is long and spiked, like the hair of the American students who arrive here with backpacks after hiking the cliff path between the villages of Cinque Terre, who eat their bread and cheese on the church steps or on benches along the boardwalk.

In New York, it's still too cold for that; but here you can walk along the harbor without a coat.

And sit on ancient stone steps warmed by sun.

Or decide that tomorrow you'll hike up to Nozarego.

Floria avoids the auto road, walks uphill on ancient footpaths that weave past the back doors of farmhouses. Built of stone, some of the buildings are set into the hillside. Feeling like an intruder, she follows overgrown paths that lead into steps, steps that lead into paths that haven't been used lately, though they've twisted for centuries through these hills above the sea.

The air is tinged with the smells of salt and earth. She feels limber and strong as she hikes along terraced olive groves and vineyards. From her father she knows that the soil is rocky, hard to work. Without these stone walls it would surely wash down the steep flanks of the hills. From close up, she can see the irregular pattern of the stones set into these walls, but whenever she looks up, she sees the green hillside sectioned off by toothlike borders. Below her: the glint of the sea and the tile roofs of the simple buildings she's passed. In an olive grove, sun streaks through the trees, settles on something shiny on the path. Beads of water? A spider's web? No. As Floria bends, scents of rosemary and thyme rise toward her. Silver . . . a ring. No, two rings . . . smooth, worn. One a wedding band. The other a band of four woven knots, tarnished on the inside. Someone must have lost them here, someone with small hands, because they're too tight for Floria's ring finger.

She wants to return them to their owner, or at least leave them within the village. *The priest. The priest will know.* To keep from losing the rings, she slips them on the little finger of her left hand and, instantly, is aware of someone else's unhappiness and joy next to her skin. Still, she keeps them on her finger as she follows the path toward the church. Huge and still, a bell hangs in the opening of the tower. In front of the church is an intricate mosaic of pebbles—white and black and gray and reddish brown—that form a circle with a crown at its center, surrounded by larger circles with diamond shapes, and within those diamonds are small circles. A huge circle of white stone blossoms borders the pattern. Floria has seen mosaics like these outside several churches, each one unique and yet simple. Taken from what the land has yielded, they've been laid with skill and patience, and they're far more exquisite than mosaics assembled of gold and precious stones that impoverished the parishioners.

Eight panels, tarnished brass and flashes of amber, make up the church door. But it's locked. And there's no priest. In back of the church rises the cemetery where she has promised her father to go.

Perhaps that's where the priest is. Touching the rings—*someone else's unhappiness and joy, not mine*—Floria starts up the stone path, counts twenty steps till she reaches a landing. The rest of the steps are deeper. Thirty-nine. Then three more to the side, where a gate is set into the cemetery wall.

Inside, watering cans hang from a rack next to a faucet. Floria pictures mourners in black coming here alone to visit a dead spouse or child. Filling those cans from the faucet and carrying them to the niches for the dead that are built into the walls, sealed cubicles identified by plaques and photos of the dead: a woman whose lips are thin and whose white hair is pulled into a severe bun; a man in a black suit and a tall hat sitting on a horse; a woman in her fifties who looks like a good-time girl. Quite a few of the dead have photos that don't match the years they've been alive: unlined faces and full hair, yet a lifespan of seventy or eighty.

Though some of the flowers are fresh, most are fake, their petals so faded by weather that they seem wilted, real. A few cubicles are still empty, long enough for a body. *That cavity waiting for you. Not in the earth like Bianca. What is worse, to be buried or to be sealed off? Darkness, either way. Confinement. Do you buy these final cells ahead of time, the way you buy burial plots back home? Do you visit your still-empty cubicle, staring inside whenever you climb up those steps to visit your already-dead? Do you pick the photo you want on your plaque once you're sealed within? Which one of Bianca's pictures would you choose? So hard to separate her from Belinda. Always together: in your womb; in the crib; touching each other as they sleep.*

Most Sundays, Floria takes the train to Gate of Heaven and sits on the stone bench across from Bianca's grave. Malcolm goes seldom, Belinda almost never, though she used to come with her.

A bare-chested man grins from his plaque, an aging gigolo type with a golden chain on his tanned chest. *I'm the only one here who is alive. No mourners. No priest.* She stops in front of a plaque with photos of an old man and a young man—both named Giulio Mastino. Although one Giulio was born in 1891 and the other in 1945, their death years were the same: 1972. A grandfather and grandson? Did the two Giulios die together one day? In an accident?

From the same illness? Or did their deaths merely occur the same year? And if so, then, who died last? It's crucial for Floria to know. Because of her father and Bianca. Because it's far more tragic for a grandfather to live through his grandchild's death. She hopes the Giulios were spared the loss of each other, that they died together.

And then she finds the plaque her father described to her. "A landmark . . . easy to find because it's so fancy." Chiseled into white marble, a sailor rides a dolphin toward a cross in the sky. "Once you see the sailor, count three plaques toward the gate. That's where your great-grandparents rest. They met when he was hiking through Liguria, and they got married a week later in Nozarego. And stayed there forever." A joint plaque with one photo of a woman and a man, both old; but his image is right above her engraved name, and her image above his name. For eight years he survived her, certainly long enough to have the negative reversed so the photo would match the names. Did he consider doing that? Or did he enjoy the switch?

When Floria walks back down to the church, she finds an alcove with two statues in the low wall near the brass door: a girl kneeling in front of a Madonna, who has two rosaries dangling from her folded hands. Floria pulls the rings from her finger, lays them at the feet of the Madonna statue. Someone, she expects, will see the rings and—in a village this small—recognize them. She imagines that person telling others. And others yet.

And out of imagining, then, rise troubling questions. What if a woman dropped those rings on the path because she was done with her marriage? What if that woman mistook the rings in front of the Madonna as a sign that she's meant to stay in her marriage? What if the entire village interpreted this as a miracle?

Floria doesn't want the burden of a miracle.

And she isn't certain enough about her own marriage to impose a life sentence of wedlock on someone else. To think that a simple fact—like finding these rings and placing them in front of the Madonna—may be misinterpreted as a miracle. She reaches for the rings. Stops herself from picking them up. Maybe that's what miracles really are: misinterpretations. But what if there were no misinterpretations? What if finding the rings made her part of the miracle? And what, then, are miracles? Events we can't plan or maneuver to suit us? Events that wrest belief from us and make us pay with our devotion?

Miracles . . .

Restoring something lost: health; life; two silver rings.

In bed that night, Floria wishes she'd left the rings where she found them. Perhaps someone placed them there intentionally. Still, why then on an overgrown path away from the village? Not the kind of place where you keep what you value. Unless, of course, you no longer value it. But then a foreigner finds your rings, puts them in front of the Madonna, and you now have to believe that it's a damn miracle, a miracle you don't want, a miracle that, because of witnesses—your entire village—obligates you to stay with this man you've been wanting to get away from.

Early the next morning, she hikes once more to Nozarego, determined to retrieve the rings from the Madonna and return them to the olive grove. But the paths all look alike, fig trees and olive trees and mossy stone walls. When she gets to the church, the rings are no longer at the feet of the statue. Startled, she looks around, up. Someone has hung them around the Madonna's neck by a golden ribbon, the kind of skinny ribbon used in stores for free gift-wrapping. As she touches the rings, Floria can feel the possibility of miracles. Maybe that's all faith is: the belief in the possibility of miracles. Even if you become the instrument of that miracle, that doesn't make it a false miracle: it just comes together from different elements. And perhaps, then, the real miracle is what it turns in you, what it evokes, changes.

Faith was the breath of her childhood, and miracles were as ordinary as weather or speech or hunger. *If you fall into faith that early, you can never totally free yourself. You may dismiss the rules of the church, but mysticism will stay in your blood. Because that is how it all began, where all religions touch—within that mysticism,*

*within that kernel of knowledge of something greater than you. It
goes beyond belief, beyond doubt, beyond your objections even.
And maybe that is good because it moors you in an awareness beyond your own, a communal awareness fed by centuries of belief
that withstood challenges and doubts. But how then—within that
tradition of belief—to account for the death* of a child? *How you
tried to lose your voice to God, raged against the habit of belief
that enveloped you like a nun's habit.* The habit you didn't choose
for yourself. *Odd. Habit. The habit of belief that courses through
your body, more potent than the habit of sexual desire. Because it
is far older, has lived within you longer.*

Above her a sudden movement—a tiny gray-haired woman
sweeping the balcony of the parsonage. Avoiding Floria's gaze, she
slowly pushes her broom across the same surfaces. Then the front
door of the parsonage opens, and an old priest emerges, walks
across the mosaic in the churchyard. Though he pretends not to
look at Floria, he's probably making sure she's not stealing the
rings. For an instant, she wants to ask the priest if he knows about
their owner; but that question belongs to yesterday, and too much
has happened since yesterday: the rings have been absorbed into
the legends of the village, the religious lore. To disturb them would
be sacrilege. She's done the part assigned to her by some capricious
God, and all she can do now is let the impact of the miracle sweep
forward without her.

꘎

That night, the sudden blush of her body is strong enough to wake
her, and she throws off her covers. Her calves ache from climbing
the hills. Lying bare, still drowsy, she rotates her ankles, flexes her
toes, lets her sweat cool on her skin. Staying calm makes it pass
sooner. It stays the longest high on her forehead, where the roots of
her hair meet her skin. In the early years of marriage, she and Malcolm were often awake at this hour, one of them murmuring, "Are
you awake, too?"

How she remembers his persistence—tender and laughing and

rough—the first night they were together, at the hotel where Malcolm was staying because his landlady was furious at him for trading her bicycle for a set of golf clubs. Floria took off her brassiere, but she kept on her girdle that entire night, even though part of her longed to strip it off in the heated back-and-forth between them.

As a young man, Malcolm was restless, full of schemes and enthusiasm, and while that made him an exciting lover, it also made him irresponsible. After they married, she found he was always reaching beyond what he had at home and at work, reaching beyond the law till the law punished him. Still, each time he returned from jail, he snared her, charmed and embarrassed her with his eagerness—initially just eagerness for her, but soon eagerness for the next scheme that would guarantee him the easy forever-money. But though he was an operator, Floria knew he was faithful to her. For years she tried to keep him within the laws while he searched for openings. What she wanted was a husband without that restlessness, yet with the same ardor; and for years she didn't understand that his ardor and restlessness sprang from the same impulse, and that without them his blood would thicken, clot. It came about gradually, a quieting altogether, and she was so pleased by how dependable Malcolm was becoming, how settled as a husband and father, that she tried not to mind that he turned to her less often. After all, he was willing enough when she started the sex. After all, he was working harder. After all, he came home to her every evening. Until, gradually, she was the one who became restless.

Floria straightens the sheet that has tangled itself around her. She could easily be the kind of woman who strips her wedding ring from her finger. Who flings it on some overgrown path. Who leaves her husband behind. Who sets out for the life she wants. Who implores God and all angels that some fool won't come along and find her ring and try to restore it to her. She isn't quite sure yet what it is, the life she wants for herself, only that now—here, alone—she feels closer to it than she has in years.

To think that the husband of her youth would have been the ideal partner for this middle span of her life—a man who would hold his palm beneath her breasts, rub the cooling sheen toward her aureolas. But perhaps only another woman would do that, would take joy in a moment like this. For an instant she imagines a woman's hand on her breast and feels aroused. The first time she felt drawn to a woman was in eighth grade, when she had a crush on Sister Francine and couldn't concentrate in class because she was imagining the Sister walking toward her, touching her hair. Always her hair—nothing below her forehead. Her fantasies wouldn't go lower than her forehead. That was her sweetest crush ever, because it brought her some knowledge about being a woman. Nothing physical happened, of course.

And nothing physical happened with Emily-from-the-fabric-store. It all happened in Floria's fantasies. At first she enjoyed going to the fabric store, getting Emily's opinion on her sketches of styles; but then Emily nested herself in her soul, a danger to Floria's concept of herself, to her marriage. To evict Emily from her soul, she bought fabrics from different stores, got rid of Emily's patterns, aimed for what was familiar and safe within her family, familiar and safe within herself. But Emily's absence was stronger than her presence: it hollowed Floria out, nested deeper, as though a greater space had been cleared for her. Now, dancing with Leonora felt confusing. What if she sensed Floria's longing for Emily? What if she misread it as being directed toward her, God forbid? Worse yet, what if—once triggered—that longing were to leap from Floria like a flea and attach itself to any woman, including her brother's wife, God forbid.

Outside the hotel window, night is fuller than at home with its street lights and neon signs. Floria touches herself, lets herself sink into the fantasy of a woman's hand on her breast—*that's-me-that's-me-that's-me*—and suddenly wonders if it's like that for Aunt Camilla and Mrs. Feinstein. And is amazed she hasn't wondered before. Maybe because the entire family seems determined to see the relationship between the two as a friendship, a convenience of sharing space and interests. A friend to live with. To go to the movies. To restaurants.

The one man Floria would like to touch is Julian Thompson, and the instant her mind veers toward him, it's his hand on her belly, on her breast, touching her sweat with pleasure, with reverence. What would Julian think if she were to send him a postcard from Italy? Or if she were to call him once she got back home to the Bronx? Would he say: "Oh, yes, I remember you," or: "I fell in love with you the day you married Malcolm." But that won't happen until after she leaves Malcolm—and she suddenly knows that she will. In time.

—◌—

Another dusk, and Floria waits for the old woman who feeds the pigeons. When she emerges from her stairwell onto the roof—slowly; achingly—Floria is careful not to move. The old woman does not linger, just feeds those birds without haste or fondness, as if she were ironing handkerchiefs, say, or setting plates on her table. Soon, she disappears down the well, only to return with a watering can. She tilts its long spout to fill several bowls. And then she's gone once again. Another chore completed until tomorrow. Her days funneling into a sequence of days just like this day.

How little I know about her, Floria thinks when she goes out to buy her dinner. At the corner shop, where dried fish hang on hooks behind the counter, a white cat—sleek and well fed—nudges past Floria's legs and through the door before she can close it. The proprietor shakes her head, tosses slivers of food to the cat. Behind the glass display simmer long trays with pesto lasagna, broccoli rabe, breaded veal filets, layered slices of *melanzana*. . . . Floria points to the tiny sautéed zucchinis. To cheese focaccia. To *torta di acciughe*—baked anchovy pie.

In her room, she unpacks her food, peels off her black stockings, and unbuttons her dress. Feeling deliciously decadent, she sits on her mattress in her black slip, eating, while watching the Italian shopping channel: bracelets, frying pans, gowns, a set of knives.

When she first considered taking this trip, she was fearful of being alone. That's why she had to go—it's that easy; that complicated—to prove to herself that she can still enjoy traveling alone; to learn once again to let her aloneness clothe her; to remind herself not to cling to her surviving daughter; to fill the pockets of time with herself, not others as she can at home, stopping at Victor's

Festa Liguria, marketing with her mother on Castle Hill Avenue, having coffee with Leonora at Sutter's.

With her fork she pushes the anchovies aside. Too salty. She drinks a glass of water. Pulls the pins from her black bun and lets her hair fall down. Switches to a channel that's showing rescues. Though she can't understand the words of the newscaster—concerned eyes, bug eyes—she patches the stories together from images of people who are stranded: stranded on shipwrecked boats; stranded in burning buildings; stranded in snowbound cars. Though each hazard is different, the people are alike, because they survive situations that could have killed them. Not just simple survivals by averting disaster. No. These are survivals of disasters that have happened. The kind of disasters that have killed others. *Who then chooses? I would have done that for Bianca, taken her death for myself. In whatever form.* Like the mother superior in *Dialogue of the Carmelites,* who dies a long and terrifying death though she has meditated on death all her life. Yet, she bears it, because she believes it's a death that belongs to someone else, and—in return—that person will have a peaceful death. Floria saw the opera with her father, who flinched each time one of the nuns walked toward the platform of the guillotine.

She sets her food aside. Leaning against the headboard, she rubs her arches with her thumbs, implores the newscasters to bring her the story of a child—any child will do—who has survived falling from a sixth-floor window. She has heard of incidents like that, and she yearns for evidence that the story of her daughter could have ended differently.

My own story, too.

What would I be like if I were living the life of a mother whose two daughters grew up and moved out? Perhaps I'd be impatient with them to find their home in a world outside my walls, to return to me only for celebrations and emergencies.

As it is, she has to be so careful not to do too much for Belinda, not to expect confidences from her. That would only make Belinda bolt. Belinda has kept her dead twin present for Floria, for everyone in the family, especially Anthony. At family gatherings, when Floria catches him observing Belinda, she knows in her gut he's

really seeing Bianca, and it's that focus she and Anthony share—
not being able to see Belinda without seeing Bianca. Moments like
that, she's afraid to know what he's thinking, in case he's in one of
his talking moods, as frightened as she was of the psychic Leonora
sent her to the summer before Bianca's death, an olive-skinned
woman from some mid-European country, who could see Bianca's
death by touching one thumb to Floria's throat, but refused to
forewarn her.

—⌒⌒—

When Floria turns off the television, the screen glows for a few seconds, then dims. She takes her dirty laundry into the tub with her.
Like long grasses, blouses and stockings and underwear float past
her hips, between her thighs, light, so light. Scooping shampoo
foam from her hair, Floria rubs it into her clothes, rinses till she can
no longer squeeze any foam from them. Overnight, they will dry,
and come morning, they'll smell of apples, like her hair.

The high rim of the tub fits the curve of her neck and spine, and
as she sighs with contentment, she feels the cats out there in the
night, listening, purring. She adds a steady trickle of hot water, reminds herself to stay awake, but already she is drifting off, drifting
and warm, warm and dreaming. *Dreaming of traveling on a bus. In
some foreign country she can't identify. Saffron dust sweeps across
the landscape, shrouding donkeys and temples, while the bleached
road is already pulling the bus forward into the next scene of the
dream, tires bouncing, blue rectangles of sky bobbing in the open
windows. Inside, warm so warm. Two long narrow benches are
bolted against the sides of the bus. Most of the passengers are farm-
ers, faces olive-brown and lined. Floria can't understand their language. The men wear frayed jackets, and hats pulled low over their
foreheads. The women have knotted scarves beneath their chins.
Layers of skirts, once colorful, are now faded and smudged with
red and yellow. Blood and pus? Stains from vegetables and fruits?
In the hollow of skirts and spread knees the women balance wide
baskets. What Floria carries is small enough to fit in one hand: an
open box padded with pink cotton, the kind Woolworth displays*

*with jewelry. On top of the pink lies Bianca, barely two inches long
and perfectly formed. It's absolutely normal that she is that size.
Sun bakes the metal roof of the bus on the long stretch of road bor-
dered by open fields. Hot, too hot. Then the slamming of brakes.
Baskets tumbling—tomatoes, onions, peppers . . . rolling beneath
seats. Floria holds her small box, safely. But when she looks closer,
Bianca is no longer inside. Frantically, she checks beneath the pink
cotton. Nothing. She can't breathe. Other women, already on the
floor, scoop vegetables from beneath the benches. Floria drops to
her knees and tries to make them understand she's lost her child.
They beam at her, nod, pile tomatoes and onions and peppers into
their baskets. Sit back down. While Floria is still crawling through
the bus trying to get breath inside herself, crawling and staring past
legs into the shadowy spaces where—*

Water—

In her eyes—

Her mouth—

Hot water. Soapy water.

She spits it out. Coughs as she slides herself upright and turns
off the faucet that's hot to her touch. Her throat is aching, and she's
terrified of being pulled back into her dream. Because she knows
where it will lead her: to never being able to find her daughter
again. To that certainty. That history. That fear of the sadness. But
she doesn't succumb to it, gets out of the tub, dries herself, searches
for something to soothe her throat. Hoping to find some of the
blood-orange juice she gets every morning, she slips on her black
raincoat, walks barefoot down the flights of stone steps to the
lobby, empty now, and into the breakfast room.

Already, the tables are set; but the altar is still empty except for
one vase with an arrangement of flowers so fresh as if someone had
just picked them in the moonlight. In the courtyard, the air sur-
rounding the fountain is blue, and thicker than air gets during the
day. Behind the netting, the scaffolding looks surreal, airy treads
leading beyond the roofs and melting into one shimmering path
above the town, where ancient gods might choose to walk.

A shadow separates itself from the wall by the marble altar. The
signora. "You want I get you something?"

"*Grazie,* no. When do you sleep?"

Lips closed, the signora smiles her mysterious smile as if to say, "*Who needs sleep?*" She motions to a chair, and when Floria sits down, she steps in front of her.

The strawberry jacket sways against Floria's face as the signora rests both palms on her shoulders, palms that feel calloused even through the fabric of Floria's coat as the signora kneads her shoulders the way she might cause bread to rise beneath her touch, steady and spare and competent, each hand followed by the weight of the signora's body as she leans forward, her jacket releasing smells of church—myrrh and dust and candles—that evoke the crushes Floria felt as a schoolgirl, crushes she believed were her secret alone. But she's no longer the girl who envied the postulants on their walk to the altar. She's the woman inside a convent in Italy with the palms of another woman on her shoulders, weaving with the motion of that woman's body.

Nuns used to pray in this space. Did those who had more imagination than other nuns reach higher levels of immersion with their bridegroom? Was it only that lack of imagination that kept her from becoming a nun?

But now Floria has the imagination. "What have you lost?" she asks.

The hands of the signora rise to stroke her neck.

"What is the worst you have ever lost?" Floria insists.

As she tilts her head to glance into the face above her—unique, and yet so familiar in its combination of features: nose; mouth; eyes; ears—she longs to know language that would link her to the signora: yet, instantly it comes to her that they don't need words between them, that they can rely on touch, on sight, and that, if the signora were to open the buttons of her strawberry jacket, take Floria's hand, and pull it to the skin beneath her breasts, Floria would touch her cooling sweat with joy, with recognition. Not unlike the cat who carries the markings of a wilder cat, Floria sometimes feels wilder on the inside than she lets others see, wild and bold and—though it's vain to think so—gorgeous. Already she knows that what feels like a tug toward the signora measures far more; and this time she is not afraid of where it may take her.

For now, she takes in the mystery of her sensations as the signora sits down next to her. Side by side, they gaze out into the quiet
courtyard, where for hundreds of years nuns walked, following the
square outline of the court, lips murmuring prayers and exclama-
tions of enchantment. And perhaps, one dawn, two nuns sat here in
this chapel, and as the stone floor released the ancient and cold
smells you only find in places of worship, one of the nuns reached
across to the other the way Floria is now laying one hand across the
folded hands of the signora as they both contemplate the changing
light between the columns.

BELINDA 1979

Ordinary Sins

In my family, priesthood was valued. While my cousin and I were growing up, the relatives sometimes speculated that he'd become a priest. Not that Anthony ever spoke of such an inclination. But his magnitude of guilt was an ideal start for a priest who'd strive for redemption. Not redemption for himself—that request would be judged as greedy by God and had to come last, in the proper sequence, and only as result of his prayers for others—but requests for redemption for those close to him. Meaning: the relatives. Who did everything except line up.

But Anthony did not want to be a priest. Anthony wanted to be a chef. And he applied to cooking college, got in, seemed more content than I'd seen him since we were kids, even laughed when my mother and Riptide harassed him about being too skinny.

". . . beyond skinny."

"Extremely skinny."

"Don't you taste the recipes you make in school, Antonio?"

"Let's hope he finds work in a restaurant where part of his job is to taste everything."

"In great quantities."

Halfway through Anthony's first year of school, Papa snared him. "Just a few hours a week," he coaxed, "something temporary . . . while I'm restarting my business."

That was EZ Roofing. Though Papa lost that company soon, he launched it again as Ideal Roofing. New starts. New names. Dis-

count Roofing. Empire Roofing. Anthony's few hours became a few
days. Became full-time. Overtime. Wholesale Roofing.

Then I met Franklin and took him away from Jesus, and now
we had two men in my family who should have belonged to God,
who should have led the relatives in the rigorous and perpetual
climb to the one heaven that was exclusively for Catholics.

—☙

But Franklin believed in a God who let others into heaven, even
Protestants and hot-tub salesmen. A more generous God, altogether. Franklin also believed in miracles, which was fine with me,
since he considered our first meeting a miracle. It happened at a
picnic to welcome him to St. Raymond's, Riptide's parish, and he
was eating barbequed ribs with blissful concentration, his lips and
fingers so dark with the spicy sauce that I wanted to taste him. I
didn't really understand what the word "rawboned" implied till I
saw Franklin, who was defined by bones: by their length; by their
grace; by the lack of flesh to hide their exquisite shapes. Rawboned.

"You're staring at the priest." Riptide nudged me.

The priest raised his face toward me, flipped his red-kinky hair
from his forehead.

"Belinda? The priest knows you are staring."

Riptide was the one who had dragged me to this picnic though
she rarely managed to drag me to mass. She also was the one who
figured out about me and Franklin, when she noticed me at early
mass every morning that week. Since I lived just a couple of blocks
from St. Catherine's Academy, where I taught music, it was obvious
I'd made quite a detour to be here. To avoid her questions, I rushed
off right after Franklin touched my tongue with the communion
wafer.

But the Wednesday of my second week, Riptide stood waiting
for me on the steps of St. Raymond's, robust and trim, purse hinged
on her crossed arms. "The thing is to see that attraction for what it
is," she announced, "to enjoy it for what it is, to feel it through
your entire body."

"Whatever are you talking about?"

"We had handsome priests in this parish when I was young."

"Good for you." I walked away from her.

But she stayed alongside me. "To confuse your lust with love would be naïve."

"Jesus Christ, Grandmother. The man is a priest."

"True."

"You're shocking the hell out of me."

We were at the corner of Castle Hill Avenue, and I stopped to say good-bye to her; but she headed with me in the direction of Westchester Square, where I had to catch a bus to school.

"When I was your age, Belinda, I thought I invented sex."

"You did. It's in all the encyclopedias of the world: 'Natalina Amedeo invented sex in the year of our Lord 1920.' Wasn't that the year you married Grandpa?"

"Yes, but I invented sex three years before I met him."

"Not *with* Grandpa?"

"Don't be fresh." She kept to my pace without sweat, the result, I was sure, of swimming her mile a day in Great-Aunt Camilla's pool.

"So here's a correction, then: Natalina Amedeo invented sex in the year of our Lord 1917, when she—"

"—believed her parents were forever finished with sex."

"They probably were."

"All young people want to believe that. So naive about everything else that they convince themselves they know more about sex than their parents . . . at least sex the way *they* do it. As if there were so many different ways."

"Eighty-two, actually."

She peeked at me from the side.

"Just testing."

"Enjoy the lust, Belinda."

"Really, Grandma."

"Really. Lean into the lust."

"You make it sound like . . . sailing."

"Funnel your lust into your passion for music. Balance it there on the highest note. Know it's normal and don't flagellate yourself over it."

"How do I lean and funnel and balance and flagellate all at once?"

"Keep your lust on the highest note." She grasped my sleeve, stopped both of us. "Remember, you're not taking anything away from the church. As long as you don't complicate this by making it physical. Let that lust feed you. Have fun with it. Your mama—she was like that the moment she first saw Julian, like you with that priest. Five thousand candles burning at once. Should have left Malcolm at the altar and driven away with Julian. Except then she wouldn't have you and Bian— Except then I wouldn't have you. Or you wouldn't be you then, would you?"

"Are you saying she had an affair with Mr. Thompson all along?"

"Of course not. She only lusted for him. Sad thing is, she didn't keep a sense of humor about lusting. She should have enjoyed it. Too serious . . . You're more like me. But she'll get even."

"Even for what?"

"We all get even with our children. For leaving us. We get even by stealing our grandchildren's love from them. You wait, as soon as you have children, your mama will wrestle their love from you."

"There's nothing to wrestle, then. Because I'm not having children."

"Then you'd better stay away from this priest. If he quits priesthood, it won't be for a woman alone. He's the kind of man who'd want children."

"I just said I was not—"

"And take this for your encyclopedias of the world: Natalina Amedeo invented sex in the year of our Lord 1917, and not necessarily with the man she would eventually marry."

—◠

Franklin didn't know he was ready to quit priesthood till four months later, when I was no longer content to enjoy bliss with him in my imagination—funneling and leaning and balancing and flagellating in amazing configurations—and told him during confession that I couldn't sleep.

"And why is that?" he asked from the dim alcove behind the carved partition, willowy fingers linked across his eyebrows.

The confessional smelled of stale incense and musty velvet. As a girl I used to imagine most smells from what others told me, until I had my sinuses operated on and understood what it was like for scents to move freely through me.

"Why can't you sleep?" Franklin asked.

I shivered. Stared at the pale skin of his wrists where they vanished into the black cloth. I imagined his bare shoulders against my palms, the skin there smoother than on his upper arms. And, as often, imagining replaced doing, became stronger than doing, changed the air between him and me.

Turned his voice urgent and cautious when he asked, "Why?"

As I wondered about the texture of his back, the cold of the stone walls pressed against me, reminding me I was inside the church where this man—this priest—drank the blood of Jesus every mass. I hadn't been to confession in years, though I'd accumulated a list of sins, guaranteed to trap me in purgatory for a dozen life-times—even slam me into hell, judging by what I was about to do. And still . . . Still I said it, though a hundred voices inside were trying to hold me back, the voices of the relatives, of my ancestors, of all of Italy.

I said: "I can't sleep because I keep thinking about you."

—♋

When I took Franklin to the relatives, some of them flinched if I touched him—frequently, intentionally—to get them used to us being together. They didn't quite know if they should ask him to say grace before dinner, an honor they'd offer any visiting priest. But this priest was a disgraced priest, and I was Maria-Magdalena-minus-redemption, who'd caused his tumble from virtue into my bed.

Except so far Franklin had not tumbled into my bed.

Franklin slept on my couch.

Though willing to quit priesthood, he was unwilling to quit celibacy, keeping to Catholic rules there, and he consoled me by swearing he was trembling to make love to me. And I held back, didn't rush him. In the meantime, we spent quite a few evenings with other ex-priests and ex-nuns. They must have been out there all along, but they were not at all like the nuns and priests of my childhood: some wore shorts or smoked, and his friend Ruthie swore worse than my Aunt Leonora. From Ruthie, I was learning to spot ex-nuns from five hundred feet away by their sensible walking shoes and their short hair edged along their earlobes.

Franklin was fascinated by people who had *not* decided by age twelve that they had a calling. "How old were you the first time you let a boy inside you?" he asked one morning when we met by the coffeepot. Branches crowded against the windows, turning the kitchen into a tree house, a secret place where you could live without curtains.

"Fifteen."

"Where?"

I pointed to my crotch.

He laughed aloud.

"At Freedomland," I said. "Behind the New Orleans Mardi Gras ride."

"You're so brave."

"You tell that to all the teenage girls who come to you for confession?"

"Only you." Franklin pulled me toward him, hip against hip, as if we were about to pivot in a ballroom tango across the landlady's yellow-and-orange linoleum. "Remember that jingle? 'Mommy and Daddy take my hand, take me out to Freedomland, two ninety-five is all you pay in Freedomland all day. . . .'"

Franklin was twelve when he fell off his horse, hit his head on the neighbors' stone wall, and rose to his knees, unhurt and certain that God wanted him for the priesthood.

"And he wasn't even Catholic," his mother told me when Franklin took me to White Plains to meet his parents. "He'd just seen too many young-priest movies."

His father nodded. "After his riding accident, Franklin insisted on switching to Catholic school. Very uncharacteristic for our Franklin, that level of insistence."

"Very uncharacteristic," his mother said.

"Not really," Franklin said. "You taught me to always be looking for signs."

His parents glanced at each other, startled, then set their features into expressions of tolerance. Since they were Unitarians, they knew they were supposed to be tolerant. Yet, in the weeks leading to our wedding, they thanked me at least three times for talking Franklin out of being a priest. "We attempted to prevent it." So much for Unitarian tolerance.

Still, it was more tolerance than Franklin and I got from my relatives—except from Aunt Leonora, of course, who advocates tolerance. For the relatives our marriage was unthinkable—imagine, a divorced woman and a disgraced priest—more unthinkable even that we weren't allowed to marry inside a Catholic church. And yet, the ceremony, held at the VFW hall that Uncle Victor liked to rent for Festa Liguria, felt weirdly Catholic, not just because our guests included several ex-nuns and ex-priests, but mostly because I was terrified someone would step forward when the justice of the peace asked if there was anyone who had final objections. Every Catholic bride I knew had feared that disruption, and our wedding was made for a legion of bishops to intervene.

But the justice of the peace didn't even ask that question, and when Franklin said clearly, "I do," all I could think was how, when Jonathan said, "I do," Franklin was still in the seminary, praying in the chapel at dawn, studying the history of belief.

After we ate the food Uncle Victor had catered as his gift to us, after we danced to the accordion band, after Anthony went outside, after we cut the wedding cake, Papa asked us to help him think of yet another new company name.

"It should include 'Roof' or 'Roofing' in the name. Something people will remember."

"CRTDL," Aunt Leonora said without hesitation.

"CRTDL . . ." He looked intrigued.

"That's right." She tapped one crimson fingernail against the white tablecloth as if typing out the letters for Papa.

After his fifth roofing business, Wholesale Roofing, had collapsed, he'd briefly owned a gas station, the only gas station I'd ever seen that had a dry cleaning store with a flashing sign: "Your favorite jacket cleaned for free with fill-up. Minimum 7 gallons." Then came another combination business: a cavernous bicycle shop that transformed itself into a movie theater at night. Eventually, Papa returned to roofing: it was what he'd learned, what he enjoyed. And since he had Anthony—who'd graduated from cooking school but didn't work as a chef—to handle his office and occasional employees, Papa got to work on the roofs. When Anthony suggested the Yellow Pages, Papa picked names at the beginning of the alphabet, so that potential customers would find him right away—A-Okay Roofing; Affordable Roofing—except both times the name had already changed before the new Yellow Pages were published.

"CRTL . . ." Papa built a rectangle with his fingers and peered through them as though they framed those letters. Then he shifted them until they framed Mama, who was all in peach, one of the few times I'd seen her wear anything but black. She'd dyed the white gown she'd bought last year, when she married Mr. Thompson— *Call me Julian, please*—and she'd designed a peach colored lace vest to float over it. Her hair was still shorter than it used to be from her wedding haircut on Madison Avenue, the cost of ten Bronx haircuts.

"What do you think of CRTDL?" Papa asked her.

"Depends on what it means."

Papa nodded energetically.

Ever since their divorce, he and Mama had shown more ease and pleasure with each other than during marriage. Since he was the one who'd been left, I sometimes felt angry at Mama; and even though he had started dating, that too felt like her fault.

With Mr. Thompson I'd felt awkward the day I met him, because he was so eager to leave Hartford, to relocate his furniture shop to the Bronx so he could be near Mama. For me, it was all too sudden. I felt awkward with him the day he married Mama, and I felt it again on my wedding day, that awkwardness, even though Mama and I both were twice-married now. But the way they were sitting there—she all in peach, one shoulder against his as if she couldn't wait to get into bed with this man who'd decided that she wasn't allowed to smoke. I'd argued with him about it, but he said it was so she would live longer. He didn't want to hear that women in my family lived to be old and smoked all they wanted.

I felt Mama looking at me, and when she winked, I thought of the two of us sneaking cigarettes on her fire escape or hunched across her stove, taking quick puffs while the fan sucked up the smoke, chewing cough drops to disguise our breath. As conspirators, Mama and I did well; but our natural stance was flight and chase. I still fled from her sorrow, because I didn't want it to ignite mine. I couldn't be her substitute for Bianca; and yet I was the only one who looked like Bianca. In the mirror, however, it was just me—minus Bianca. *The me that confirms her absence. My likeness rotting beneath the ground. How long does it take? Is there anything left of us? Rib or skull or femur? The heart will already be gone. Perhaps the heart is always the first to go. With Jonathan it certainly was. And the body just has to follow it.* As a small girl I was hefty—Bianca and I both were: hefty and tall— and yet I ended up skinny, as though my twin's death had taken the flesh from me.

Once in a while I hated her.

Because she was dead.

Because they were in love with her absence.

And yet, to taste Mama's excess love, I sometimes let her turn me into Bianca, greedily became Bianca for her, and fed on love not intended for me though I'd never be enough for her, though she couldn't look at me without sorrow. How I fought for that love of hers, tried to make it match the intense and confusing love I felt for her. And how I kept losing, because a dead daughter was more powerful than a daughter still alive. Once, I think, Mama understood what it was like for me, because she cried and hugged me tightly and said, "I don't ever want to do this to you, make you be both daughters to me." And I stepped out of her arms and said, "I don't know what you mean."

—☙

"CRTDL . . ." Papa was saying slowly. "It's catchy, Leonora. But what does it stand for?"

"Cheap Roofs That Don't Last." Aunt Leonora did not blink.

Just then, Anthony came back in. He hesitated by the door, as if about to leave again.

Franklin's parents glanced at each other, startled, then set their features into identical expressions of tolerance.

"You got that from one of your crossword puzzles?" Papa asked Aunt Leonora.

"I made it up."

"An original. Of course."

My grandfather started coughing, and Anthony was holding himself tight, wary, as he often did. With him it was either that silence or outrageous banter, when he'd talk on that sharp edge of ribbing as if he wanted us to slap him down.

"We have a few more pieces of wedding cake," Uncle Victor announced. "Unless anyone would like more stuffed veal breast or—"

"Yes," Franklin said. "Veal for me, please. I'd also like some more of your spaghetti."

We all stared at my bridegroom as he cut his spaghetti into two-inch sections, and when my grandfather was the first to glance away, I vowed to myself that I'd teach Franklin to twirl spaghetti around his fork in the curve of his spoon.

"Another toast," my grandfather suggested in his gentle voice. "Sit down, Anthony. Join me in a toast to our lovely bride and to her—"

"I bet you have other original suggestions," Papa prompted Aunt Leonora.

"Well, if you prefer a shorter name . . ."

"Something shorter, then." As usual, he was punctuating each word with his hands. But only his hands moved. The rest of his body looked stiff. He used to deliver words with his entire body, but ever since the Quality crooks had broken his hands, Papa had seemed without full speech. Playing his accordion had been part of his language, but he'd never played again.

"You could drop the *D* and just go with CRTL," Aunt Leonora said.

"Cheap Roofs That Last?" He grinned at her like a schoolboy, eager to be praised for the right answer.

But she corrected him. "Leak."

At least four of the relatives were silently mouthing the words, "Cheap Roofs That Leak," and that instant I knew we all felt some joy at Papa's dilemma. Along with guilt for feeling that joy. None of us came to Papa's help. Not even I. Because Aunt Leonora had a right to her fury.

Fury at Papa for exploiting her son.

Fury at her son for letting himself be exploited.

I'd never really understood why Anthony would choose work that put him on roofs; but as he sat at my U-shaped banquet table, spookily quiet, observing his mother—each of her words a weapon in her fight to reclaim him—I wondered if he found some odd redemption by trading Papa his labor for my sister's life. Even if Papa was hatching some strange revenge, Anthony had become an accomplice to being used.

Suddenly I was tired of his silence, his miserable silence. I used to think it was a game, daring himself to make it through a family dinner without speaking. One afternoon at Jones Beach last summer, when I offered him my suntan lotion and he shook his head, I decided to find out how that kind of silence felt. I continued to look at him quietly, fully knowing that, unlike Papa, who took what he could, Anthony had trouble accepting even compliments or a second cup of coffee or my suntan lotion. He'd rather burn. Suffer some more.

I continued to wait. Quietly. But I lasted barely two minutes. "You'd rather burn?" I finally yelled at him.

He looked pained.

"What do you want, Anthony? Suffer some more?"

Still, he wouldn't speak.

"Hold still. Goddamn you." I jumped up from my towel, opened the bottle, smeared lotion on his back; and when he flinched I said, "Just hold still."

Anthony wasn't there the morning my twin was put into the earth with her favorite toys and sweets in her coffin, with Nik-L-Nips and Bazooka bubble gum and paper candies and Chuckles, with her Tiny Tears doll, who could cry real tears, but not with the Superman cape that had failed her so.

I tucked Papa's domino game into my sister's coffin, because he wasn't allowed to be at her funeral. On the phone from jail, he'd cried, and I'd promised to find something that was his and send it with Bianca.

Afterwards, at my grandparents' house, where we were staying for a while, Anthony's father whispered to Great-Aunt Camilla that Anthony had stopped speaking the day Bianca died. The sight of food made me queasy, but the grown-ups piled linguine and beans and a slice from Riptide's Christmas turkey on my plate. I carried the plate upstairs, and as I hid it under my grandparents' bed, the sudden roar of an airplane taking off startled me; when I glanced up, the Jesus with the summer tan and the curious eyes was spying on me from the painting above the dresser.

Quickly, I picked up the plate and took it outside, where the air was as gray as the siding. Its ridges looked like the ridges in cardboard, but when I pressed one fingernail against them, it didn't leave a mark. I opened the lid of the milkman's box and set my plate inside. Against the drab sky, my grandparents' wrought-iron banister looked like an ink drawing. So did the empty wrought-iron flower boxes that were bolted to the walls below the first-floor windows, from where I heard voices, laughter even. How could anyone laugh today?

All at once I had to pee. But if I went back inside, they'd only fix me another plate. I searched for something tall to squat behind. But what if another airplane came by, lower? I decided to pee standing, like a boy. Halfway down the alley, next to my grandparents' side of the attached house, I slipped my fingers beneath my black skirt and bunched myself up so that my pee had to squirt out front. Still,

I got my hands wet. What astonished me was how warm the pee was, something you don't find out when it just runs down some toilet bowl.

I didn't get to see Anthony the next day or the day after.

For twenty-three days I didn't get to see Anthony.

Not on New Year's Eve, which we didn't celebrate.

Not when school started in January.

His parents didn't send him, kept him at home, as if his heartache were bigger than mine. I felt cheated because I had to go to school though it was *my* sister who'd died.

From what I was told, his parents were taking Anthony to doctors because he still did not speak—not one word—and when one of the doctors suggested it would be best for Anthony to be somewhere else for a couple of weeks, his father and our grandfather took him to Canada.

"Why they'd think of a hunting trip, I don't understand," Riptide said. "Or why they'd figure a trip with men only will do the boy good. It's crazy."

"Perhaps we're all a bit crazed right now," my mother said.

Though I was a year older than Anthony, I wasn't allowed to come along to Canada. It bothered me that I missed him more than my sister.

During those twenty-three days, we moved to furnished rooms on Ryer Avenue, and I was transferred from St. Margaret Mary's to St. Simon Stock. In each place I'd lived so far, the furniture had been different, and I thought of it as the landlord's furniture, because all landlords merged into one person, who had the power to keep our deposit if we scratched or stained furniture more than it already was. "Careful with the landlord's furniture," Mama would remind me, because it was crucial to get a refund of our deposit, which would become the deposit for the next apartment. And there always was a next apartment. Sometimes we moved secretly, in the middle of the night, because the rent was overdue. The only pieces of furniture that moved with us were Mama's sewing machine; her dummy that followed us like an extra child; and the television that Uncle Victor had given us.

I loved the television bishop, Bishop Sheen, who'd walk toward me as if about to step from the screen, hands folded, to inspect each new apartment. Then he'd open his hands and remind me, "Believe the incredible, and you can do the impossible," and I'd look around and suddenly notice all Mama was already doing to improve the apartment, washing walls, rubbing tables and chairs with lemon oil, concealing even the nastiest upholstery beneath clean slipcovers—striped cotton for summer, green velvet for winter— that had ties and folds to adjust to any size sofa and chairs and made each apartment instantly familiar.

Most of her fabrics she bought on sale at Pring's, where the bolts were stacked so high that I couldn't see beyond them. Since new fabrics made my eyes burn, Mama would wash them, and if that was not possible, at least air them before she started cutting and sewing. Miss Pring—Emily-from-the-fabric-store, Mama called her—looked so pleased when Mama showed her new sketches or thanked her for special fabrics she'd saved for Mama in the back room. Emily-from-the-fabric-store talked with Mama about who was getting divorced, about how people liked Mama's wedding gowns. Emily-from-the-fabric-store said Mama had exquisite hands and showed me what she meant by taking Mama's hands into hers till Mama pulled away. In each new neighborhood Mama found new friends quickly, and I liked those women better than Emily-from-the-fabric-store, whose breath clung to the fabrics, bothering my eyes.

Fabrics that Mama could afford on her own were never as expensive as those she worked on for her customers, whose scraps she kept to make something for me. Sleeveless blouses took the least fabric. That's why I had several expensive-looking blouses that Mama didn't let me wear when customers came back. Though I couldn't recall which customer had brought which fabric, Mama always knew, because she believed anything that ran through your hands settled in your memory. "It gives me a lift seeing you in good clothes," she'd say.

Great-Aunt Camilla had good clothes, elegant clothes; and I craved that elegance, craved not being poor. "Camilla is fortunate," the relatives would say, "to have a friend to share apartment expenses with. That's why she can afford to live on the Upper East Side." Did any of them understand about the love between her and

Mrs. Feinstein? It probably didn't occur to them. They'd tell her to bring Mrs. Feinstein to family dinners, but she seldom did. "Mrs. Feinstein is visiting her own family," she'd say. They'd tease each other about visiting Camilla, because Mrs. Feinstein had antiquing kits and antiqued everything in sight with streaks and golden flakes. "Watch it," they'd say, "you'll come home looking antique."

— ⸙

Knowing that soon, once Anthony was back from Canada, I'd have him all to myself, was not the only good thing that happened when I no longer had a sister. I also had my own room. And my parents appreciated me more than before. I also liked the building on Ryer Avenue better than our last one, because its bricks glittered when the sun hit them, and because I no longer had to be scared of taking the trash down to the cans in the cellar but could throw it down the chute to the incinerator. The super would set the ashes on the curb for the garbage truck. Some nights you could see smoke rising from my chimney, and once a flaming piece of paper floated on the smoke and burned for an instant like a wishing star.

Whenever Mama's sadness came, I kept my leftover family together, running to the store for groceries, winding the alarm clock, boiling water for hot dogs and spaghetti. Those were the two things I knew how to make, and I'd mix them, slice the hot dogs and stir them into the spaghetti while it boiled. Margarine kept it from getting sticky, but we didn't always have margarine.

One afternoon, early in January, I found Mama crying on her bed, facedown, skirt up to her garters. I rubbed one hand between her shoulders. "I'm here," I said, "I'm here."

When Papa came home, he tried to turn Mama around.

"Don't," she whimpered.

But he pulled at her till she stood in the circle of his arms, swaying.

"Floria," he whispered. "Hey, girl—"

She coughed. "I can't."

"Take my breath." Papa blew into his palm, cupped it lightly across her mouth. "Pretend it's yours."

"I—I—"

"Swallow it. Pretend it's yours."

"Do it, Mama. Swallow," I cried. Already my family had changed from four to three, and though we'd been three before, whenever Papa had been Elsewhere, we'd always become four again. Only now we wouldn't. Because it was Bianca being away, not Papa, which meant that if he went Elsewhere again, there'd just be two of us for a while, Mama and I, and if Mama choked from coughing and died and got buried, I'd be all alone. "Swallow," I yelled at her. "Swallow Papa's breath. I said: now."

"I'm sorry." Mama's face was slippery, her mouth open.

"Belinda," Papa said, "turn on the shower. Hot. And keep the door closed."

I ran into the bathroom, scooped my rabbit from the bathtub, settled him in his cardboard box next to the toilet, and waited for the water to get hot. Odd, to see water running from the shower without anyone standing underneath it. Puffs of steam like white flowers. Aunt Leonora said white flowers were not as strong as flowers with color. I liked Aunt Leonora even though Riptide Grandma had told me that Aunt Leonora was pretty selfish; but all I could see was that Aunt Leonora was pretty, and if pretty was the same as selfish, I wanted to be pretty selfish, too. The white steam flowers were spreading their blossoms around the lamp, hiding cracks in the ceiling, curling edges of wallpaper. There'd been white flowers around Bianca's coffin. At least she was not a pagan baby.

When Papa came in, he was carrying Mama across one shoulder. One arm locking Mama's legs against his chest, he sat on the toilet lid, nudged the rabbit's box aside with his shoe, and slid Mama forward till she was sitting on his knees, leaning into his arm. "Steam will make it easier," he said. "That's it, good, Floria girl, keep breathing."

Grasping my rabbit by the folds in back of his neck, I settled him into my arms. "That's it, good, Ralph. Keep breathing." I'd had lots of pets, when all I'd really wanted was a dog. But we never had enough space. Still, Ralph was the largest of my pets. And there were small dogs that were the size of Ralph. I sneezed.

"Bless you." Sweat trickled down Papa's forehead. His chin rested on her hair.

As I crouched on the edge of the tub, I wished I could sit on his knees.

"Let's practice numbers," he said.

I scuttled closer to him.

"So, then . . . imagine you have twelve chocolate snaps. You want to keep half of them for yourself and give half to—"

"But I want to keep them all."

"Division is about sharing."

"I don't like to share."

"But knowing division helps you to make sure you don't ever get cheated."

"You wouldn't cheat me."

"Not you."

"I'll share them with Anthony."

"So, after you give half of the chocolate snaps to your cousin, how many do you have left for yourself?" Papa's voice sounded fuzzy as the steam flowers wrapped themselves around each word. Where the mirror had been was a milky square.

"Six."

"Right. Twelve divided by two equals six. Twelve chocolate snaps shared by two children equals six. Now, what if you want to share those twelve chocolate snaps with Anthony and Uncle Victor?" He raised one hand from Mama's thigh as if shaking a pair of dice that would spill the correct number across Mama's skirt.

"Four."

"Excellent. So that's twelve divided by three equals four."

I sneezed, and when Papa motioned to his shirt pocket, I reached inside. As always, his handkerchief was fresh, folded, because he only carried it for me. I blew my nose.

"I know you can do it, Floria girl." His voice and the flowers became Mama's breath—filling and leaving her without struggle—until her sadness melted into the hot mist. All at once her breath popped, gurgled.

I laughed, and right away felt bad for laughing, because of Mama's sadness.

But Papa winked at her. "I bet you didn't know mothers burped."

"She isn't crying anymore."

Papa's hand below my chin, he tilted my face, and in the center of his light brown eyes, I found my own real self, not Bianca, who was no longer here but who'd left her clothes, so that, for a while, I had doubles of skirts and blouses and dresses and nightgowns. But most I had outgrown, except for the green skirts and striped cardigans. Now when Mama sewed she made only one outfit. For me. Except sometimes she made a smaller outfit for the doll that stayed the same size forever, just as my twin stayed the same size in photos and in my dreams, larger than the doll, but still the same size she'd been before her funeral. Sometimes I loved the doll, because she looked almost like Bianca. And sometimes I was spooked by the doll. For the same reason.

When Papa bent his neck, his hair tumbled across his eyes, hiding my reflection. He ran his fingers between his collar and his throat. Where his shirt clung to his body, it was wet.

But the heat didn't seem to bother Mama. One side of her face was resting against Papa's chest, and her lips were half open, curled. When she spoke, her voice was sleepy. "You forgot to change out of your school clothes."

I knew she was better, because she always reminded me to take off my brown uniform as soon as I got home from school

"I'm . . . soaked. . . ." Her face moved against Papa's shirt. Bunched it up.

"Set down that rabbit, Belinda, and dry yourself off. Give me one of those towels, too." He dried Mama's face and neck. Her wrists and arms. "I'll make you some hot milk and honey."

I followed him as he carried Mama into the kitchen.

Before he lowered her onto the green couch, he tightened his arms around her. "You want the radio on?"

"Close the window, quickly." She started to cry. "I can't believe I left the window open." Usually Mama opened the windows at dawn, when everyone else was still asleep, and closed them before I got up. But today the window was open. "I can't leave windows open and get everyone killed."

"Hey—" Papa shut the window and took her by the shoulders. "Hey, girl. You've got to stop this. You've got to stop being afraid. Belinda, get a cigarette for your mama."

As I reached for her pack, my thumb snagged on the chipped table. Where the white paint had worn off, the wood was dim and grainy. I lit a cigarette for Mama.

"Schaefer is the one beer to have when you're having more than one," someone sang on the radio.

To cheer Mama, I sang the rest of the advertising jingle, though I didn't like the taste of beer. If I did, I'd drink Rheingold, because of Miss Rheingold. In grocery stores were voting boxes with pictures of girls who wanted to be the next Miss Rheingold on the radio and on the television for one whole year. Mama and I had voted for a girl with hair like ours, thick and dark. "My beer is Rheingold, the dry beer," the sign on her picture said. I hoped the dark-haired girl would win, because if she could then maybe I, too, could become the Miss Rheingold girl once I was finished with high school.

Already, I could see my picture in grocery stores for people to vote for. "My beer is Rheingold, the dry beer," I sang.

"Listen to her, Malcolm," Mama said.

———&

When I finally saw Anthony, the middle of January, he said his ear was hurting and gave me two surprises: pink bubble gum with trading cards of foreign flags; and wax lips in cherry flavor with a licorice mustache. But when I pressed them over my lips, I felt someone else's teeth marks in the red wax.

"They're used lips."

"I tried them on. Just once."

I sucked at the ends of the mustache. "I got a surprise for you, too."

Behind our building, where the bricks were gray with frost, I reached beneath my plaid skirt, shoved my crotch forward, and created an astonishing arc of yellow that made a funnel in the snow. I thought Anthony would be impressed, but he just kicked at a clump of frozen weeds, their spines curled and brittle.

That night I got spanked for playing nasty with Anthony. I didn't explain that I'd just shown him how I could pee, didn't protest the punishment, because I understood it was old punishment that belonged to me and was finally catching up—not for peeing, but for stealing the onyx giraffe. "Which hand?" Great-Aunt Camilla had asked, but Bianca had gotten the giraffe, because she'd chosen swiftly. In the other hand was an onyx bull, clumsy where the giraffe was graceful, but Bianca wouldn't take turns, wouldn't trade. What was I willing to trade? To lose? What I lost, I believed, was my soul, when I hid the giraffe inside a pair of socks and hiding turned into stealing because Bianca died. I wanted to return the giraffe to her, tuck it between her pillow and the domino game, but I was never alone with her coffin. Scared that someone would see me with her giraffe, I kept it in my pocket and only laid purple and pink paper-candies next to her elbow.

Those years after her death, Anthony and I became more like siblings than cousins—the only children in a family of adults. We both liked movies, and we had the same favorite DJ, Alan Freed on WINS, who introduced us to rock and roll, to Elvis, to Bill Haley and the Comets. We didn't talk about my twin. No one talked about my twin. The day she had fallen from our lives, she had taken along all stories of herself, leaving me with fragments of myself that didn't feel true. Stories about our first communion became stories of *my* first communion. Stories of how we learned to walk the very same day became stories of how *I* learned to walk.

Till then I'd loved stories, because the relatives would spur each other on. "You tell that part." "No, you. You do it so well." In their stories, even people long before my time became real for me. Stories often gave me bits of additional stories that might not be finished until a week, say, or a month later. And not even finished by the same person. But always finished. Except for the story of Bianca falling. That story had no ending. Because only Anthony knew.

So many ways of falling. Walking from Mama's hollow screams that follow me like screams of long-traveling birds. Now I'll have Anthony all to myself. Already, I can see Anthony and me building a snowman, training my rabbit to stand on its hind legs, riding bi-

cycles come spring. To see if I'm still the same, I climb on the sink in front of the mirror. My face is flat. All my bones have melted, and there's nothing behind those melted bones. Frightened, I touch my jaw . . . ears . . . cheeks . . . neck . . . chest . . . waist . . . belly . . . legs . . . relieved I'm still there behind my melted bones. "Now you can let Bianca come back," I pray.

—☙

Franklin and I had a long weekend for our honeymoon, and we drove along the New Jersey shore in the Oldsmobile we'd borrowed from his father. As a child, I'd yearned to live in New Jersey, because I'd pictured it as one endless meadow speckled with chicks and turtles and rabbits. From there it was quite rational to envision my twin in New Jersey, too, getting ready to fly back to the Bronx.

When Franklin and I got to Cape May, we found a swanky hotel at off-season rates right on the beach, with an indoor pool and those little rip-off refrigerators. Franklin was thirty-one years, two months, and eleven days old, and he had never been fucked. He wanted to reclaim what he had yielded to God all those years— yielded willingly, granted—and he reclaimed it with such fervor, such ecstasy, that fucking him felt holy.

Outside: waves and the half-light of moon; salt in the watery air. Inside: so many things this new husband and I didn't know about each other yet. He had an innocence about him that made me feel immeasurably wiser, though I was just two years older. As I let my hands study the landscape of his skin, where it felt rough, where it felt silken, it occurred to me that already I was learning what I'd wondered about that day in the confessional—the direction his hair grew on his back; the four small moles between his shoulder blades—and I thought, This is what it's like to discover an unfamiliar neighborhood during your first year there.

After we made love, I nestled one side of my face against his shoulder, one palm low on his flat belly. "Is this what you meant when you said you were trembling to make love to me?"

"This. Yes." He kissed me. Hard. Loving me with his soul and with his body, and I could feel that he didn't regret leaving priesthood for me. He had told me so before, but feeling it inside my body transformed it into belief. I wasn't jealous of him missing priesthood—it would have been odd if he hadn't—but there was a difference between regretting and missing, and being with other ex-priests and ex-nuns helped him through the missing.

"Fifteen? Your first time . . ."

I dipped one fingertip into his clavicle, rotated it, lightly. "I have a history of doing things early. It goes back to when I was a kid and opened presents ahead of time. I have a talent for sniffing out presents ahead of time. For a week before my fifth birthday . . . I played with a burp-me doll I found in my grandpa's music room. Whenever Riptide caught me with a gift she'd hidden, she asked, 'Wouldn't you rather be surprised?'"

"Surprise me . . ."

I stroked his pubic hair, his erection. "When I told Riptide I'd rather know than be surprised, she came at me with the same story . . . how she was seven and still living in Italy and sneaked into her parents' bedroom and opened a present intended for her first communion and got cramps at mass and threw up her first communion wafer in the aisle."

"Maybe—" Franklin raised himself toward my palm. "Maybe the priest gave her a rotten communion wafer."

"Tell that to Riptide."

"I'll give her the Vatican's statistics on rotten communion wafers. . . ."

"I felt like a thief."

Franklin's head came up, his Adam's apple a sculptor's final touch. "Opening a present ahead of time does not make you a thief."

I thought of the onyx giraffe at the bottom of the file box with old tax returns. But I told Franklin, "A thief for stealing you. Away from Jesus."

"That's not my interpretation." Franklin tunneled one arm between my thighs. Cupped me.

I pressed myself down. "I don't know much about thieves. That's not true. Papa always—"

"Here, now—" Franklin swung himself atop me.

I pushed up, against him, felt him inside me, urgent and deep. "Riptide Grandma—"

"—who is in this bed with us this very moment—"

"—grew up all tangled in guilt, and she's done her best to pass it on to Mama and me. The way I see it, you've got to keep yourself free of all that shit. I mean, when something starts feeling heavy or cross, I shake myself loose. While Mama holds on to the same kind of thing and tries to figure out what it was she has done wrong."

"This is not a . . . time to think of . . . guilt." Almost. He was almost there. Heavy and swift and almost there.

"Slow . . ." I was swaying against him. "Slow . . . Think of Riptide Grandma."

"That'll stop me altogether."

"When it comes to sex, she's quite radical."

He was thrusting himself faster.

"What I've figured out, conscience—her kind of conscience—is what makes you feel bad."

"I think of conscience as . . ." Faster now. ". . . something to figure out choices. Something instinctive."

Instinctive . . .

In-stinc-tive . . . a pulse now, the word *In-stinc-tive . . .* an echo throughout my body.

In-
stinc-
tive . . .
In-
stinc-
tive . . .
In—

"Franklin? I love you—" But it was Jonathan's voice I heard. *"You instinctively find the sun and lie in it. Like a cat."*

stinc-
tive . . .
In-
stinc—

. . . an echo throughout my body, urgent and sweet—

"You're like a cat, Belinda. You instinctively find the sun and lie in it." Another husband, same bed—"You inspire me, Belinda. You mind if I write it down? 'Like a cat, you instinctively find the sun and lie in it.'"

tive . . .

In-

stinc-

Days, Jonathan works for the IRS, but evenings he designs greeting cards. "I know I'm getting closer," he says whenever Hallmark rejects his cards, and—

"I love you," my other husband, this new husband, was saying, throat arched. "I love—"

tive . . .

In—

Franklin. Reaching between us, thumb stroking my clitoris—

In-stinc-tive . . .

In-

stinc—

tive . . . an echo, a pulse—

In—

"Franklin? I love you—"

Jonathan buying yet another one of those ridiculous books: How to Turn Your Hobby into a Career Without Leaving the House. Jonathan daydreaming of becoming eligible for the IRS home-office deduction, of designing his greeting cards while watching our children. How often—

Franklin, kissing the sweat from my temples.

stinc-

tive . . .

—do I tell Jonathan that I can't see myself with children of my own? And how many nights does he go on about our children—chil-dren, always plural—while I let him talk himself to sleep? Until one night when it feels dangerous to listen to him about chil-dren because he may convince me, outlast my will.

"Too much of myself is still missing in Bianca."

"What does that mean?"

"I don't want to talk anymore."

"I think it means you use Bianca as a scapegoat for everything you don't want to feel."

"Not with me. You cannot have children with me."

But he does his patient voice: "You'll want chil-dren before too long. It's a biological thing, Belinda."

I fly at him. "Don't tell me what I want."

He's quiet then. For almost an entire minute, he is quiet. And then accuses me, "You only do what feels good to you."

"I kissed Franklin. "He wasn't like you."

"Who?"

"Jonathan."

"I guess one more person in bed with us doesn't really matter. We already have your grandmother here."

"Let's buy a new bed."

"To make room for a few more people?"

"It's still from that other marriage."

"We'll get a new bed."

"Jonathan said I only do what feels good to me."

"Why would anyone not do just that?"

"You're cold like a cat." That's how Jonathan summarizes me when he finally believes I do not want chil-dren.

"What is it with you and cats?" I ask him. "First you go on about cats and sun, and now all of sudden cats are cold."

But he slings the last words. "Some cats eat their young, Belinda."

———❦———

Franklin was shy around cats. Our landlady had adopted two strays, and they slunk against Franklin's legs when we returned from our honeymoon. He got alarmed because he'd grown up with horses, and anything smaller seemed at risk to be harmed by his wide hands. Though he felt gangly because of his size, I found such beauty in the way his bones were linked. With most people you first noticed hair and eyes, but with Franklin you saw bones. Raw and harmonious. Rawboned. When he stroked the cats' backs, it was gingerly and with one finger; yet they sought him out, leaned against his finger as if to train him in caresses he hadn't considered yet.

In our bedroom, he unpacked dozens of tiny liquor bottles from that rip-off refrigerator in our hotel.

"When did you take those?"

"While you were in the shower."

"See . . . you use what you like, but then you tell them and pay when you check out."

Franklin looked green around the nostrils, as if just convicted of first-degree altar robbery. "I thought they were complimentary . . . like the soap and towels and notepads."

"Soap, yes. Towels, no. Notepads, yes. You didn't know. It's probably a seminary thing."

Of course, then he had to call the hotel and confess. And of course they already knew about the bottles, though not about the towels, and told him they'd mail us a bill for ninety-four dollars.

"More than the room cost us." Franklin looked stricken.

"Thank God you left the curtains."

All of that week he fretted about what things cost, about getting a job, and it became obvious how little experience he had handling money because he'd gone right from his parents' care to the care of the church.

"How's the job search?" Papa asked when he stopped by a week later.

"Franklin is applying for teaching positions," I said quickly.

"Nothing, so far," Franklin said.

Papa nodded. "Because this whole area is heavily Catholic." He was studying Franklin closely. I'd seen that look before: on Papa and on predators in *National Geographic*. And, sure enough, he said to Franklin, "Let me know if there's anything I can do."

"Thank you," Franklin started. "I—"

"Franklin doesn't need any help."

"I'm talking about advice, Belinda."

After that, Papa called every other day with offers. "We'll schedule something easy for you. . . ."

Franklin and I had fights. The same fight: he'd insist Papa was helping him; I'd insist it was all manipulation, the sincerity of the con man.

"Something temporary . . ." Papa suggested.

But already two generations were propping him up: first Uncle Victor, pitching in not for Papa's sake but to make Mama's days easier; and then Anthony, for almost fifteen years now. If I let Papa continue, he'd lure Franklin and future generations, making each exploitation sound like an opportunity.

In my family we were accustomed to him presenting his failures as successes; but there was also that other side to him, the generous side that made him be first in line when the Red Cross asked for blood donations—never mind that he might sell a business opportunity to the person waiting behind him. It was Mama's theory that his generosity was directly linked to play and profit. Like Chocolate for Jesus—those chocolate bars wrapped in red-and-silver foil with a picture of Baby Jesus that Papa helped me sell door to door, earning me first prize, a holy-card collection of saints who were both virgins and martyrs, for selling more Chocolate for Jesus than anyone in the history of St. Simon's. He also used to volunteer for the Lenten clothing drive, and he was a regular chaperon for our school trips to the Museum of Natural History and to the Central Park Zoo, where we'd wait for the hippo to charge down the concrete ramp and lunge into the murky water, splashing the wall of glass that separated us from the hippo. I worried the hippo might hurt itself on the edges of the pool that was barely large enough for four hippos, even if you crammed them in there, side by side.

When Franklin had worked for nearly a year as a roofer, his ladder slipped while he was sealing the flashing on Our Lady of Mercy. For two hours he was trapped on that pitched roof, till the nun, who was changing the water of the altar flowers, heard him shouting for help.

"It's a sign," I told him, "that God is scheming to get you back."

Franklin laughed. "You and your imagination, Belinda." His Adam's apple rode high in his elegant throat.

"That's what the nuns always told me in elementary school: 'Belinda, you have too much imagination. You fill in the blanks of what you don't understand with your imagination.' And look where it's taken me."

"Where's that?" His red hair fell forward.

"To you. When I met you at the St. Raymond's picnic, I imagined us together."

He nuzzled my neck. "It's not like you did it all alone." He smelled of tar and shingles and sun and sweat.

Though I fretted about him working on roofs, I loved that smell on him. Jonathan used to smell of soap and toothpaste, and I swear that's what killed the loving in me. When we met at NYU, we had work-study jobs in the music department. He was peculiar about smells, but I thought it was limited to food, because he complained when one of us brought in lunches with a potent smell—tuna or garlic or peanut butter. To tease him, I'd buy hot dogs or fish from street vendors. I was still not entirely sure how Jonathan and I got from those pained glances to the altar, except that some of it had to do with his voice. He and four other music students, who called themselves the Grand Concourse Troubadours, sang operas without staging them, and when I took my grandfather to *Daughter of the Regiment,* he said, "Your friend Jonathan has the kind of voice that makes you forgot where you've parked the car." The only other voice Grandpa ever said that about was Mario Lanza's.

It amazed me that Jonathan's mouth made those sounds, considering how he barely moved his lips while eating or kissing. He definitely was a better singer than kisser. But his voice was rich, generous; and he was also generous with surprises: socks with musical notes; stationery with a velvet accordion in one corner; panties with a violin embroidered on the crotch. . . .

—◌—

"Did you see any birds while you were on the church roof?" I asked Franklin.

"What does that have to do with—"

"Think. Any birds at all?"

"A pigeon."

I yanked cellophane from a head of iceberg. Dropped it on our orange-and-yellow counter. "Would you hand me Ruthie's bowls, please?"

Without stretching, Franklin reached for the top shelf and got two large bowls, an Easter present from Ruthie. Easter presents were popular with ex-nuns. Most didn't do much for birthdays, but Easter stimulated extravagance. Same with ex-priests . . . hell-bent on celebrating Easter, especially Marv, who lived with a policeman, Chris. Last Easter, they'd given us eggs they'd stenciled, and Marv had read from the Easter liturgy.

"I guess I saw a few pigeons on the roof," Franklin admitted.

"That proves it. In pictures the Holy Ghost looks like a pigeon. He even has the name of a bird—parakeet."

"Paraclete."

"Whatever you want to call it—it's scheming to get you back. And it's using my wise-ass father as some divine instrument."

"Somehow . . . I find it challenging to envision your father in the role of a divine instrument." Franklin lifted me off the landlady's linoleum. The landlady liked yellow and orange, not just on the floor, but also on the walls that were papered in frothy sunbursts that had no resemblance to the low-slanting sun of this late afternoon. "I like working for your father," Franklin said, though he knew of Papa's struggles with the law—not conscience—while Papa stalked the lucky-money, the forever-money; sniffed out deals too special to be legal; borrowed from friends and relatives without paying back; coaxed others to do his work for him.

"Church roofs are not safe." I tore the iceberg lettuce apart.

Franklin picked up the crispy core and bit into it, chewed, eyelids half shut, his body's habit of showing bliss. "I'm discovering how much I love working outdoors."

"All part of the manipulation." I dribbled blue-cheese dressing on the lettuce, sliced the portion of stuffed veal breast Uncle Victor had dropped off. It smelled every bit as good as when he'd made it for our wedding—of rosemary and bacon and hot sausage and garlic—and whenever he had any left over from a catering job, he saved it for us. We all ate off his Festa Liguria, even Mama, though she had a responsible husband now. At least twice a month, Uncle Victor got to everyone in the family. I was wary of sacrifices, but I could tell he enjoyed feeding us, and I enjoyed his generosity, enjoyed what was freely given: food and laughter, an hour together.

I set down Ruthie's Easter bowls. "You know what I like about Marv and Chris? That they sin against the pope in at least one additional way than you and I."

"How did Marv and Chris get into this?" Franklin picked up a piece of sausage and veal. "I love this stuff."

"Ruthie's bowls . . . lead to Easter presents . . . lead to ex-nuns . . . to ex-priests. . . ."

"It all follows." He licked his fingers. "Your courage to engage in skirmishes with the pope—however imaginary they may be—awes me." That was how Franklin talked at times. Distinguished. Lofty. That was why I still thought he'd make an inspiring teacher.

I reached for the top button of Franklin's denim shirt. Opened it. "The pope has won too many skirmishes already. All through my childhood. Throughout centuries."

"I had no idea he was that old."

"It doesn't matter what pope." I covered his lips with my left index finger, ran one index finger down from his beautiful throat, keeping it evenly between his nipples on its journey toward the next button. "It's the pope's office. The power. All those beliefs you're forbidden to question."

"A lot of beliefs are culturally and historically driven. And really inconsequential. Like the virgin birth." He kissed me.

I worked my hands to his next button. "All that training in guilt . . . Why, then, do I still get seduced by the hymns, the smells?"

"Maybe for you the rituals persist although the faith has waned. For me it's the opposite, really. My faith is solid as ever, but I choose my own rituals."

"Like confession?"

"Yes, but not as a sacrament."

"No, but the listening." Leaves showed their bellies to the sky, predicting rain, seeking rain. "I think Great-Aunt Camilla sees you as a father confessor without the direct line to heaven but with more compassion. That's why my grandpa confides in you, too. You don't judge. And you appreciate the mystery of faith."

"It's what drew me to priesthood. To marriage. The mystery."

"I promise to remain mysterious." I leaned into him. "My nipples—touch them."

But the phone rang, and Franklin answered just as I said, "Don't."

"No, not at all . . ." he said. "I'm always glad to hear your voice."

"Nipples," I whispered.

"What a great idea . . . But I'll let you talk about that with your daughter." He handed me the receiver.

"Not nipples."

"Would you and Franklin like to go apple picking with us at that orchard in Southampton in a couple of weeks? We'll take the train, and I'll bring a picnic and—"

"I hate apple picking."

"No, you don't."

"I know." I used to like taking the train and returning in the evening with bags full of apples, and—if the ocean was still warm enough—dried salt water on my shins.

"But I don't know if we have time. Can I discuss it with Franklin?" I asked.

"Sure . . . Julian and I'll be here all evening." Mama's voice was husky with sorrow that I was not elated to hear from her.

Sorrow like that could control you as much as the excessive teaching of religion. I'd learned that from Aunt Leonora, who'd come to us from the outside; who still felt like outside, even though she'd been family since long before I was born. But I came from within the family. As did Anthony. I think Aunt Leonora never quite belonged because, in addition to being from outside, she was not a believer—at least not in the Catholic God of my family—and she liked to flaunt her disbelief, as well as her suspicion of politicians who said they were doing God's will. Family could mean many things. Warmth and love and food and church. Church and punishment. Church and threats. Family togetherness was the best of what

I knew and the worst. Worst, I think, for my Aunt Leonora, who contributed ten dollars each year to Madalyn Murray O'Hair, who'd managed to get the Supreme Court to ban prayers in public school. Aunt Leonora was as allergic to organized religion as she was to the smell of camphor, while to Mama and Riptide camphor signified that you were taking care of what belonged to you.

I got off the phone by promising to call back, and for an instant, I missed Jonathan, who could deliver excuses with such sincerity: sprained ankle; rehearsal; flat tire. But with Franklin, any excuse became an embarrassment, because he got too flustered to recall details. Still, I tried to coach him. "Let's tell Mama out-of-state friends of your parents are visiting the day she wants to pick apples."

"What am I supposed to tell her if she asks their names?"

"She won't."

"But what if—"

"Pick any names."

"Or if she asks what kind of jobs they have? Or how many children?"

I set both palms on his shoulders, shook him lightly. "Your choice."

"But what if I say three children—"

"Franklin!"

"—and you say four children, and then—"

"—then I'll tell her I don't know them well enough, because they're your parents' friends. Then you can say whatever you think of."

He looked so terrified, that I knew we'd go because his reluctance to lie was greater than my reluctance to spend a full day with Mama. To end his agony, I called her back. Told her we'd both go with her.

"I'm glad," she said.

Still, after she hung up, I could feel the questions she hadn't asked aloud: *Why don't you visit more? Why don't you call more?* Franklin's parents had different questions, questions that were all in their eyes. Whenever we visited them, they scrutinized my belly for their much-wanted grandchild. Franklin's family was tiny: no siblings; no aunts and uncles; no grandparents. His parents' fixation on my belly could easily get crazy-making, but they were relatives now, and from relatives you put up with more than from regular people.

With relatives you appreciated. And I was on my way toward appreciating their clumsy kindness, their efforts to be flexible.

— ᦉ —

Franklin reached past me, swept aside the phone and salad, curved his hands around the back of my thighs, and raised me onto the counter. "Doing work you love," he said, "has nothing to do with manipulation."

"I need that phone. It's not a coincidence Papa has sent you on a church job."

"Are you worried about me wanting to return to the church?"

"No. Just suspicious of the church snagging you back. And that's where Papa comes in."

"Are we back to the divine instrument?"

"You bet." As I dialed 464-4664, I almost heard Papa coaching me: *Easy to remember, Belinda, my new number—only fours and sixes. You have four once. And then six once. After once comes twice, right? So you have four twice. And six twice. And then you're back to four.*

An answering machine came on—a minute of his new wife's dippy harp music. Rude. None of the other relatives had answering machines. Last February, Papa had married a woman half Mama's weight and half Mama's age, as if to win double in this game of remarriage. Dippy Diane. Whose voice floated through the receiver: "Please, do let us know who you are . . ."

I rolled my eyes at Franklin.

More harp music. ". . . and we do appreciate that you are thinking of us. . . ." Harps. ". . . and we do intend to talk with you very soon. . . ."

"Listen, Papa," I said quickly when I made it past Diane and her harp to the beep. "I want to know what the hell you think you're doing with Franklin. Pick up if you're there. If not, call me. Okay?"

Then I called Anthony, who made more business decisions than Papa anyhow, and when I reached him at the bookstore where he moonlighted most evenings, cooking Italian food in the bookstore café, I told him, "I'm taking you out to lunch Saturday."

"But I—"

Before he could say anything else, I added, "HoJo's at noon. And I won't accept 'too busy,' or 'I need a root canal.'" Not much of a challenge, really, because I was a faster talker than my cousin. I hung up. "And you—" I said to my husband, "you promise me to stay away from that parakeet."

"Paraclete."

"I got a parakeet from the five and dime after our rabbit went to live in New Jersey. It had a green breast."

Franklin touched my breasts.

"Black-and-white wings. Now you're going to find wings on me, too?"

He nuzzled me, lightly, flicked his tongue, eyes half closed.

"I called it Cuddles. Except you couldn't."

"Couldn't what?"

"Cuddle it. It would nip at your fingers if you held it. We had to let it out of its cage twice a day and let it fly, get some exercise. Mama sewed a cover from wedding satin, and we tossed that across the cage at night so Cuddles would sleep. But one morning he didn't wake up. Aunt Leonora buried him. The next day she took me to the five and dime, and we came home with two white boxes, the kind they use for chow mein. One box had birdseed inside and pictures of birds on the outside. The other had a bird inside, a parakeet with a blue breast. Guess what we named that one?"

"Cuddles?"

"He was the Cuddles who didn't last long." My voice went light, and I found myself laughing, the way I often did just before I got to something sad. "He crashed into the mirror."

Franklin looked stunned. "Why are you laughing?"

"It wasn't that bad."

"Maybe that's what you need to tell yourself."

"What's this? Confession 101?"

"Right. How to postpone sorrow. Anyhow, I'm sorry Cuddles flew into the mirror."

"There were other birds. The third Cuddles came from the pet shop. Uncle Victor bought it for me and said parakeets from the pet shop were supposed to be better than from the five and dime. It was green and had a bad disposition, bit Mama when she changed its water, came after me and got its wings into my hair . . . made me feel like Medusa. We were all glad to see that Cuddles go."

"Do I dare ask what happened to that one?"

"Papa took it to our milkman in New Jersey. He liked pets and always took ours when they got too big or too messy to live in an apartment. I believe that all my pets had a better life in New Jersey. Listen to me. If that doesn't sound Catholic—some weird notion of heaven, New Jersey."

"A personal notion of heaven. We all have that."

"Not the Santa Claus God on the clouds for you?"

He shook his head. "How many more Cuddles?"

"One more. The fourth Cuddles. From the pet shop."

"I hope that one lived for a long time."

"It did."

"I'm relieved. I don't think I could handle another dead parakeet."

At HoJo's, Anthony ordered Dr Pepper and a BLT, "heavy on the B." I got coffee and onion rings. Like his mother, Anthony was short and skinny; but where she got by as petite, he was scrappy. A runt. He made up for it with green eyes and drop-dead eyelashes and a mouth the size of Pelham Bay Park. That was, *if* he decided to talk. And with Anthony, you never knew.

"Listen, Belinda," he started off, "when your father got you that job for Frankly, he—"

"Franklin," I corrected Anthony, who obviously was in the mood for outrageousness. Good. "My husband's name is Franklin. And don't tell me Papa got that job for me. Because I surely don't want it."

"Well, he did it for you. Out of gratitude."

"Gratitude for what?" I scowled to warn Anthony I knew him inside out.

"For not having to sit through another Sunday dinner with Jonathan."

Ever since Papa met Jonathan, he'd teased him by offering him only the most pungent food. He'd make chipmunk faces behind Jonathan's back, twitchy nose and buck teeth. Curl his fingers close to his mouth—fussy little paws. Mama would tell him, "Don't be so childish, Malcolm." *Childish.* From early on, Papa was my concept of what childish meant: not being able to count on someone to buy you school supplies, to teach you an entire song, to be there when you die. Childish meant that promises were no more than teases.

"Okay, then," I told Anthony, "I ditched Jonathan entirely for Papa's sake. Now that we've established that—what's this with Franklin and those goddamn church roofs?"

"Your father gave Frankly the choice of working in the office."

"Then why didn't Franklin tell me?"

"Because, quite frankly, Frankly—"

"Will you stop calling him that?"

"—wants to be on the roof and does not want to tell you everything. Why is it so difficult to understand that he likes working for your father? Or that I like working for your father?"

"You wanted to be a cook."

"And your husband wanted to be a priest. But then the priest wanted to be a husband. And now the husband wants to be on the roof."

I had to laugh.

"So—let me decide what I like. Let Franklin decide. And maybe assume that your father is good at what he does. Why do you think Franklin didn't tell you that your father offered him an office job? Because you would make him take that office job."

"You're damn right I would. Because I don't want him stuck on some church roof."

"I don't see why they're different from other roofs."

"Because Franklin used to be a priest."

"You really want your father to turn down jobs because you snatch priests from altars?"

"I snatched him from the confessional. If you care to be accurate."

"I always care to be accurate. Listen, your father and I have trained Franklin for a job he had zero training for. I mean, we get very few confessions on the roof, and so far we haven't had requests for him to bless water. As for last rites—"

"You'll be needing those for yourself if you don't keep him off church roofs."

"We've all gotten stuck on roofs. Just a few weeks ago, I was cleaning gutters on a three-story in Queens when the hose looped around the ladder and pulled it down, so that—"

"I'm so fucking sick of that story."

"I've never fucking told you *that* story."

"I've heard it. Believe me. Countless versions of the same fucking story."

"Well, this one's a different fucking story about a different fucking roof."

"Watch your mouth."

"You talk filth like that around your priest."

"Sure."

"And you still pee standing up?"

"Eventually I figured it wasn't worth it."

"Good. Because otherwise—" Anthony grinned his smutty-little-boy grin.

I could guess where he was heading with that one, and I quickly took it from him. "Because otherwise I would have grown balls."

"You got balls."

"Takes balls to grow balls."

"So that's how it works. Balls to go with that make-believe pecker. Which leads to make-believe-pecker envy."

"The only time I get pecker envy is when it comes to peeing outdoors."

"I hope you're not corrupting your priest with any of this."

"*You* would blush."

"Church isn't what it used to be."

"Thank heavens and the parakeet for that."

Though Anthony and I no longer threw rabbit droppings at each other or elbowed each other in the backseat of his father's car, we still liked to go at each other with words as we did when he called my sinus problem "ugly boogers," and I convinced him he would turn into a cocker spaniel because the liver-tasting spread on his sandwich was Alpo. While he kept spitting and crying, Bianca and I danced around him, told him if you ate dog food you turned into a dog.

"A cocker spaniel."

"All cocker spaniels are really children who ate Alpo."

"That's why they look so sad."

We could barely hear each other over Anthony's howls.

How easily he cried. Bianca and I tormented him, fought over whom he liked best, fought each other while we fought over him. We negotiated a schedule for when each of us could play alone with Anthony, and we got jealous if one of us was friendly to him during the other's time. Secretly, I knew I was his favorite. Even when I broke his belt buckle. Even when I scratched his leg. Whenever I wished I had a brother, I'd imagine him like Anthony, and then he'd be around anyhow and I wouldn't need a brother of my own.

⸻

Anthony grabbed one of my onion rings. "So I was waiting on that roof in Queens, hoping for someone to hear me. But no one did."

I resigned myself to listening. As I'd listened when Papa had come home with his stuck-on-the-roof tales.

"It was an uncommonly steep roof, Belinda."

"Amazing how the roof gets steeper and higher whenever one of you tells that story."

"It was steep."

"A big steep treacherous roof."

"You got it. And all along, the owners' dog was watching me—a Dalmatian mutt."

"Not a Great Dane?"

"Different roof. Anyhow, I finally managed to lasso that hose around the ladder and pull it up. I had to miss dinner."

"You and Papa—" All at once I was furious. "Missing dinner. Missing—"

"Your father wasn't even with me."

"Missing dinner. Missing a school concert. Arriving weeks later, breathing apologies . . . lies."

Anthony raised both palms toward me. "Hey—"

"You know how many versions of that roof story I've heard?" I could barely swallow. "The breed of dog changes. The pitch of the roof. The size of the ladder. What remains the same are the lost hours . . . days. And then he'd try and charm me by letting me win at dominoes."

"Eat your onion rings," Anthony said gently.

I slid my plate toward him.

"Dominoes . . ." He sighed. "Games . . . I don't see you often enough to stay in practice." He slopped ketchup all over my onion rings. "If you weren't my favorite relative . . ." He shook his head, suddenly serious. "What have I done to you?"

I felt that old question between us, giving me power, too much power. *What if it had been me by the window?* I'd come close to asking him before. But not this close. "Anthony—"

He looked at me, startled.

My heart was tilting. The question felt too dangerous, because knowing could be worse than what I imagined, could change what I was accustomed to seeing: *Anthony by the open window, keening the way wind will trap itself in rain gutters. While Mama leans out and screams, "BiancaBiancaBianca—" While Uncle Victor races down flights of stairs as if he believed he'd catch my twin before she'd hit the sidewalk. While Aunt Leonora grips Anthony by the shoulders, her eyes wild, but what she sees in his face she hides from everyone—from herself—by yanking him against her bathrobe, moaning, rocking with him as if, together, they were the kind of rocking toy that's weighted on the bottom and will eventually right itself.*

"What is it?" Anthony leaned back, away from me.

So many ways of falling . . . I gripped his hands.

He tried to tug his thin fingers from mine.

But I held on—tight, so tight—held on for him and for myself. And asked him: "What if it had been me, Anthony?"

He shook his head.

"By the window? That day?"

He shook his head.

"You're the one who was there with her. What if it had been me, Anthony? By the window? Would you have pushed me out instead?"

"I didn't push . . ." Something in his eyes shifted. "That winter . . . ?"

"That winter." I held my breath.

"That winter I learned to hunt. I was seven," he said, his voice suddenly that of a seven-year-old. "I went to Canada and came back with an earache. Remember?"

"I know what you're doing." By offering me his hunting story, he was dodging my question, mining for sympathy.

"I shot three rabbits."

"Did they bleed?"

He blinked.

I felt queasy. Still, I pushed. "Did they bleed, Anthony?"

"First time you cry for ten minutes. Second time you whimper. After that it's nothing." He stalled while the waitress filled my coffee cup. Then he said, "Most of that trip I cried."

"You just said you stopped crying after ten minutes."

"Crying about the rabbit, yes. But I kept crying because of the cold. Dad and Grandpa . . . they took me hunting for hours in icy weather. When I told them how my fingers and feet were hurting, Grandpa said that was good."

"Grandpa? I can't picture him saying that to a child."

"He said it was good because . . ." Anthony's scrawny face grew hollow—"a man has to understand that killing is *not* fun. I already knew that."

I felt all stiff through my neck, my shoulders. "I'm so sorry," I said, and as I looked into his frog-green eyes, I had other memories of tormenting him—*how easily he cried*—memories that made me uneasy. Bianca and I wrestling him down, sitting on him, tickling his armpits and crotch. Maybe we had to see where he was different from us. Where he was like us.

I pressed my fingertips into my shoulders, drummed them into the muscles to loosen them a bit.

"I like that Franklin of yours."

I felt him across from me, the closest I ever had to a brother, and in that instant he became every man who'd moved through my life: Papa; Franklin; my grandpa; Uncle Victor; my third-grade teacher; even my first husband. At first I didn't like it that anything about

Jonathan should remind me of these other men, considering his despicable comment about cats eating their young; but then there was that other side to him, too—familiar and tender and generous—that linked all of them. It was definitely there in Franklin and in Papa. It was also there in Anthony, despite the crap and the bluffing, and as he looked at me and nodded, I knew I could trust that he'd keep Franklin off church roofs even if he couldn't quite see why. It was enough for him that it mattered to me.

"Sorry for the Alpo," I said, "for the tickle game, for stealing Bianca's giraffe, for—"

"I knew all along you had it."

"I'm still afraid of throwing it away, of being found out."

"You could bury it—" He grimaced. "No. That's too weird."

"Bury it where?"

"In her grave. But—"

"It's not that weird."

"If you want . . ." He bent toward me, no longer keeping me away.

"But I'd need you to do this with me."

"Maybe some weekend when—"

"Next Sunday?"

"Today." His eyes locked with mine.

I nodded. "You mean get it now."

"You know where it is?"

When I said, "Yes," it was with the certainty that Anthony and I would restore the onyx giraffe to my sister, today, and I felt toward him as if we'd already done so—relieved and grateful and amazed—felt as though I were already remembering the two of us *kneeling at my twin's grave site, the onyx giraffe in my hand, smooth veins of green within other greens. Opening the earth above the coffin feels odd. We reach into the ground, not to tuck the giraffe into Bianca's coffin, but into the earth that yields to us though we have braced ourselves to come upon bone: rib or skull or femur. Yields to us.*

BOOK THREE

FLORIA 2001

The Weight of All That Was Never Brought Forward

Floria is dying. Her husband has darkened the living room where she lies on the couch, and he's holding her hands. Julian's fingers are softer than hers

sinews and bones and mottled skin that's been burning ever since Julian peeled strips of gauze from her, miles and miles of white gauze, paring her down to this last layer of herself, to her lungs half transparent with the lace her mother taught her to crochet as a girl. White on white

light and voices hanging above her

rubbing against her

"Try this, Mama." Bianca . . . a spoon against Floria's teeth. "Anthony cooked this soup for you."
"It'll be easy on your throat." Julian. Standing between her couch and the china cabinet he made for their dance trophies. Cherry and aspen

blood and light

inlaid wood, like all the furniture he builds in his shop.

Soup like seaweed . . . lukewarm and salty on Floria's tongue. Her nostrils feel bruised from the oxygen. A spoonful is all she can swallow. For nine days she has been dying—ever since Julian carried her out of Montefiore Hospital, his tweed coat flapping around her flimsy johnny. She made him bring her home because of the promise they made when they married, more than two decades ago. They were both fifty-five then, both old enough to consider their deaths despite this fierce-blooming passion that astounded them.

"Imagine, at our age," she would marvel as she'd reach for him once again.

"Imagine . . ." he'd sigh as his mouth searched her skin.

Their promise was not to let each other die among strangers. "You'll be dead first," he'd scold when he'd find her on their fire escape at night, sneaking cigarettes, or when he'd taste tobacco on her despite the cough drops after smoking.

"I'm smoking less since I married you," she'd protest and remind him of her compromise—no smoking in their apartment or in front of him.

But Julian wanted her to stop altogether, swore he'd take her for a visit to a convalescent home in Washington Heights where smokers—mouths eaten away by cancer—sucked on cigarettes through tubes that stuck from the front of their necks. "Is that how you want to end up?" he'd ask.

Every argument they had—even arguments she started whenever he repaired the furniture of her relatives for free in his shop—ended with Julian predicting she'd die of lung cancer. Not that there were many quarrels in their marriage. Amazingly easy, getting along with Julian

> the way she explains it to Belinda and Julian's son, Mick—both past thirty when their parents marry— is that she and Julian left their thorns in others before they came together.
>
> "Makes me queasy," Belinda says, "to think of Papa with any of your thorns."

"Jesus Christ, Belinda," Leonora says. "Your mother is not talking about some bleeding Jesus with a thorn crown hanging from some bleeding cross."

"It means the older we get," Julian explains, "the more your mother and I know what's worthy of fight."

But then Julian is proven true about the cancer, and he's not even the kind who likes to be right. Except about knowing as a young man that he loves her. Knowing on the day she marries Malcolm. Just as she knows. Telling her—when she calls him after her return from Italy—that he thinks of her often.

"Quite often . . . every day."

Stunning her into admitting how she watched his eyes in the rearview mirror of the limo and imagined driving away with him.

"I almost did," he confesses, "I almost drove past that church with you in your wedding gown. God, I wanted to—so much."

"When I was in Italy," she tells him, "I decided to leave Malcolm

"Malcolm . . ."

"It's me, Julian." Julian. His face above her. Gray

Years of marriage to Julian before he admits that Malcolm borrows money from him. Julian doesn't want her to know, but she prods because she recognizes the discomfort in his turned-away eyes. Long-borrowed money will cause that discomfort. Never-returned money. It's the look she's seen in the faces of her brother, her Aunt Camilla, her father, various neighbors

". . . his . . . most developed . . . skill is coaxing."

"Malcolm coaxed me, too, sweetheart."

"I'll pay . . . you back."

"It's not yours to pay back."

"Open your mouth, Mama."

"Nothing wrong . . . with . . . my mouth."

"Your mouth is just fine, Aunt Floria." Anthony

> *who cooks but is not a cook. Who is a chef. That's what Leonora reminds everyone to say. Chef. Though he learned his recipes from Floria and Victor, who learned them from Riptide: layers of eggplant with sauce and cheese, manicotti or ravioli or lasagna so hot you can't touch them for minutes, just watch the cheese dribble down the sides. It's food Floria loves. Not like Julian's anniversary food, when he takes her to gourmet restaurants—brandy sauces and whole fish with eyes—where you always pay extra for the salad*

"Chefs are . . . smarter than cooks. . . ."

"Thank you, Aunt Floria."

". . . especially if they . . . are chefs . . . in a bookstore."

"Ida and Joey send their love."

> *Half that bookstore Anthony's now that he's married to Ida*

"Old . . . to be a . . . father. All . . . that waiting."

"Floria doesn't mean it." Leonora's voice.

". . . waiting makes . . . you . . . cautious."

"True enough. Ida says I'm the kind of father who buys safety gear before choosing athletic gear for Joey."

"Sad . . . you sound sad . . . always sad when Ida moves out. . . ."

> *Some people have several marriages. Some have one marriage. But Anthony and Ida have one separation that's disrupted by intervals of marriage*

Floria has two marriages. And two wedding dresses. The first one she sewed. The second one was store-bought and too expensive

> "You're always sewing for others, sweetheart."
> But the saleswomen don't understand, even though Floria clearly says "a wedding dress," and then "a dress to wear to my wedding." A bride her age is beyond their imagination.
> "Are you the mother of the bride?"
> "Are you a guest?"

"I'm it . . . the bride. . . ."
"Mama?"
"She said something about being a bride."
"Laughing . . . gas . . ."
"Everyone is here, Mama."

> "Oh," the saleswomen say. Congratulate her. Lead her to mother of the bride outfits. Outfits to be buried in.
> "Beige is not a good color for me."
> "If you just put on some lipstick. Some eyeshadow."
> "I'd feel funny with all that smeared on my face."
> They suggest different shoes, a higher heel, straps though she's already wearing the shoes she plans to wear for her wedding. New dress. But time-proven shoes.
> "Here is your way out," she tells Julian that night.
> "Saleswomen have trouble seeing me as a bride."
> "I've always seen you as a bride. For over thirty years I've thought of you as a bride."
> When the photos of their wedding are developed, Floria gets out the album of her first wedding, looks with her new husband at pictures of herself as a much younger bride. "I was there," Julian says, "see, I was there, the best man," as if he'd

been with her from that day forward; as if Malcolm had been no more than a switch in her life, an idea, an inconvenience; as if she could rewind her memories and relive them with Julian. But those years of being with Malcolm are part of her life, too, and brought her two daughters

"Good. She's swallowing."

"Hot . . ."

"I'll blow on it for you, Mama." Bianca's voice.

Hot, Floria's face is hot

from playing in the schoolyard, rescuing ants she hides in the pocket of her blouse till she sneaks them into the castle she made for them from clay. She hides the castle beneath her bed so her mother won't find the ants and kill them. "What do you think you are doing, Floria, bringing vermin into the house?" To her mother, any animal you don't buy in the pet shop is vermin

"Vermin . . ."

"We don't have a problem with that, sweetheart."

"I can give you the name of a reasonable exterminator, Julian."

"Here is another spoonful, Mama."

"The . . . castle has . . ."

two turrets and tunnels that Floria pokes through the clay with her pencil. When the lead breaks, she fixes it with her brother's pencil sharpener. But Victor gets huffy because his sharpener is gummed up with clay. Victor can get so huffy. Gets huffy and wants to divorce Leonora, but then stays, while Floria divorces Malcolm

"Because of the . . . sweaty sleep . . ."

"Sshhh—Aunt Floria is saying something."

"Mama?"

"Because of what?"

"Sweaty . . . sleep . . ."

> *and Julian loving her while silk-sweat blossoms on her neck, spreads into her hair, slicks her breasts, her thighs, while her body is cooling itself, making her grateful for its wisdom*

"She says she's hot."

"Malcolm . . . won't touch . . ."

"What about Papa?"

"I want to . . . pay Julian . . . back."

"For what?"

"What . . . he borrowed."

"But we're married." Julian. Old man . . . so old. A glimpse into the future Floria doesn't want. "Besides, whatever you paid me would still belong to both of us."

Tears in her eyes at the relief of money not being such a problem anymore—

"Don't cry, Mama."

> *the relief of Malcolm no longer wasting money with his schemes; relief of not just owning her sewing machine and dummy, but every piece of her furniture, most of it new—store-bought or made by Julian—except for inheriting her father's Victrola. Things she wants. No more furnished apartments. No more slipcovers. No more landlords who keep her deposit. Still, first time she and Julian move, she feels she's stealing the landlord's furniture, that she should move during the night. So accustomed to furniture staying behind, to starting out with different old furniture like that brown couch on Ryer Avenue with the musty-sweet smell*

Fanning that smell away with her hands. ". . . awful . . . smell—"
"Mama—you'll tear off the tubes."
"Get a hold of her arms."

> *musty-sweet smell of the brown couch, too big for*
> *her slipcovers, brown and too soft, with divided pil-*
> *lows that swallow spoons and babies and coins*

"Hold still, Floria."
"Coins. I . . . want—"
"She's getting even more upset."
"Yes, Mama? What do you want?"
". . . pay Julian . . . back."
"Just tell her she can pay you back, Julian."
"You can pay me back, sweetheart."

> *Her father tucks money into her palm the way he*
> *does with the twins. Forgetting bills and coins in his*
> *pockets just so he can enjoy finding them*

"Now she's crying."

> *and giving them to her. Bills and coins to pay Julian*
> *back*

"Floria—"
"She's in pain."
"Quiet."

> *Quiet, first she must be quiet, because her father is*
> *wiping dust from a record with a folded undershirt.*
> *When the voice starts, he becomes flat as he leans*
> *into the breath of the voice, voice high and thin like*
> *a wail*

"Can't we give her something for the pain?"
"When's that doctor supposed to be here?"

Floria closes her hand

hides the money from them all

"Mine—"
"Of course it's yours, Aunt Floria."
"Mine—"

and it's the pebble in her palm. Days and months and years thinking of her pebble in Slattery Park, there if she needs it to remind her she wants to stay alive. Or make it possible for the not wanting to live. She knows the shape of the pebble, touches it every day with her thoughts, pictures Malcolm taking her to the park, digging his fingers into a crevice between two large stones, shaking his head, trying another gap, and pulling out her pebble. But one Sunday when she's no longer afraid and asks Malcolm to take her there—he leads her to a pebble larger than hers, brighter.
"What did you do with it, Malcolm?"
"You're holding it."
"No."
"It is just a stone."
"What did you do with it?"
"I tossed it. All right? Into some bushes."
"But where were you those hours?"
"What does it matter?"
"Because I felt safe thinking of you finding a place for the stone. And now

"—it's all . . . false."

Malcolm comes running toward her, and her mother is clicking photos, and it's no longer Slattery Park but Central Park, where her mother is making her and Malcolm run toward each other on the snow-

*covered lawn, click-clicking at the bride and groom
running toward each other, one standing still while
the other runs, arms extended. "More exuberance,"
her mother demands. "Motion." They have to repeat their run, click-click, repeat their embrace till
Floria is stiff. Frozen. Her brother's new girlfriend
offers her red cardigan. Leonora, half her size. Tries
to button that tight cardigan over Floria's satin
breasts. Good luck. The camera click-clicking.
Warming herself inside Leonora's tight red cardigan
till her mother makes her take it off before she runs
toward Malcolm again. Running toward Malcolm,
again and once again, till it's only the running*

"Julian? Let me help you change her sheets."
"Thank you."

*and the running is toward Julian, such a long time
to get there, to him, but still early enough in her life
to test him—sudden heat and silk-sweat blossoms—
and Malcolm is fading . . . one of his pranks. He can
be so childish, Malcolm. Childish and spoiled. Aunt
Camilla says he promises clouds and gives you dirt.
One trip abroad every year for Aunt Camilla, always farther away than Italy*

"Italy . . . is not far . . . enough for . . ."
"I'll take you to Italy, Mama, once you get better. We'll visit that island where they make lace."

*Lace and weddings.
"Are you the mother of the bride?"
"Are you a guest?"*

"Guest . . ."
"Yes?"
"At . . . my own . . . wedding."

"You were the bride, Floria." Leonora's voice. "A stunning bride."
"And you've already had many anniversaries with Mr. Thompson." That's Bianca.
"Do you thinks she understands what you're saying, Belinda?"
"Frogs . . ."
"What about frogs, sweetheart?"
"Julian likes . . . frogs . . . my secret."

> *The day before their first anniversary, and she's putting the frog tattoo on her butt while he's working at his furniture shop. But it won't stick, the tattoo, because she's forgotten to remove the plastic on the decal. The second frog she does just right: places it on her butt, wets it down, waits thirty seconds before pulling the backing off. And there it is—she can see it in the mirror, smack on her left buttock. To keep it from rubbing off against her underpants, she walks around bare-assed, cooks bare-assed linguine. Then pulls on a skirt just before Julian comes home.*
>
> *"I know that smile. You're up to something."*
> *She shakes her head. Grins. "My secret."*
> *Five in the morning she's awake, rolls on her right side, fits her back against his belly, burrows herself into the warmth of his half-sleep spooning, sweet spooning, till they begin to make love, and he's waking fully, and she positions herself so he has to see the tattoo.*
> *"My God." He touches it. "Does it hurt? Why would you do that?" Then the relief in his voice: "It's on top of your skin." And they're both laughing. "You're my wild woman," he says*

"Wild . . . woman." Floria feels wilder now than when she was a girl.
"Now I remember, sweetheart. That tattoo, right?"
"Cats . . . the wilder . . . cat . . ."

"What cats, Aunt Floria?"
"Did your mother have a cat, Belinda?"

> *Wilder. Wilder than she feels at twenty-two and walks tilted back to carry her huge belly. Crocheting silky white thread into her baby's christening gown. White on white. Half transparent. One gown because she doesn't know she's carrying two. That's why one twin has to wear that store-bought christening gown. Bianca. Who doesn't last. Is that why?*

"Remember . . . the gown?"
"We are all praying for you." Irish Spring and fried food. So it's the priest standing above her

> *and she's fretting with Julian about their letter to the Irish-Spring-Priest after their friend Maxine's funeral mass, where the Irish-Spring-Priest only talked about man's relationship with God, man-this and man-that. Is it too rude to tell him so? Julian says their letter is necessary. "How else will he know to do it right at another woman's funeral?"*
> *At my funeral. We just didn't know it would be this soon*

"We . . . didn't know . . . it'll . . . be this soon."

> *Maxine. Radical and conservative, outspoken on both, sending donations to Planned Parenthood and the Vatican. Whenever Maxine gets too militant, Floria stays away from her for a while. Like when their super is gossiping in the lobby about his niece. "Got herself pregnant."*
> *Maxine fixes her hot gray stare on him. "You mean she held up a sperm bank with a gun?"*
> *He laughs, uneasily.*
> *"The only fair way is to have every boy, by the*

time he's fourteen, freeze his sperm at a sperm bank and get snipped."

The super gasps. "Snipped?"

"Snipped." Maxine nods. "Once he marries, he can withdraw from his sperm account if his wife agrees. The sperm will be released to them if they both sign an agreement that they'll take care of the child resulting from his sperm. Long term it keeps your taxes down."

The super is shaking his head. "And how is that?"

"Because part of that agreement is that he pays child support if there's a divorce."

Floria and Julian like Maxine's feistiness, and that's why they have to write that letter to the Irish-Spring-Priest, who's washing Floria's legs with a sponge that's almost dry. Priests and doctors. Spoiled men, all of them, expecting your instant respect and obedience while, already, they're rushing away from you. Floria's doctor calls her "Kiddo" though she's old enough to be his grandmother. It amuses and annoys her. When she has her eye infection, he tells her to soak her eye in front of the television, as if that's all women do. When her fingernails keep breaking, Dr. Kiddo prescribes prenatal vitamins. She's not about to take them, and when the pharmacist agrees and suggests gelatin capsules instead, Floria starts to ignore much of Doctor Kiddo's advice, even makes fun of him when she comes home to Julian. But Doctor Kiddo gets even. Finds her cancer

Against her thighs, the sponge makes harsh whispers.

She doesn't want the hands of the Irish-Spring-Priest there

"Don't." She tries to raise herself on her elbows.

But it's the girl from Hospice, dipping the sponge into a basin of tepid water, wringing it out more than Floria likes.

Whispers . . . people knock at her door. Smother their steps on the rug. Neighbors murmur their I'm-so-sorries

"What can we do to help?"

"She's much too thin."

Neighbors . . . each with one nose and one mouth and two eyes and two ears, but the arrangement so different

> *nose mouth eyes ears watching faces in stores and subways, in crowds, always amazed how unique each of them looks, given how many people there are in the world and that each has the same four ingredients. Nose mouth eyes ears . . .*

"How is she doing, Julian?"

"My father-in-law's aunt had the same thing."

"Sleet. That's what they're forecasting."

"Chocolate, a two-for-one special, but only till Friday."

Floria likes Barricini's better than Loft's. " Not . . . Loft's . . ."

"We don't think of Al Gore as being handsome, but he is not a bad looking fellow."

"Too well-behaved. He should have fought for the votes that belonged to him."

> *A thief will steal more if he isn't stopped. If the law didn't stop Malcolm, he'd move her into The White House. Instead he tried to move her to Co-op City, built on swampland, on failed Freedomland. Half of the Concourse moved to Co-op City, changing the neighborhood. Mustache Sheila liked it at first, then kvetched about structural problems*

"Not for . . . me."

> *Floria knows what it's like to be the wife of a thief. Making nice though you're ashamed of his bragging*

and grabbing and coaxing. But Malcolm likes new-
ness, likes moving on. "It's in the country beyond
Pelham Bay Park," he said. "And it's affordable. At
least take a look." But looking confirmed what Flo-
ria knew—that Co-op City was ugly, and that she
didn't want to live in tall skinny boxes so near the
clouds, that you couldn't see your children playing
in the grass. In Mustache Sheila's apartment, a gap
opened as the building spread while settling, and it
got filled in with concrete

Franklin . . . praying over her. Franklin who is Belinda's priest and
became a history teacher when Malcolm died and his roofing business caved into itself, only held up by Malcolm's schemes. Franklin
prays two hours every night, and Belinda is jealous. Jealous of her
husband's God. Jealous of Bianca.
Floria closes her eyes so she can hear their voices more clearly and
tune out the breath of snow that presses against the windowpanes,
snow

> *on the day she meets Julian but marries Malcolm.*
> *White on white*

"You're so brave, Julian."
"Problem with my daughter is that she's set on having this one be a
girl."
Floria likes Franklin better than the Irish-Spring-Priest. Better than
the television bishop

> *"Believe the incredible, and you can do the impossible."*
> *But two men carry the television from her apart-*
> *ment. Repossessed*

"No television . . . bishop . . ."
"That show was the ultimate Catholic kitsch." Leonora. Of course.
"It may not be kitsch to someone else."
Leonora. At it again, she and Franklin, about religion

Leonora. At it, she and one of the nuns at Anthony's first communion. "With all that Catholic prudishness, there's the myth of Immaculate Conception, justifying a woman giving birth to a child that is not her husband's."

"It's not a myth. It's a miracle. Because of Jesus."
Leonora's neck grows longer, straighter.

"Jesus always helps when I feel nervous," the nun says. "All I need to do is pray: 'Oh Jesus, Jesus help me.'"

"I believe in an openness to other beliefs . . . to other possibilities."

"But Jesus teaches us that his is the one true religion."

"All religions give us symbols, things that help us to imagine something beyond ourselves."

The nun gets all flustered. "But Jesus—"

"It's too literal. Catholics want it all spelled out, right down to the buttons on the robes of the angels. And then they claim their images are better than the images of others. That's how the Catholic church controls us. Even sin is controlled by the church."

"How can you say that?"

"Because sexual thoughts and feelings are labeled impure. Children are made to feel unclean for enjoying the nature of their bodies and touching—"

"Tell me, Sister—" Floria's father interrupts Leonora and steps forward to block her view of the nun. "I have always wondered about the meaning of holy water."

The nun blinks.

"How did it originate, Sister?" he asks, listening attentively as she explains about baptism and Jesus and other sacraments and some more Jesus. . . .

Floria hasn't seen him like this before, her gentle father, who doesn't like to interrupt others, but here he is, taking the conversation away from Leonora,

*keeping Leonora away from the nun. And it comes
to Floria how, with his mildness, he holds the power
in the family.*

*Afterwards, Leonora tells him, "Thanks for saving
my ass."*

"Is that what I was doing?"

"You know you were."

He laughs.

*"I guess this was not the occasion to discuss reli-
gious tolerance."*

*"If you fight for too many things," he says to her,
softly, "you won't have anything."*

". . . never too . . . young to . . . believe." But too young to fuck. As
if God really cared. Of that Floria is sure. "Fuck . . ."

"Did you hear that—"

"Is she saying what I think she—"

"Fuck fuck . . . fuck . . ." The older Floria gets, the more she enjoys
that sound and how it shocks

*not for her the gaunt, sexless Jesus who waits on his
cross for the postulants, but the brown-limbed Jesus
in her parents' bedroom painting, the Jesus with his
deep-deep eyes that reveal human passion*

"Maybe she said luck or duck or—"

". . . fuck."

"Floria clearly said fuck."

"Do you have to encourage her, Leonora?"

"What do you have in mind? Send her to reform school."

"It's not funny."

". . . fuck fuck . . ."

Leonora laughs.

"Supposed to drop to the low twenties tonight."

"Mohair."

Floria tricks them by not letting on she can hear them.

Like tricking the dentist. "I can't feel the laughing gas. Is it on yet?" If she lets on how much she loves it, he'll turn it down. Laughing gas gives her the most delicious orgasms that swell through her body—slow and sweet and steady

"How much longer do you think she—"
"Could you . . . turn . . . that up a . . . bit?"

Floria asks the dentist, reminding herself to keep her hips from bucking up with bliss

"What is she doing now?"
"It's the pain."
"Mama, you want us to turn you on your side?"
"It's not . . . working . . ."

"The gas is up as high as it goes," the dentist tells her

"What's not working, sweetheart?"
"Tell us what we can do, Mama."
Laughing gas is the reason Floria understands addicts. Addicts much worse than cigarette smokers with holes in their throats. All at once she's sure her dentist knows

that all dentists know and plan orgasms for their patients at dental conventions, and what she thinks of as her trick is actually the dentists' trick to lure patients back to their drills

She has to laugh

and without any gas, imagine

but her tongue only pushes against her gums.
"Aunt Floria is choking. Look—"

A wide hand beneath the back of her neck. Julian's.
She nestles her tongue against the roof of her mouth.

My secret.

"She's quieting down."

*Secrets. Leopardman. Ants in a castle of clay. Se-
crets Leonora's psychic can't see.*
"I know this psychic on Burnside Avenue."
"I don't like psychics. They make you afraid."
*"This one's different. I've been to her twice. Mus-
tache Sheila goes to her, and the psychic has warned
her about a loose tire on her husband's cab. And it
was true."*
"So what has this psychic predicted for you?"
"That I'll have another man in my life."
"They all say that. You're too gullible."
*"Gullible . . . Now, there's a word to consider.
Naïve. Innocent. Trusting. Unsuspecting."*
*Still, Floria goes to Burnside Avenue, stands in front
of the psychic with her collar open.*
*But the moment the psychic touches Floria's throat,
she snatches her hand away. "I won't charge you
anything."*
"What did you see?"
"I can't tell your future. Or your past."
"Why not?"
"Don't worry. I won't charge you."
"Tell me what you saw."
*"I didn't see anything. That's why I won't charge
you."*
*"I don't care about you charging me. Just look
again. Please*

"Look . . . harder . . . please—"
"Look where, Mama?"
"Aunt Floria?" Anthony. Hovering

> *Floria is furious at the psychic for not warning her.*
> *Because she sees me carrying Bianca's death, as*
> *much part of me as the womb Bianca lived in. Car-*
> *rying both life and death in my body. But what if the*
> *psychic warned me? Would I watch my daughters*
> *every second? Keep all doors and windows closed?*
> *Tie them to me day and night? Yes. I would. Easier*
> *to be furious at the psychic than at Anthony who's*
> *hovering, trying to help. Always there, right there.*
> *By the window the day Bianca fell*

and now by the couch. "Aunt Floria?"
"Hovering . . ."
Someone is crying, a woman Floria remembers seeing somewhere

> *in a store, maybe. Or in a movie. And it is for the*
> *crying woman that Floria pulls the breath of snow*
> *from the window and into her voice*

so she can say clearly what she knows they all expect of her: "I
do . . . not want to . . . die."

> *Death. Raging against death, howling her terror*
> *against Malcolm's chest, wanting their love to last,*
> *believing she can't go on if he dies. One evening, the*
> *first month of their marriage, he's eating chicken*
> *cacciatore across from her at the table, and she's*
> *suddenly terrified he'll choke and die. Or go to sleep*
> *that night and die. If not now, then tomorrow. Or*
> *next week. Or that he'll collapse on a roof and die.*
> *Or have an accident on the way to work. And die.*
> *Die. But then it comes to where distance from Mal-*
> *colm is the most desirable part of their marriage,*

and she vows to herself she'll never again let herself
get that afraid of losing someone. Because if that
wish of always being with Malcolm came through, it
would be hell. And yet, with Julian, daring to hope
that forever is what they'll both want and have

"Just one more spoonful, Mama?"

"Soup . . . time . . ."

"Sshhh—she's saying something."

Floria's mother calls everyone to the table according
to what she has cooked—"Pancake time . . ." "Lin-
guine time . . ."—and her voice carries the memory
and scents of the last time she cooked that food: fish
or pancakes or linguine or chicken. After the Sunday
meal, while the men sit on the sofa for their little
naps and the children play outside with marbles or
jumpropes, that voice floats from the kitchen win-
dow: "Cheesecake

"Cheesecake . . . time . . ."

Her mother's hands, stroking her hair

no . . . the girl from Hospice. It embarrasses Floria, this stranger
touching her matted hair. Washing it. Rinsing hair in a basin never
gets it clean

Floria lies in the tub, swishes her head back and
forth underwater till her hair sways with a momen-
tum of its own. Gorgeous hair

"Joelle . . . ?"

The lean boy steps behind her, spreads his fingers,
holds the base of her skull as if in a cradle. Joelle.
A girl's name on a boy. Swiftly, gently, he fans his

fingers upward through the weight of her hair till, it
ripples toward her shoulders. "You have gorgeous
hair

"Gorgeous . . . hair . . ."
"Please, hold still. I'm almost done."

Two days before her wedding to Julian, and she en-
ters the expensive salon on Madison—on impulse
and ready to flee—to ask an opinion on what style
would be best for the shape of her face. His face in
the mirror behind hers. Joelle. Square jaw and the
eyes of an artist. His shoulders uneven, a bit too
high. Again, he fans his fingers upward. And sighs.
"You have gorgeous hair." Already, just by touching
her hair, light and full and again, he's making her
hair gorgeous, and of course she stays, lets him cut
it. Too expensive to ever come back here. With tip
the price of a really good dress. But for her wedding
she can justify. And forever fantasize being back
here with Joelle, fingers upward through her hair,
telling her, "You'll be surprised how little shampoo
you'll need now that your hair is shorter. At first it'll
feel weird, like not enough on your head, but you'll
get used to it." Joelle gives her a good-bye gift, a
chamois cloth for her face, reminds her, "Rinse,
rinse, rinse. I hope you'll come back."

The woman is still crying.
"I . . . hope you'll come . . . back," Floria tells her to make her feel
better.
"But Mama, I've been here all day." Bianca.
"Rinse, rinse, rinse—"

Bianca running ahead at the zoo, dance-running,
arms stirring the air, shouting how she loves the big

animals. "The gorillas and the hippopotamuses, rhi-
noceroses . . . and elephants especially."
And Belinda, following her, leaping. "I like birds
better. With the big animals, you know right away
where they are. But with the little ones, you have to
look forever until you see something moving. And
then you think, There's an animal. But maybe not

"Wait . . . wait for me . . . girls—"
"No one's leaving, Aunt Floria."
"We're all here, Mama."

"At least the big animals you don't lose," Bianca
shouts. "You always know where they are."
Smaller, getting smaller, her girls. Easy to lose.
Crawling through the bus. Onions and legs and
pink cotton. Hot. So hot and dusty. Baskets. Getting
smaller— "Wait . . ."
"Birds are the lucky animals."
"Not if they are in cages."
"Sparrows and swallows. Regular kinds of birds.
Birds outside."

"Wait . . ."
"I'll wait for you." Julian. Pulling the afghan to her shoulders, col-
ors of church floors, three shades of gray, two of terra-cotta.
But Floria wipes the afghan away

miles of gauze

". . . too heavy . . ."

and follows her girls, who're dance-running toward
the mist, bobbing like marionettes

"Everyone is here, Mama."

"That's . . . good, Bianca. . . ."

"But I'm Belinda."

"Sshhh. Let her."

> *closer, getting closer to her girls, but not seeing*
> *them, just hearing them chant the eletelephony*
> *poem from school, rapidly as if all one sentence:*
> *"Once there was an elephant who tried to use the*
> *telephant no no I mean an elephone who tried to use*
> *the telephone anyway he got his trunk entangled in*
> *the telephunk the more he tried to get it free the*
> *louder buzzed the telephee I fear I better drop this*
> *song of elephop and telephong*

". . . and telephong . . ."

"Aunt Floria says she wants to use the phone."

"Would you like me to call someone for you, sweetheart?"

"Why don't you just let her hold the phone?"

"Here it is."

"Now she doesn't want it."

Warm hands on Floria's ankles. Thin hands with long fingernails. Leonora's. "Let me rub your feet."

Floria feels shy. "I want Julian . . . to . . . it's something . . . special . . . between us . . ."

"Of course." A quick kiss on her forehead. Leonora. Lips that cool Floria's burning skin.

Then his hands. Julian knows instinctively where she wants him to touch. How

> *after the dancing. Rubbing her ankles, her heels, the*
> *fleshy balls behind her toes. Just so. His tongue be-*
> *tween her toes. Behind her toes. His hair*

gray now, gray and wiry. Tall, he is, Julian, tall and moving with greater ease than his son, Mick *there'll be women who'll want to take up with Julian*

"Go ahead . . . Don't . . . wait too long. . . ."
"Remember how long I waited for you already?"

Looking good on the dance floor, she and Julian, limber and young for their age, so everybody says, dancing in city competitions—the cha-cha-cha, the waltz, the tango—winning trophies. The tango, dancing the tango with Leonora. Julian is the only man who's as good a dancer as Leonora. At Floria's first wedding, he dances with Leonora. At her second wedding, Floria watches them closely, amazed how jealous she is despite and because of her love for both of them: her love for Julian immediate; her love for Leonora slow-growing, widening ever since the Sambuca night

". . . Sambuca . . ."
"Do you have any Sambuca around, Julian?"
"Leopard . . . man . . ."
Laughing. Leonora. "So that's where you are hiding out? Enjoy . . ."
"But Mama is not allowed to have alcohol with her medications."
"Does it really make a difference now?"
"Don't say it like that, Aunt Leonora."
"I just want Floria to have what she wants."
"Thank . . . you . . ." Floria knows she and Leonora would do anything for each other. Out of love for their children

one lost to death; one lost to suspicion

Rubbing her feet, Julian

readying her feet for dancing. Now. Light. So light when she dances in the mist that's half transparent,

lace and gauze, white on white, leaving him behind.
Cancer has snagged her into utmost age, a genera-
tion ahead of Julian, and now he'll never reach her.
She feels sorry for him. A voice talking close by, so
close Floria feels the humming of that voice inside
her temples . . . about spoons and cracked glass and
having to hurry. Humming

her own voice, humming about spoons, though she doesn't know
what it means except that it's important and is pushing to come
out.
"What is it, Mama? What are you saying?"
". . . spoons . . . wait for . . . me . . . Bianca?"
"I'm here."
But Floria can see that it's Belinda.
"I'm listening, Mama."
"Now you want . . . to listen. . . ."

Belinda doesn't listen the day Floria borrows Vic-
tor's car to drive her to her dorm. College only a few
miles from home, and yet Floria keeps talking . . .
talking—though she knows she must stop—as if
these forty minutes in the car are all she'll ever have
to pass every bit of her wisdom to her daughter who
won't look at her. How hurt she feels in the lobby
when Belinda says, "None of the other mothers are
here."

". . . plenty . . . of other mothers . . ."
"Mama?"
"Plenty of other mothers, for sure . . ." Julian, one hand lightly on
her sore belly, eyes so afraid. "There now. There, sweetheart."
Whispering to the visitors: "Best to agree with whatever she says.
To keep her from getting agitated."
"Agitated . . ."

There are things Floria can tell that'll agitate all of them . . . secrets that lie inside her and sometimes flicker as if on the screen of the RKO, startling her with the sudden that's-me-that's-me-that's-me. Secrets. The signora who teaches her one February dawn where women gather their pleasure. Curlicues of black iron along the steps to her parents' front door. Her mother's clay pots, geraniums, pink, set into black curlicues beneath the windows. A pink garden, her mother likes. Pink as the cave in Floria's soul when she uproots Emily. An emptiness waiting for the signora

"You can't see . . . the . . . pink in winter."
"Are you cold, sweetheart?" That afghan again

Belinda has trouble breathing in fabric stores. It's the sizing that clogs her sinuses. Emily looking at the sketchbook: lines and colors from stores, from magazines, even from the street. Styles and swatches and techniques. A certain fold. Designs Floria has sewn and designs she'll never sew. Emily . . . Moved away? Dead already like nuns in the opera house?

"And whose . . . death . . ."
"Mama? Don't go yet, Mama."
". . . am I . . . dying?"
"But you're getting better, Aunt Floria."

Nuns waiting for the guillotine. A harder death than the one I'm dying. The slam of the blade, while leftover nuns stand in line, singing hymns: ". . . the telephant no no I mean an elephone who tried to use the telephone anyway he got his trunk entangled in . . . ," their voices tapering till only one is left. Silence, then. In the ladies' room a buzz of voices tapering as stalls empty

*and others step inside. Doors slamming like the slam of
the guillotine. Floria almost says aloud how they're all
like nuns waiting. But she feels shy. On the subway, her
father says, "You should have told them." Different
ways of dying. A guillotine. An open window. Dance-
running up the hills above the turquoise bay, skipping*

"Be . . . careful, girls . . ."

*dance-running up paths the colors of dunes and earth,
past donkeys and rocky ledges, trampling thyme and
rosemary. Far below them the harbors of Santa
Margherita and Rapallo. Gates to olive groves and vineyards, to farms and sheds. And the echoes of pigeons, following girls falling or drowning or dance-running from
the smell of fish and mangoes and animals toward the
glint of rings that look like one, not two rings*

"Don't touch . . ."

someone else's unhappiness and joy next to her skin

"Just checking your oxygen, Kiddo."

*back from Italy, and asking others what they would
have done with the rings. Leonora: "I would have kept
them." Her father: "Once you pick up a young bird,
you've done harm. Because of your scent, the mother
won't feed it any longer."*

"Birds . . . young birds . . . rings are not—"
"Right, Kiddo."

*leaving the birds alone on the deserted path in the olive
grove. But what's deserted to you is a significant place
to someone else*

"Not . . . disturb . . ."

"Sorry if I disturbed you, Kiddo."

". . . the pattern."

"Make a fist. Here we go."

"Is the priest coming back, Julian?"

Priests and doctors. Spoiled men, all of them, demanding obedience. Not letting her girls touch the rings

"Someone . . . placed them here . . . intentionally."

Rosemary and thyme and your great-grandfather is hiking through Liguria, a young man hiking through an olive grove, sun streaking through the trees, settling on something shiny on the path. Beads of water? A spider's web? Silver . . . a ring. No, two rings . . . smooth, worn. One a wedding band. The other a band of four woven knots, tarnished on the inside. Leaving the rings in the next village he comes to, at the feet of the Madonna statue. A day later he hears of a miracle in the church- yard of Nozarego, how the Madonna restored two lost rings to a young woman just hours after she prayed to that statue, wedding rings of her dead par- ents, rings she wore on a chain around her neck be- cause her fingers were too large for them. Your great-grandfather returns to Nozarego, knocks at the door of the priest's house, tells him how he found the rings and left them with the statue. But the priest doesn't want to hear. Tells your great-grandfather it's a miracle, and that he is the instrument of that mira- cle. Warns that it would be a transgression to undo this miracle, that your great-grandfather must let the miracle be. The priest takes him to meet the young woman's family, and your great-grandfather marries her the following week, believing the real miracle is how the rings led him to her

"Hold still, Kiddo. You can open your fist now."

*Your girls running up the path, hair flying, stone
arches and steps and walls. Shoes in a window*

"Don't go . . . in there. They—"

*No reason to scare your twins by telling them the
saleswoman would rather cut off their toes than let
them leave without buying tight tight shoes*

"They expect . . . you to . . . buy."

*Buying prune yogurt, two in a package that's purple
with wrinkled prunes. Vitasnella. Con pezzi di prugna*

"My recommendation is still to have your wife in the hospital." Dr.
Kiddo.
"It's not what Floria wants."
"Your wife would be a lot more comfortable. And so would I."
"Not . . . about your . . . comfort . . . Dr. Kiddo."
"Floria and I have discussed this." Julian. "It's not what we want.
Anthony? Will you help me carry your aunt into the bedroom."
"I'm here."
"Lift her legs. Careful. Like that. I'll take her shoulders."

*Two men to carry one skinny woman. Years of want-
ing to weigh less, and now you miss that gravity.
One more kind of aloneness. Whenever you figure it
out, this aloneness, it tricks you, takes you one degree further. And yet the more alone you are, the
closer you get to yourself*

Julian turns off the light, and it's night again, his shape next to
yours, his sorrow. His cool fingers graze your neck, then your forehead as if you were brittle. What you need is the bulk of his body on
yours

anchoring you, searching with you for your girls in the monkey house that opens into the church where the Madonna is forever and before nursing the infant who's already the man nailed to the nearby cross, then out into the mist of the piazza—"Steam will make it easier . . . that's it, good, Floria girl, keep breathing . . ."—silver mist, and through that mist a girl dance-running toward you without help, no longer limping, but playful, Bianca, dance-running exquisitely, and Belinda right behind her, skipping, both in velvet coats, both restored to you, and once more time is forever and before. Forever and before Bianca falls

forever and before Julian fits himself against your side, cautious not to crush what's left of you

forever and before rising from the signora's bed. How much warmer the signora's body is . . . Floria does not regret it. For years it felt like something she had to bring forward, talk it and rest it and go from there. Except she didn't confess. Not with Malcolm. Not with Julian. There's something loyal about secrets—they're yours, all yours, holding on to you when nothing else will—and Floria no longer feels that anyone, even a husband, is entitled to them. If anything, she wishes she had more secrets, because the weight of all that was never brought forward has become so precious, so familiar, that to part with it would make her lighter yet

ANTHONY 2002

Acts of Violence

My mother is taking self-defense classes in the basement of a pawn shop on East 149th, the roughest neighborhood in the South Bronx. Of nine students, my mother is the oldest. The only other woman is half her age and owns a massage parlor near what used to be Alexander's.

So far, my mother has studied how to free herself from a choking hold; assault someone who comes at her with a pool cue or broken bottle; break her attacker's nose and elbow. When she visits Joey and me for the weekend in Brooklyn, she brings us fresh mozzarella from Arthur Avenue and wants to practice her maneuvers on the patio, where I'm setting the table.

"Come here, Joey, choke me from behind."

At eleven, my son is already a head taller than my mother, and when he steps toward her, he moves with a grace I certainly didn't have at his age. He has Ida's build, long and narrow.

I catch his elbow. "I don't think choking your grandmother is a good idea."

"Then you choke me, Anthony," she says.

"Let's eat. I cooked Dad's minestrone for you."

"We can eat after you choke me." White hair swings around my mother's mottled face, transforms her into a photo negative of the mother I grew up with, the mother with hair all black and skin so white it glowed. When her hair faded, it began along her left eyebrow till all her hair was white, as though, all along, it had been her true color, waiting.

"But pool cues?" I ask her. "Broken bottles? Where does that man expect you to fight? In bars?"

"He used to work as a bouncer."

"Cool," Joey says.

"Not cool."

"Cool," he repeats, defiance in his eyes—that first flare of hate?—and even as I wonder what I've missed noticing, I know he'll look at me like that again.

"The instructor says—" She drops her voice. Makes it go choppy. "'Hit hard. Then get out. Courts give criminals more rights than victims. Someone can sue you if you don't finish him. Don't leave your calling card. Go home. Read about it in the paper the next morning. Say to yourself: So a mugger got killed. . . . Hmm . . . How about that?'"

"'How about that?'" Joey imitates the accent. "'So a mugger got killed. Hmm.'"

I envy their excitement, their bond. Nudge my way in. "What is that man's background?"

"He's in his forties, about ten years younger than you, Anthony. Came over from Norway when he was a boy. Still has a face like a boy, with those—"

"That is not what I asked."

"But that's my answer."

"What is his educational background?"

"A bit of everything."

"I bet."

"He has a black belt and teaches other classes, too."

"Classes in how to hold up a liquor store? A bank?"

"Karate classes. Judo classes. Kickboxing classes."

"You could sign up for a women's self-defense class. I'm sure the YWCA has supportive programs . . . with other women there."

"If I get attacked—" My mother raises herself to her full height of five feet and one inch. "—it's unlikely that my attacker will be a woman. So I may as well train against men. And this instructor knows a lot. He even trains firefighters."

"Thugs, too, I bet."

"The week after 9/11 he started two classes that were only for firefighters."

"You really believe what he's teaching you can stop terrorists?"

"It's far more complicated than that, Anthony."

"You saw what Ground Zero looked like."

"And I'll never forget it." My mother was with us last October, when Ida and I took Joey to Ground Zero and stood on a sidewalk crowded with people from different cultures, all speechless, all grieving across from what had become a mass grave. Many of us cried. No one pushed.

Until, all at once, a young woman with brassy hair and a brassy voice started shoving, yelling. "People, move. Walk. This is a side-W-A-L-K."

I was stunned. All along I'd been reluctant to come here, to let Joey see this; but he'd told Ida and me that, before he could enjoy any part of Manhattan again, he had to cry at Ground Zero. And that's what he was doing.

"Get it, people? A side-W-A-L-K." Cheap leather jacket. Cheap makeup. A voice that could rattle a continent. "Get it?"

"Quiet," someone said.

"So . . . walk, people."

But as she went on like that, I had to smile—for the first time in weeks—because she was the one spark of life and energy here: she was the real New York. We talked about her afterwards, as we walked through Washington Square where jugglers were surrounded by audiences, where couples sunned themselves in the grass. Normal. As always. Life continuing as it was before the attack.

———⟋⟍———

"I need you to practice with me, Anthony," my mother tells me.

"I don't want to choke you."

"Will you at least grab me by the front of my collar?"

Cautiously, I test an edge of her silk collar between my right thumb and forefinger.

"Not like that." She rolls her eyes to the sky. "Jesus Christ. You're not buying fabric."

How can I tell her that we draw toward us what occupies our passion—what we dread or love or want or hate intensely—and that I'm afraid of her drawing violence toward us with those classes of hers. The same way I have drawn violence to my family. As a boy I was pushy—skutchy, she called it—until I became afraid of wanting. If wanting anything as simple as a stencil kit could kill, I resolved, I'd stop wanting altogether. But inside me, the wanting grew, a voracious beast. My life's work: to keep it caged.

My mother is watching me closely, so closely that I wonder if I've thought aloud. "There are things we need to forgive ourselves, if we are to continue breathing," she says slowly. "Certain things we . . . did as children, Anthony. Especially if we did them to keep our family intact."

We?

"But I did not keep us intact," I remind her.

"You tried."

"So . . . what bad things did you do as a child?"

She won't answer, has no sins to offer me; yet in her eyes I see a legacy of sins no son should have to imagine for his mother.

"I don't understand."

"Forgiveness," she says, "comes in the shape of a red umbrella. Comes in the canter of a horse."

"I still don't understand."

She nods. Sits down. "Can we eat now?"

"But— Of course." I give her what I'm good at. Food.

She takes a spoonful. "That little bit of ham . . . just a hint, the way your father made his minestrone. Wonderful. How is Ida?"

"All right."

"Are you talking?"

"Yes."

"To each other?"

"Of course we are talking to each other. We have to plan our visits with Joey."

"Don't call them visits." She unrolls her napkin. "Being a father does not mean visiting your child."

"Don't you think I'd like to live here with Joey all the time?"

Ida and I take turns staying in this house and in the apartment above our bookstore, so that Joey can live in one familiar place. At work, she and I navigate around each other—pleasant and helpful, from what our customers must observe—she in the bookstore, I in the attached café where, enveloped by scents of garlic and cheese and rosemary, I re-create the meals I loved as a boy. Most of what I know about cooking comes from my father and Aunt Floria: his skill; her passion. "Italian comfort food for solitary readers," one of the food critics wrote. I like to think of people coming here to be alone, satisfied as they eat and read. Watching them makes me less afraid of being alone. And so I feed them, coax them with my cooking into wanting to return.

I bought into Ida's business the year before we got married. Before that, I used to help her with the café after roofing all day. That's how we first met, when she advertised for a part-time cook. It's hard to be near Ida all day. Nights I'm haunted by the concept of Elsewhere I figured out as a boy—that men did not exist without marriage. I used to dismiss it as a child's misunderstanding, but away from Ida, Elsewhere—not belonging, not being rooted—is exactly how I feel. It makes me think of Uncle Malcolm, and though I haven't been to jail, I, too, have moved along that edge of respectability. After I started helping Uncle Malcolm with his roofing business, I didn't know how to get away from him until he died, and I was released to do the work I loved. When I married Ida, I felt myself opening myself to her as much as I knew how to. And then to Joey. But there are parts of me I can't show him or Ida. The least I deserve is the loneliness of that.

For myself. But not for them.

—ᏅᏄ—

Weeks I'm at the house, I often invite my mother, because she softens Ida's absence, the only other woman who has loved both me and Joey. But there's been nothing soft about my mother lately.

"The instructor showed us how to drive a fist into a groin," she tells us. "'Like holding an ice pick.'"

"Whenever you quote this man, you speak in this phony accent . . . some low-budget spy movie."

"'Like holding an ice pick.'" Joey is trying the accent. "'Like holding—'"

"That's just how the instructor sounds," my mother says in her own voice.

"I don't want Joey hearing this stuff."

"You're too protective of Joey."

"I never expected I'd have to protect him from you."

"From me?"

"From your influence."

"Don't say that." She looks shaken.

"Not from *you*. I'm sorry. From your self-defense stories."

Behind her are the purple wisteria vines Ida and I trimmed back so radically when we bought this place a decade ago. Vacant for years, the brownstone was crumbling in a yard so overgrown with poison ivy and wisteria and trumpet vines that we kept Joey out of there. The third time Ida left me—six separations and five reunions so far—I bought industrial-rubber gloves and went after the poison ivy with weed spray and clippers, amazed at the satisfaction I felt while yanking out those long vines. My revenge. As a boy, I'd touched poison ivy deliberately to prove that, just like Kevin, I was immune to poison ivy and sin and punishment, but the hot rash of blisters only confirmed that I couldn't get away unscathed.

Beneath the tangle of vines in back of our house, I found a deep hole covered with rotting boards. A root cellar, I figured; but when I got the ladder and climbed down—grateful we'd kept Joey out of the yard—the hole was lined with cinder blocks. An abandoned fallout shelter from the fifties, about eight by eight. Olive-green canisters of water. Two corroded flashlights. A metal crate full of hardened packages. On one of them I could still make out letters: "General Mills." Survival rations that, if indeed a nuclear bomb had struck, wouldn't have saved us any more than cowering under our desks in school, chins down, arms pressed against our ears, fingers linked behind our heads in prayer, the way Sister had demonstrated, so we'd bypass purgatory and go directly to heaven. *Duck and cover.*

Where I tore out the poison ivy and filled in the shelter, lilacs and peonies grow now; roses and trumpet vines. I understand that, given its roots and the nature of our land, some of the poison ivy will reappear; but I've learned to identify it during any season—even without its shiny leaves—by the brown centipede hairs on the vines that suckle themselves to trees. I've learned what I must do to destroy it.

Our backyard is safe now: I have made it so.

But it's not that simple with conflict. Here's the prevailing struggle between Ida and me: she wants to climb into my darkness and understand me, while I fight her with silence to shield her from my darkness. Sometimes I still long to go without speaking for days. But I can't anymore. Not as a father. For Joey, I've learned to pull words from myself.

The last time the three of us lived together was after the attack on the World Trade Center, when Ida and I raced to Joey's school, horrified. We took him home, but even there we no longer felt safe. Not in our house. Not in Brooklyn. Not in the world. After a few days we stopped watching the news on television and listened to NPR instead; yet images of the twin towers crumbling—forever and again—replayed themselves inside our minds when we closed our eyes.

Ida and I didn't sleep well, and whenever one of us woke up, the other lay already awake. One night I heard her slipping out of bed, her slow bare feet on the wooden floor, the flush of the toilet. Then she burrowed back under the quilt. Shivered. Four in the morning, and the house was cold.

"Maybe we should," I said, "you know, get a gun?"

"Maybe . . . But would we shoot it?"

"I would. If terrorists broke into our house, I would."

"Terrorists need bigger targets than us. Targets that make the news."

"Buildings . . . Bridges . . . Your feet—"

"My feet?"

"They're like ice."

"That's why I need to warm them on you, Antonio." Ida called me Antonio, the way my grandparents used to. She used to say the Italian version of my name was sexy, but I hadn't heard that in a long time, not since she'd accused me that I didn't desire her. And when I'd said I did, she'd insisted she didn't feel any desire coming from me.

"We'd have to keep the bullets in a separate place," I said. "Hide them from Joey."

"You believe it's going to happen again?"

I hesitated. According to Ida, I was tentative. Timid. "Some day," she liked to say, "you may finally have to decide something, Antonio." Now, as I felt her waiting, I told her with a certainty I didn't feel, that, yes, I would shoot, and that I'd aim for the legs.

"What good would that do?"

"Stop them."

"Too easy to miss." Ida used to watch *Cagney and Lacey*. "Besides, if you get one leg, someone can still come after you. Not to mention the other terrorists."

I thought about hiding places for bullets. Thought about getting shot. Reached down and rubbed my wife's feet between my hands.

Ida sighed. Shifted closer. "What are you . . . doing?"

I traced the delicate bone spurs above the ridge of her left foot. "Warming your feet," I said and stroked the tender spots between her toes, the rough skin above her heels.

My mother sets a bakery box with Florentines on the counter, and when I kiss her cheek, she leans into my arm. "Let's just look at him." She motions toward Joey mowing the lawn, carving his own trails.

He's wearing his red jacket with the decals of all the teams sewn on it, and the red leather cap that goes with it. When he notices us, he waves. Skips. Walks two steps and skips again.

"What a performer," my mother says affectionately.

"He has that from you."

"Early training." She waves back to him, and a whiff of basement pool rises from her—chlorine and mildew and dingy lockers—a smell I used to find on Ida some days, and I'm right back *there in the water, with Riptide Grandma, both of us silly and wild, exuberant, as if we were the same age. She's floating on her back, showing me how to: "Once you believe you can rest on water, you'll never be afraid of sinking."* My mother inherited the key to the pool from Riptide, who inherited it from Great-Aunt Camilla, and the building is large enough so that others assume my mother lives there, including the doormen, who appreciate the generous tips she gives them the week before Christmas.

"Every week Joey mows a different pattern," I tell her. "Figure eights; diamonds; a grid."

"That means he enjoys it." She's delighted to have a grandchild after years of pointing out to me what she called "daughter-in-law material"—in restaurants or in stores or on the street. "This one is intelligent," she'd say. Or: "Such a kind face . . . definitely daughter-in-law material." Or: "Not daughter-in-law material. Greedy eyes."

Joey glances over his shoulder, walks taller, faster, as he cuts diagonal stripes into the grass. When we step outside, toward the buzz of his mower, he stops the engine.

"I want to learn kickboxing, Grandma."

"Kickboxing is dangerous," I tell him.

"Grandma does it." Green eyes like mine. Frog-green, my cousin Belinda says.

"It's dangerous for your grandmother, too."

"Not if you do it properly," she corrects me. "The instructor uses the best of each form, whatever is most effective."

"How did you find your instructor, Grandma?"

"The Yellow Pages."

I groan.

"I called four numbers, and this man was the only one who had a class starting the day I called. He said: 'Come and watch and try if you like.'"

"What's the urgency?" I ask.

She expands her lean shoulders, frail wings that won't get her anywhere, and I want to wrap her into my arms, keep her sheltered. "I used to think you could leave fear behind if you chose to. But lately I've been feeling afraid again. Of what's happening in our country. Almost every day, we're warned of terrorist attacks, and—"

"But 9/11 did happen," Joey reminds her.

"Absolutely." She nods. "And it was terrible. Monstrous. That's what makes this fear so real—9/11 happened, but it has become increasingly monstrous, because the government is using it to take away our rights . . . supposedly for the sake of our protection. 'Huddle closer. Only we can protect you.'"

"You need to be careful," I say. "Saying these things aloud—"

"Let's look at it on a smaller scale, then . . . at a family where one of the parents—the father, say—beats the child . . . makes the child afraid. Afraid of him *and* of telling. And all along that father promises: 'I'm the only one who can protect you.' He teaches the child to fear. Reminds the child of what happened and can happen again."

Joey is nodding. "Just as we are reminded of 9/11."

"Right. It's not that terrorists attack us every day. But we're taught to be afraid it will happen again. The government color-codes our fear, tells us how afraid we need to be today. Tomorrow. And we're promised that the only one who can protect us is the person warning us. And so we draw closer to that leader. Let him govern us with fear."

"It's not wise to say these things aloud."

"True. And that fact, alone, must show you how many rights we've already lost. Remember those three firefighters who were suspended the week after 9/11 because they wouldn't fly the American flag on their engines? A lot of people are still being harassed for not flying the flag. It means you're not patriotic. Listen, I've lived a long time, but this is much worse than the McCarthy years. And it'll only get worse if we don't stop it. If we don't reclaim that absence of fear."

I glance at Joey. "Not in front of him."

"Joey can think for himself. With this whole 'axis of evil' thing, I'm far more afraid of our government than of terrorists."

"I don't want Joey repeating any of this in school."

"If his teachers are any good, they'll get the students thinking . . . discussing nationalism . . . its impact on other countries, too, throughout history. Aren't you worried we'll lose freedom of speech altogether?"

"Not really."

"Well . . . I am."

"Do me a favor," I tell Joey. "Let's keep this discussion in this house, all right?"

My mother laughs. "You sound like your father, Anthony. 'Whatever the Amedeo family talks about in the car, stays in the car. And whatever—'"

"'—the Amedeo family talks about in the house, stays in the house.' My father was a man of great wisdom. But really, now . . . what do those classes of yours have to do with any of this?"

"Learning to defend myself is one thing I can do to protect myself right now."

"It won't protect you from terrorists."

"No."

"Or from the government."

"No."

"Then—"

"It protects me from the fear."

"That man's ethics worry me."

"Absolutely."

"He's an opportunist."

"An opportunist. I'm glad you're seeing that, Anthony."

"How can I not? Just consider how he pounced on 9/11 to promote himself."

"He's a dictator."

"Hel-lo . . ." Joey waves both hands to interrupt us. "Hel-lo . . ."

"I wouldn't call him a dictator. But scheduling classes for firefighters and capitalizing on—"

"We're not talking about the same person, Anthony."

"Hel-lo . . ." Joey's hands are still up. "That's what I was trying to tell you."

"No wonder we agreed," I say.

"Let's keep going like this. Let's talk about government and religion on the same mattress. I know we agree on that."

"Yes. I'd rather have them fighting each other than combining powers."

"Agreed."

"Now let's talk about the *instructor's* ethics."

"Oh . . . his ethics worry me, too, Anthony."

"Finally."

"No. All along. But I'm not going to him for the study of ethics."

"It's street fighting."

"That's what I plan to learn."

"Cool," Joey says.

I give him a warning glance. "Not cool." I have feared for him since his birth. Even before his birth. That's why I waited to be a father. Too long. Ida wanted two children at least; but I know that terrible things happen.

That I cause them to happen.

⎯⎯ ☾

All Ida knows is that my cousin died as a girl.

Early in our marriage, at a family dinner, when Ida asked my mother how Bianca's death happened, everyone stared at me; and in that brutal moment—that brutal and eternal moment without sound—it came to me that family is the most violent unit, and I felt certain that retribution would come from within my family.

Aunt Floria was the first to glance away. Her daughter's death is one huge ripple—a tidal wave, rather—that seized all of us and flung us down in strange formations from where we've struggled to come back to what once was familiar. It was different for every one of us. There was no clarity, no common focus, only conflicting angles of vision, colliding and aligning in a mosaic, chaotic and orderly, shifting whenever one of us seized upon some measure of guilt to keep us linked to Bianca: for my mother that it happened while I was alone with Bianca in the kitchen; for Aunt Floria that she wasn't in the kitchen to prevent it; for Belinda that she hid the onyx giraffe.

For me, of course, it's that last minute by the open window.

Sometimes I dream the story of my family, the dream-story in which Bianca is still alive. Most of it is without texture and color, as if I were watching shadow dancers through a translucent curtain, flat shadows that shrink or loom depending on how close they come to the lights, one suddenly twice as large as the other, the way people will loom inside your mind when they fill your thoughts. When one of the dancers moves in front of the curtain, she's suddenly her regular size, three-dimensional, and wearing colors: red and yellow and purple. In my dream-story, the only moment that stands out like that—sharply; vibrantly; irrevocably—is when Bianca climbs from the chair to the windowsill. Countless times I have touched that moment just as those dancers touched the gauzy curtain between them, when it looked as though the dancer in front were reaching up toward the hand of the shadow giant behind the curtain, who was reaching down. Countless times I have revised that moment when Bianca stands up on the windowsill, and I usually manage to freeze her the moment *before* she flies away.

I can. As long as I cease to want anything. As long as I remember this: wanting is a reason for not having. I practice not having many things. If things accumulate, I give them away.

I'm so consumed by the effort of keeping Bianca there, on the windowsill, that sometimes I wish I could let her fall, hear her scream as she plummets to the ground, stand by her grave, and watch her coffin sink into the ground. And live through that.

No one asked me: "How did you trick her into flying?" And because no one did, I could not assault my family with the truth, could not trade confession for atonement. My penance: to keep my family braced with my silence. At first I kept the silence to protect myself. Then to protect my parents. Then Aunt Floria. And now my son, although I suspect that what continues to harm long beyond the act of violence is the silence. No one mentions Bianca when I'm around. Still, I'm sure any conversation that breaks off when I enter a room has to be about her. I believe they want me to forget Bianca ever existed. But I want her to exist. And some days, I manage to persuade myself that she flew off on her own. That I was only teasing her. That we both heard the long-drawn sighs of an accordion. That she said, "There's Papa." And that I tried to stop her.

When I offer to pay for cabs to my mother's class, she refuses and continues to walk from her apartment to Jerome Avenue to catch the Woodlawn IRT to 149th, then walk across to the Hub. And that's while it's still light. To think of her coming back after dark by herself makes me sick with worry.

"I like to walk," she tells me.

"As far as I'm concerned, that class is the most dangerous thing in your life."

She assures me the students hold vinyl bolsters between them when they team up to rehearse their kicks and punches.

"That's not what I meant, but even that could injure you. Some of those types must be twice your weight. At your age—"

"The only bad thing so far is a rash on my feet."

"What if one of those types followed you from that neighborhood?"

"The carpets there . . . But now I wear socks."

"You told me your legs were sore."

"Only the muscles in my calves. It means I'm getting stronger. Now, quit skutching me, Anthony."

I search the *New York Times* instead of skimming it. Suddenly there are more reports of blood and violence in the world, stimulating further violence.

Wednesday evening, I call my mother to make sure she's back from her class. But no one answers. Ten minutes later, I try again. Nothing. By now, Ida will have tucked Joey in for the night. It's what I miss most when I stay at the apartment, the ritual of saying good night to my son, turning his reading light so we can cast shadow animals against the illuminated wall, asking him, "Are you quite settled?" and hearing him say, "Quite settled, Daddy."

If only I could keep him at this age, where he's content to find the shadows of animals in the configurations of his hands. Whenever it's Ida's turn to live in the house with Joey, I call frequently, because the apartment feels bleak after the bookstore and café downstairs have closed. I make plans with Joey to ride bikes or go to Yankee Stadium. I get us good seats, though somehow I still like the cheap seats in the top bleachers.

Traces of Ida are everywhere in this apartment. In our house, too, but at least there I'm with Joey and don't need Ida quite as much.

At nine-forty-five I finally reach my mother. "Tell me something—"

"Hold on, Anthony. I just got in."

I hear her setting down the phone. A man's voice in the back. Something clunking. I'm ready to call the police.

A click. "Can you hear me?"

"Is someone bothering you?"

"Yes. You."

"What was that noise?"

"My shoes. I kicked them off so I can sit on the bed and put up my feet while I'm on the phone with my son, who—"

"I also heard a voice."

"Now, *that* is low-budget movie stuff, Anthony."

"I can hear someone there with you."

"Probably just the television."

"It doesn't sound like television."

"Oh . . . you must have heard James Hudak. He's replacing some wiring." She has always felt sorry for James—used to feed him dinner now and then during those months my father stayed with Elaine. After James' grandmother died, he took over her lease, and he's lived on the first floor since, never married, working as a waiter a couple of days a week, trading repairs for my mother's cooking.

"Make sure you lock up after James. I fretted about you all day at the café."

"You should just cook."

"I can cook *and* fret."

"You're too good a chef to piss it away with fretting."

—⁀ꙅ

Next I call Ida, try to win her back by getting her to fret with me about my mother. "I can already see my mother crouched by a dumpster, bleeding from a knife wound in her belly. Or in a coffin, her lips painted a vulgar pink that—"

"Pink is not her color," Ida interrupts.

"I have visions of my mother kicking and punching four hairy bikers who take a broken bottle to her face."

"After she gets out of the coffin?"

"A different scenario. Altogether. You're not taking me seriously. All that *could* happen to her. I have visions of her in a coma that has lasted years, hooked up to machines, her skin the color of salt. I see her, Ida. I hear her. Even in my dreams, I see her. And now she wants me to attack her."

"Joey told me."

"Fighting with words isn't enough for her anymore, she says. Do you think she's maybe . . . you know, maybe getting senile?"

"No," Ida says firmly. "Leonora is very clear and determined." Ida loves my mother. Admires my mother. Once a month, the two of them swim in the ancient basement pool where Riptide Grandma used to do her one mile every morning after mass.

"She used to talk about plays she wanted to see, about her friends. Now all she talks about is that class. I think she likes the danger."

"I'm sure she does."

"Really?"

"Leonora needs a bit of an edge."

"I've offered to help her move to a building that has security. That old neighborhood used to be great, but now it's claustrophobic. The noise, the dirt—"

"It's been her home since she was a young woman."

"Still, I don't understand why she stays there."

"Because people identify with neighborhoods they've lived in for a long time. Leonora knows where everything is. People know her. Most of the shopkeepers have changed, but some are still the same. She's also near the subway, can get to Macy's or Rockefeller Center in thirty minutes on the D train."

"Yes, but—"

"All that obviously means something to her. Besides, the apartment is rent-controlled."

"Something is always breaking. Whenever I'm there, James Hudak is repairing stuff. She's living in an oasis of a different time, when we had our windows open and could hear violin lessons from the courtyard. Saxophone lessons. When the neighborhood was a little village and the children played in the street."

"You're romanticizing the years before you got air conditioning." Ida's voice is dry. "It was like that where I lived. We got air conditioning and closed the windows, and when we walked up the stairs, we heard the air conditioning, not music lessons."

"It isolated us . . . changed our entire neighborhood."

"And made us more comfortable."

"We could no longer hear the sounds of other families."

"Thank God for that."

"You win." I laugh.

"It's not about winning, Antonio. Unless . . ."

"Yes?"

"Unless first prize is that you'll let me go to sleep."

To lure Ida into staying awake, I beget words. Mimic feelings. Open myself to her, bit by bit. Let her reel me back into language, reel me back into existence, all along knowing I don't deserve her or Joey. During fourteen years of marriage, Ida and I have spent more days alone than together. The first time she left me was before Joey was conceived, when it still was just the two of us, and though she came back after forty-one days, and though we made and raised this child between us, I expect her to leave again.

"We all have that darkness," she told me last winter. It was evening, we were on the subway to the Brooklyn Academy of Music, and I felt so cornered by her that I wondered what it would be like to court her with my darkness. Just then, a man in a dirty coat stumbled past us in the aisle, arms like flippers, and I thought, My God, that's what it's like for me, too, day to day, marked and isolated. Where did it go in him, the dread and the fear? And then I knew. Because it broke through as he heaved himself atop an empty seat and stood up, his flipper arms thrashing the air while he shrieked, "I am the devil. I am the devil." I said to Ida, "That's me. That's what it's like to be me."

I'm afraid of what'll happen to me if Ida finds someone else to love. I don't think I can do this again with another person. People don't stay with me for long. Except for Joey. But, then, he doesn't really have a choice. The longest I was in a relationship before Ida was seven months. The kind of love I wish for is the love my grandfather and Riptide had between them. I see them *drifting in the ocean, waiting for their chance to swim out of the current, together, outlasting its path. Floating in Riptide's embrace, his hands on her body, embracing her the way she would have never let a stranger hold her, my grandfather thinks of drowning and of making love to her. And he chooses her over drowning.*

"At least you can't accuse me of pulling away from you," I tell her.

"You still misinterpret everything."

"What do you mean?"

"That you expect agendas behind the most ordinary conversations."

"My mother's conversations about killing and maiming are not ordinary."

"Sleep, Antonio. Your mother is stubborn. Strong." And she's gone, my wife, leaving beyond the leaving she has already done.

—⌒ↄ

"I wish I could kick my legs higher," my mother says, "and keep my fists up at the same time." She starts with the instructor-voice: "'Because the natural reaction is to drop them when you kick. All a matter of TSC.'"

"I'm afraid to ask what that stands for."

"Timing. Surprise—as in the element of surprise. And calm—keeping calm. 'The three major elements of effective self-defense. TSC can save your life. It did for one of the students.'" Her instructor voice is choppy. Tough. "'A rapist broke into this student's house. Threatened her. So she pretended to go along. Till he got his pants off. Then she grabbed him. By the balls.'"

Joey giggles.

"'He tried to beat on her. But she held on. Till he howled for mercy. Then she dragged him to the door. She kicked him out. He ran down the street. And she got her baseball bat. Chased after him, yelling: I'm not through with you yet.'"

"Now he wants you chasing rapists?" I'm furious. Helpless.

"That's not what he's telling us to do."

"I'd love to chase that instructor with a baseball bat or worse. For giving you a false sense of security."

"There's nothing false about it," my mother says. "And I never want to walk without that knowledge again."

Every morning, she practices by herself in her bedroom. I imagine her in front of the mirror—*still graceful, though of a slower grace. She is powerful: she observes it in her stance as she kicks and rotates and punches and stretches. But her floors are still bare and not ready to absorb a fall, as they will during the winter, when she has her rugs down.*

She still has the maple bedroom set and the family photos the way she used to arrange them above the dresser, including the one of my father lifting me high and the one of herself as a bride. Now, this is what's weird: her left elbow leans on a marble pillar that is just the height of her elbow. If I didn't remember this very photo of her with my father, I might believe she had posed like this, alone, on her wedding day. But when I was a boy, she and my father stood in this photo together, their arms linked, and I want to stop time there, when everyone I loved lived close by; when I believed my parents would be together forever, and that the entire world was made up of apartment buildings with tar beaches and fire escapes and washlines and neighbors propping their lawn chairs on the sidewalk and kids playing kick-the-can and hopscotch.

When the wedding photo vanished, it revealed a pale rectangle of wallpaper, a nothing-time before a nothing-now. It happened the day of my father's engagement party, and I was there, a witness to his uneasiness, toes hurting in my new shoes. The next morning, when I woke up, Aunt Floria was sleeping on a chair in our kitchen, smelling of licorice, her hair spread around her, while my mother was alone in the big bed, also smelling of licorice. The wedding photo was not on the wall.

When it finally reappeared to cover the nothing-now, my father was no longer in it; but since no one mentioned that change, it felt dangerous to ask, because then my father might vanish from my baby picture, too. I had nightmares of bobbing toward the ceiling fan like a getaway balloon about to be sliced by the blades, unable to return to the ground without my father's arms to pull me back.

That photo still puzzles me. Sometimes, I swear, the curtain behind the marble pillar is moving as if just stirred by a magician who has snatched my father behind that fabric; and I'm oddly reassured to think of him there—not in heaven or purgatory; most certainly not hell—but with this magician, leading a different kind of afterlife from what the priest promised at my father's funeral, waiting eagerly behind that curtain for my mother: still in his tuxedo; still with his sweepstakes smile; still the age he was when he vanished from the photo, younger than I am now, half the age my mother has reached; and still close enough if she were ever to call him back. Waiting. The way I wait for Ida.

I used to hope my mother would replace the photo with one printed from the original negative, and perhaps she planned to, eventually, once she no longer distrusted my father. I doubt that keeping him out was an act of omission, or that she no longer noticed the picture, the way she became used to the pattern of ferns on our wallpaper. I rather believe she deliberately made *him* live with his absence, just as she had lived with his absence, a reminder of what could happen to both of them again.

That day before she let my father come back to us, he asked me to help him clean the Studebaker. I said yes, but I didn't look at him. Just worked with him. Under the driver's seat, I found a quarter, a nickel, and a dried beet.

"Can I ask you something?" my father asked.

I shrugged.

My father brushed dirt from the floor mats, and one dried lettuce leaf dropped to the pavement, thin, like lizard skin. "Can I come home to you and your mother, Anthony?"

I raised the beet to my nose. It smelled of dry earth. "Okay," I said. "Yes."

"She's quite a fighter, your mother."

What I recall most about my father's return was his adoration of my mother, spoiled by caution. It's how I am with Ida whenever she returns to me. Except that she doesn't stay long, while my parents stayed together after their one rift, tugging at their marriage to reshape it into how they remembered it. Through the wall of my bedroom I'd hear him at night, talking to her more than he ever had before. *Mia cara,* he called her. It took my parents years to figure out that their marriage had become something else—stronger; more tender—and just when they settled into this new marriage of theirs and dared to cherish it for what it had become, my father had a stroke.

While he was recovering, he cooked. No longer for Festa Liguria, but for family. "Even now Victor brings food," my relatives used to say.

My mother was not all that interested in food, but after my father had his second stroke and only survived for another nine days, she was the one who started cooking, bringing food around.

Though she doesn't like noisy music—she used to claim my grandfather's operas makes her elbows hurt from pushing against the armrests while she tried to get away—she now plays rapid and thumping music whenever she goes out, so that intruders will think someone young and strong and male is in there. Instead, it's become a signal to her neighbors that she isn't home.

I have started to call my mother Monday and Wednesday evenings at nine-forty-five.

"Don't spy on me, Anthony."

"I can't sleep until I'm sure you're safe."

"I cannot help you with that."

"Usually you're glad to hear from me."

"Not when you're spying on me."

"I am not spying on you. Ever since you've started those classes, you're no longer the person I know."

The following week, I dial her number at nine-forty-five and hang up the instant she answers, though it must be quite obvious that I'm the one calling. And for the first time it does feel like spying.

That Saturday, Joey and I take the subway to visit her. When we climb up the stairs at Fordham Road, a rat hunkers on the sidewalk. A few people point at it. Walk in a wide arc past it. Except for one man with a shopping bag who strides toward the rat, grinning. The rat doesn't move. It's disoriented. Weak. Two women scream, and Joey covers his eyes; but I don't look away soon enough.

"Did he step on it from the side or from the top?" Joey asks when I pull him away.

"The Bronx was not like that when I was a child," I tell him as we pass a building with cracked windows, repaired with duct tape and cardboard. "After being downtown and arriving on the Concourse, you could breathe fresh air. With all the trees, it was like being in the country. It also was elegant, with the Art Deco buildings and shops. On weekends, women would wear mink stoles on the Concourse."

"You're trying to distract me from the rat, Daddy."

"That, too. But I also notice the changes in the neighborhood more whenever I'm with you, because you have nothing to compare this to."

"Yes I do. Your stories. The shiny doors of the Paradise. Playing mass on Kevin's roof. Your Uncle Malcolm opening the fire hydrant in August—"

"He used to aim the spray toward us with the lid of a trash can and let Belinda and me dash through the cold water."

"The ice-cream truck that came to your street . . ."

"Yelling up to my mother for money for a Bungalow Bar." As I listen to myself, I feel I'm reclaiming some of that magic with words.

"Tell me about the Kitchen Sink."

We pass the Indian-spice store that used to be the Fordham Boys Shop. Sometimes we shop here for cardamom and dried ginger. Coriander and fennel seeds. Across the street is the bodega where we buy ripe plantains. Joey loves to fry them till they're black. The last time we were at St. Simon Stock, the mass schedule outside the door was in Spanish. Most of the Jewish, Irish, and Italian immigrant families are gone from our neighborhood—some to the suburbs or Manhattan; most, like Kevin, to Co-op City—and they've been replaced by immigrants more recent than my grandfather, who used to tell us how he struggled to get by when he arrived here. Except what these new immigrants have come to is not as promising as it was for him in the postwar years, when these buildings were new. Now they're in disrepair, with outdated plumbing, and steel bars outside many windows. Hardship has become more visible.

"Maybe this will become the next neighborhood to be regenerated," I tell Joey. "You've seen it in Brooklyn. Houses like ours. Street by street. Entire blocks."

"Cool."

I think of SoHo—those vacant warehouses where even students wouldn't live, and where you wouldn't dare park your car. I've seen the East Village change. All places where hardship certainly remains but no longer defines the neighborhoods.

"Kitchen Sink? First you went to the library with your mother . . ."

". . . and afterwards she took me to Jahn's. They were famous for their Kitchen Sink Sundae. My mother said it was a rule you had to have six people to order the Kitchen Sink, because it was so big."

"That's why you never got to eat it."

"You remember everything."

"Do you remember how long that rat's tail was?"

"You want to talk about tails? I had a hat with a raccoon tail when I was about nine, a Davy Crockett hat. Kevin had one, too. He also had a signed photo of Fess Parker."

"Who's that?"

"The actor who played Davy Crockett. One day, in front of the Concourse Plaza Hotel, Fess Parker got into the cab of Kevin's father, who took him to Yankee Stadium. When he told Fess Parker that he was his son's favorite actor on the continent, he whipped out a photo and signed it right there. 'For my friend Kevin, from the king of the wild frontier. Fess Parker.'"

"Cool."

"King of the wild frontier . . ." I sang. "Davy, Davy Crockett—"

"Daddy . . ." Joey glances around.

". . . born on a mountaintop in Tennessee, greenest state—" I laughed. "I used to sing 'cleanest state.'"

Joey walks faster, embarrassed to be on the same street with me.

"Just a year ago, you would have sung with me."

"A year ago, I was a child."

"The Palisades song? 'Come on over . . .'"

"'Palisades has the rides after dark. . . .'" He runs ahead.

"Wait. We can talk about the rat."

He stops. "Did the man step on the rat from the side or from the top?"

I spare him by lying that I didn't see the man's foot coming down.

"You can sing me the rest of that Davy Crockett song now." He sounds relieved.

"You're too . . . kind." I start singing: "'killed him a bear when he was only three . . .'"

"Are you saying that killing a bear is not as bad as killing a rat?"

"You're fixated on rats, huh? All right. My father, he hated rats more than anyone I know. One afternoon, he arrived home early, yanked off his trousers, and slapped them against the wall, dancing around."

Joey laughs.

"He was sure rats had climbed up his legs. They'd swarmed around him when he walked past Smelly Alley. 'Hundreds of rats,' he said, 'a sea of rats. Rats of all sizes.' It started with one scurrying across his shoe, and within seconds all he could see were rats—in front of him, behind him. There were no cars by the curb for them to hide beneath, and he was between the rats and their protection, those bushes and weeds in the alley."

"Maybe they were afraid when this human appeared," Joey suggests.

"My father—he freaked out. Hopped up and down, certain he felt claws and fur against his legs. One rat headed toward a sewer grate. Then the others. Down. Hind ends last. A wave of hind ends, and it was over. My father took a shower until all the hot water was gone. Never wore those pants again."

"Let's not say anything to Grandma about the sick rat," Joey says as we approach the corner candy store, where my mother still buys her cigarettes and magazines, and where Joey often gets a Snickers. But today he doesn't mention candy.

Joey and I approach the building where I grew up, where the hedges have been dead for many years. In their place: hard soil. The courtyard has a steel gate. On the building old graffiti, new graffiti: "fuck you suck me lola loves tommy up yours happy eater . . ."

"Eater?" Joey asks. "Probably something to do with food, sex, or a misspelling of 'Easter.'"

"I vote for Easter."

"You're such a . . . Dad."

"To think that I got hell for drawing with chalk on the sidewalk. . . ."

"And what happened?"

"The super told my mother, and I got grounded."

"Different generations, Dad."

I glance at Joey from the side, and we both laugh.

My mother's bell no longer works, but I have a key for the gate and the front door. Six concrete steps with concrete flowerpots, cracked and gray with specks of white where the paint hasn't weathered, filled with cigarette butts and candy wrappers and cellophane. It could be so different.

As Joey and I race each other up the stairway, I smell cardamom and turmeric, schmaltz and wet plaster, urine and yesterday's fish.

Three floors up, and I'm panting. "Wait—"

Joey stops halfway up the next flight. More than four decades between us. If I were a young father, I'd be able to give him more energy. More playfulness. Less of the caution he already rebels against. He waits till I'm next to him. Side by side, we walk up to the sixth floor, where it's silent in the hallway. No loud music. That's how I know my mother is home. I knock.

When she opens her door, James Hudak is sitting on her sofa

in jeans and a sleeveless undershirt, working on one of her cross-word puzzles with the retractable pencil I gave her. Though his age is somewhere between my mother's and mine, James looks younger than I, fitter. As usual, he doesn't stay. Mumbles something about coming back later to fix the window latch. Last time it was the sink. When I was a boy, I used to see him often—too often, really—because whenever he visited his grandmother she ignored me. James and I passed a sharp and swift dislike back and forth between us until he went into the Navy, and then I was away at cooking school, and we didn't come across each other for years.

He grabs his denim shirt from the couch, gives me a brief nod. "Anthony."

I nod. "James."

"I'll call you in a while," my mother tells him.

"You need anything from the store?"

"A couple of onions for the roast tomorrow."

He whispers something, and she whispers back.

She gets out plates and silverware with the Festa Liguria logo. While she feeds Joey and me, I try not to think of the rat; yet the effort of not thinking about the rat *brings the rat into my mother's kitchen, makes the man's foot come down to crush it again and again, fills my head with the smell of wet feathers and sawdust, and I'm standing with Riptide in the poultry market, where the turkey with the shy eyes hangs by his feet from the scale.*

"Look at that turkey looking at that little boy."

"That turkey is looking at you, Antonio."

"Gobobobob . . ."

"Nice turkey. Nice—"

"Antonio has decided. Questo."

"No—"

And already I'm thinking of the rat again, *and the man's shoe is coming down, blood and violence, stimulating other violence,* and what you see inside your head, you have to say. It's like confession, where what you did or thought or said will push at you till you say it to the priest, and then you'll feel better. And so I murmur "rat" to myself without moving my lips. "Rat. Rat." Thinking this is stupid.

And I don't feel better. My mother is watching me. She seems small.
Alone.

"Alone," I whisper.

"What did you say?"

"That you spend too much time alone."

"But Grandma's got James," my son says.

"I'm talking about a different kind of relationship."

Joey is looking at me as if he were the father and I the child. He's
standing by her boombox, checking her CDs. "You got the new
Busta," he says excitedly.

"Go ahead and borrow it."

"Thanks." He and my mother trade CDs: Busta and Mystical
and The Neptunes and Lil' Kim.

"What if you started dating again?" I ask my mother.

She glances at Joey. They both shrug.

"Dad—" Joey pulls his hands through his short hair. Makes the
ends stick up. "Grandma's got James."

"I want what's already familiar," my mother says.

"He'll become familiar."

"Who?"

"Someone new."

"I don't want someone new."

"Once you get to know him, he'll become familiar."

"I would feel like a fifteen-year-old inside an eighty-year-old
body."

"There are men with eighty-year-old bodies . . . with ninety-
year-old bodies . . . who're alone and looking for a woman to—"

"Old men . . ." She waves my idea aside. "Whatever would I do
with an old man?"

"Maybe one of your friends could introduce you to someone."

Joey groans. "Dad—"

My mother winks at him. "A blind date . . . How romantic. I
can picture it already. . . . I'm getting dressed for our date, and before I even meet him, I'm ready to have him be the one who is
meant for me. But then I open my door and there he stands, barely
my height, balding or with his hair parted above one ear, smelling
of some manly cologne—"

"Anything but manly cologne." I have to laugh.

"—and I want to change him already into the man I ought to be dreaming about."

"Warts," Joey says, "your blind date has warts."

"Definitely warts," she agrees.

I'm feeling lighthearted. "Why is it that the two of you need to gang up on me?"

*   *   *

Two weekends later, my mother arrives on the train with raisin scones and wants to rehearse for multiple attackers. After dinner, she instructs Joey to hold on to her arms while I'm supposed to approach her from the front.

"Wait a second, please—" she says, when she has us in position. "I have to think what to do first." She lifts her right heel. Flexes her foot. "There are six parts to this."

I'm stunned. "Is that what you'll say if you get into that kind of situation? 'There are six parts to this. Excuse me, please, while I think of the sequence.'"

"That is exactly why I have to rehearse with you." Her voice is patient and slow, as if I were a four-year-old, a particularly dense four-year-old. "I have to rehearse with you, Anthony, so that it all becomes reflex."

Swinging her right leg toward me, she stops before it touches my thigh. "I'll do this a lot harder with real attackers," she promises, and pivots herself to the side, using her right leg—still raised—to cock back, tap Joey's knee, and from there shoot forward to graze my leg.

"Cool kick, Grandma."

"Don't you encourage her," I snap.

But my mother is beaming at him. Her face is flushed. "Once I remember the sequence, I'll be much faster."

"All you'd do with any of these antics is annoy a mugger." I hate the disapproving tone in my voice.

"No one wants to fight a wild, screaming woman. Look at Salome. . . . And if Lot's wife had fought, she wouldn't have become a pillar of salt. . . . You see, that's what we're supposed to turn ourselves into when we're in danger—pillars of salt. That's how they get us. Now, if Lot's wife—"

"Don't tell me the instructor is a preacher, too?"

"It's something I've thought out."

"Now she wants to be Mrs. Lot."

"Don't talk about me in the third person, damnit."

"I was just quoting what Dad would say: 'Now she wants to be Mrs. Lot.'"

"And I would tell your father what I told you: 'Don't talk about me in the third person.'"

"But he'd remind you that you only quote the Bible to win an argument."

For a moment, we're both smiling. And I see my father *arch his throat while she strokes his neck, see them lean close to each other, whispering, laughing. And I see him across the table from me at Hung Min's, playing backgammon, his eyes on the board and on the lined face of his opponent, while I pour tea for all of us into tiny cups, stirring three spoonfuls of sugar into each.*

"The instructor says ninety percent of self-defense is attitude . . . how I carry myself."

"Attitude? I thought it was BLT or whatever."

"Not BLT, Daddy. TSC. Timing, surprise, and calm."

"Right," my mother says. "And attitude is what leads you to TSC."

"Then why isn't it ATSC?"

"You're looking for disagreement."

"I'm looking for security. Security for you. Can't you take some other kind of class that would make you feel stronger? Something like . . . aerobics? Just make sure it's low-impact. Yoga would be even better."

"Yoga doesn't kick ass, Daddy. Grandma does."

I ignore Joey. "One of Ida's customers—she's in her mid-eighties—took up low-impact aerobics a few years ago. She bought several books on aerobics, and she's walking better now than she did back then."

"I'm walking just fine." My mother looks at me, steadily. "Please, listen. Remember the example I gave you about a parent hurting a child, making the child afraid?"

"I remember."

"I'm that child."

I am still, cold. The sky is motionless. And I stand in front of her, defenseless, while my shadow lies on her face.

"I have been beaten. Many times. Brutally."

My son is still holding my mother's arms. While I'm afraid of knowing . . . afraid of not knowing.

"It happened over the span of four years . . . before my father com— Before he died."

Joey moves one hand up her arm. Strokes her shoulder.

"Working as a prison guard changed him . . . made him brutal."

"God—I'm sorry. . . ." I want to hold my mother, but my shadow still lies on her face. "Why didn't you tell me?"

"It's not the kind of thing you tell your son." She keeps herself so straight and brittle that I don't dare touch her.

But Joey dares. Joey keeps stroking her shoulder.

"I'm so sorry."

Joey curves one arm around my mother's shoulders. And now the two of them are facing me. I feel separate from them. Linked only to this grandfather—both of us causing harm—and as I wonder what malice I've inherited from him, I feel dizzy. I've only seen one photo of him, in a uniform, angular and somber, as if getting ready for his appendix to burst. My mother rarely talked about him. But now, in telling me about the beatings, she's ripping me far open. How can I possibly hold on to my secrets any longer? I try to hear what they're saying, my son and my mother.

"I wish I had known self-defense when I was a girl."

"Would you have used it, Grandma?"

"Oh yes," she says without hesitation.

"On your own father?" Joey asks her, but he's staring at me with his new defiance.

"He shot himself," she says. "He stuck his gun into his mouth instead of going into the prison for one more day of guard duty. I didn't find out till I was twenty."

And suddenly I have my arms around her, and we're both rocking, back and forth.

"My mother said he wasn't like that when she married him. . . ."

Rocking, back and forth and back and forth, crying now.

"As a girl, I believed what had really burst inside my father was not his appendix but his rage. Because that's what I wished on him whenever I was beneath his fists, that his rage would explode inside his body and kill him. Then it happened . . . and I felt powerful and guilty and grateful that the rage had killed him. And not me. Because it could have."

I tighten my arms around her.

"Sometimes I tell myself that my father was just a poor schmuck inside his private hell, who struck at me, was afraid of being found out, and threatened. Compliance by fear. It works."

"But you don't have to defend yourself against him ever again. All that is over."

"It is never over." She steps away. "It is never over, Anthony. Because any new terror will attach itself to your earliest fear, and once you walk with fear—"

"But I want you safe."

"You don't get it, do you?" my mother says softly. She takes me by the wrist. Leads me outside. "Put both hands around my neck."

"Mother—"

She grasps my hands, studies my palms as if estimating my lifeline, and places my fingers around her neck.

Beneath my hands, her bones feel fragile.

Her skin is papery.

It might tear.

Slip off.

Her lips move. "Tighter," she says.

I feel huge.

And as dangerous as the evening I lured Bianca into flying.

My mother—my tiny, old mother—lifts her right arm. She points toward the cloudless sky and pivots to the left, breaking my hold. Her elbow swings toward me. But this time she does not stop. In her swing, I feel her rage at having lost me to the silence, and as she lets her elbow crash into my sternum and jab up beneath my rib cage, it comes to me that she knows about Bianca, that she's known forever how I pushed at Bianca with my words to fly, and that nothing since has been as thrilling and horrifying for me as that moment I knew Bianca was about to fly.

And now *I* fall.

Fall toward the smell of cut grass. Fall toward a startling release at both of us knowing, toward the possibility of going with my mother to that first fear of mine, toward the possibility of redemption, desire even. Fall into wanting.

Fall so hard that it rushes back at me, slams into me, the wanting. And I dare to want Ida. Dare to want our lost stories coming back into my family. Dare to *stand in front of our old apartment building and stare up at our kitchen windows, one open, one smeared with glass wax, while Bianca spins toward me—languid and beyond all time—spins and pivots, slow-moving like a dazed star, her cape flitting around her. While I pray. Pray for that pulsebeat of mercy when both windows remain closed while Bianca applies television-perfect glass-wax decorations. Pray that—beyond Bianca in our kitchen—my mother and Aunt Floria dance, their faces close as if they spent all their waking hours practicing together. Pray that Riptide Grandma and Great-Aunt Camilla join them, that my father and grandfather and Uncle Malcolm clap their hands and chant, "The tango . . . Do the tango," while Aunt Floria dips my mother so far back that her black hair sweeps the floor. Snow spins around my ankles while I pray for my mother and Aunt Floria to keep dancing, the glass-wax ornaments a pale flicker across their dark dresses as they reach for me and pull me into their circle,* but when I look up, it's the sun that's spinning, not snow, spinning around my mother, who stands above me, fists raised, feet planted in her fighting stance, staging her fullest and all-out fight for my soul.

ABOUT THE AUTHOR

Ursula Hegi is the author of nine critically acclaimed books, including *Intrusions, Floating in My Mother's Palm, Stones from the River, Tearing the Silence, The Vision of Emma Blau,* and *Hotel of the Saints.* She lives in New York State.